MURDER GAME

ALSO BY CAROLINE MITCHELL

MURDER GAME

CAROLINE MITCHELL

Bookouture

Published by Bookouture in 2017
An imprint of StoryFire Ltd.
Carmelite House, 50 Victoria Embankment, London EC4Y 0DZ
www.bookouture.com

ISBN: 978-1-78681-163-9
eBook ISBN: 978-1-78681-162-2

To Helen Cadbury, whose warmth, talent and humour left little imprints on our hearts x

The cruellest lies are often told in silence – Robert Louis Stevenson

PROLOGUE

The last embers of a guilty conscience made Melissa twist her wedding band free.

'Leave it on,' the man behind her murmured, his breath heavy on the curve of her neck.

Melissa arched a perfectly plucked blonde eyebrow as she gave him a sideways glance. 'Why?'

'I want you to wear it.' His hands slid down her arms, driving goose bumps on her flesh. Opening her palm, he claimed the band of gold and worked it back onto her finger. 'It shows how much I mean to you.'

Odd, Melissa thought. 'What makes you think that?'

'You're cheating on your husband to be with me. You wouldn't commit a mortal sin with just anyone, now would you?'

Melissa resisted the urge to shrug. It was hardly love at first sight. The fact that Matthew was offering no strings sex and high-quality coke was good enough for her. 'I just want to have fun,' she said, truthfully.

'I second that,' Matthew said, raising his iPhone in the air.

'No photos,' Melissa slurred after he had captured her image, her reactions slowed by the copious amounts of cocktails she had consumed. 'If my husband finds out…'

'He'd react in exactly the same way as my wife. Don't worry. What happens in *Debauchery* stays in *Debauchery*. I just wanted to remember your sexy face.' Tapping at his phone, he offered a reassuring smile. 'There, all gone. You can relax now.'

'I am relaxed,' she said, a devilish smile playing on her lips as all thoughts of her older husband floated away. 'Why don't you serve up a couple more lines while I pop to the loo?'

'Consider it done,' Matthew said, turning towards the rucksack he had picked up from the nightclub cloakroom on the way out. The scruffy canvas bag seemed out of place as he rested it on the four-poster hotel bed. Had she been sober, Melissa may have given it more than a passing thought.

'What's in the bag?' she said. 'Looks heavy.'

'Oh, just some fun and games.'

The words were loaded with promise, and Melissa felt a tingle shoot up her spine. She lifted her foot to kick off her heels, but Matthew shot out another warning.

'Leave the shoes on too, please… and the dress. I want to take it off myself.'

'Fine,' she said, her voice trailing behind her as she tottered into the en-suite. A series of spotlights lit the room, bouncing against the shiny chrome and temporarily dazzling her vision. Melissa blinked at her reflection, her eyes alight with anticipation. Her face was still flushed from the afterglow of the club, and the line of coke that followed. She swept back a lock of blonde curly hair before thumbing the mascara stains from beneath her eyes.

Matthew wasn't normally the type of guy she went for, but right now, she was beyond caring. Sex with her husband had become worse than a chore. She tried to remember a time when it meant something, when they had actually connected, but the memory would not come. His wealth could only stretch so far when it came to cushioning the harsh reality. All too late, Melissa discovered that Phillip's priority was satisfying his own needs first. A smile touched her lips. She deserved this. And the ironic thing was that her husband would be paying for her fun. Still, she would play the dutiful wife when she went home. She thought of her mobile phone, left charging on her bedside table. She knew her husband sometimes tracked her online. Who needed alibis when your phone could vouch for your whereabouts? But her second phone, the one she hid in her purse, now that was where the real fun began. The flirty texts, the dating app, all leading up to this night.

She swished her mouth with water in the absence of a toothbrush, allowing herself a flutter of excitement, thinking about what was to come. Matthew wasn't like other men. She had not expected such dominance for a start. Not that she was complaining. His online bio was extensive, and she had been promised an amazing night…

Sod it, she thought, flipping up the toilet seat before pulling down her knickers and sitting down. It wasn't as if she was having an affair. That was what she loved about *Debauchery*: being a part of such an illicit online group. Each encounter was quick and disposable. Explosive bursts of pleasure in an otherwise mundane week. After three years of marriage, she had come to a crossroads. She could either leave her husband and be penniless and jobless – or stay married and treat herself when he wasn't around. She rose from the toilet, kicking off the knickers straddling her ankles. It was a no-brainer. She chose the latter.

CHAPTER ONE

'I'm back.' Phillip Sherman's voice echoed in the spacious hall. His home was not unlike the hotel in which he had recently stayed, with its high ceilings and marble floors. Built to his specifications, it reflected his wealth; much like his wife who was still not answering his calls. 'Melissa? I'm home.' His booming voice filtered through the expansive space, carrying up the stairs and onto the top landing. He frowned at the lack of response and the strange, uneasy silence that followed in its wake. A week had passed since they had last seen each other and it had been three whole days since they'd spoken. It was a silly argument, but unfortunate in its timing. If he hadn't gone away, they would have made up by now. He had enjoyed his golf trip almost as much as Melissa's lovemaking, and he could not wait to be reacquainted with her again. True, his weight had piled on as middle age had crept in, and it was thanks to his hairdresser that no grey hairs were on display, but money paved the way to quiet acceptance as far as his young wife was concerned. It was her job to look pretty, his to keep them in the lavish lifestyle they both deserved.

'Melissa, darling, let's not sulk, daddy's home!' It was their pet name, born from a joke about sugar daddies. He knew she loved him in her own way, although he was not a big enough fool to believe she would be with him if he were destitute. He rested his hand on the stairwell, a small sliver of fear creeping through his body. It was too quiet. Yet, the friend finder tracker on his iPhone told him that she was here. She would never leave without her mobile phone. Yes, she had been upset with him but—

A sudden rap on the door made him inhale a sharp intake of breath, and he half expected to find Melissa on the other side. Perhaps she had locked herself out. It wouldn't be the first time. His face fell as a smiling postman greeted him instead. Phillip grunted as he took the white envelopes, and small padded parcel too bulky to fit in the letterbox. He syphoned through today's post before picking up more letters, littered on the floor. He frowned at the postmarks, some dated three days ago. Having come in from the garage entrance, he had failed to notice them immediately upon his return. Why hadn't his wife picked them up? A disagreement with the cleaner had left them without housekeeping, but surely, Melissa was capable of doing that one small thing? Another, more worrying thought niggled at him. She couldn't have left him, could she? Not over something so minor. Only last week she had been picking out a new car. And then there was the prenup to consider, something he knew would tie her to him for years. So why did he feel so scared? A sudden rush of acid indigestion flared. Still holding the parcel, he climbed the stairs. Perhaps she was just teasing him, dressed in one of her sexy costumes waiting to see to his every need.

But the house felt cold and unsettled, and each step upwards felt as if it were bringing him towards a terrible outcome. He thought about Melissa's Prozac prescription and her comfortable acquaintance with cocaine. He had caught her inhaling the substance through a rolled up fifty-pound note at their last celebrity bash. Her excuse that 'everyone does it' did not wash with him. His media profile was perfect. It would not do to have his copybook blotted now. As he entered their sprawling master bedroom, he half expected to find her laid out on the bed. Where was she? Her clothes were still in the wardrobe and her shoes still in place. But her handbag was nowhere to be seen. He glanced at her phone, which was plugged into the charger on the bedside table. Even the air was sterile, devoid of the expensive perfume that lingered in the air.

A sense of dread encapsulated him, his Italian leather shoes clicking against the marble floors as he checked each room in turn. Wiping away the beads of sweat breaking out on his forehead, Phillip's attention returned to the parcel in his hand. He stood on the top floor landing, ripped the package open and peered within. Almost too late, he noticed that the red splotches coming through the tissue paper were not part of the design. As he unwrapped it his eyes were unable to comprehend the sight of the finger within. His mouth falling open in a sudden gasp, he dropped the parcel onto the floor. 'Melissa?' he croaked in utter disbelief. His heart raced as he tried to convince himself it wasn't real. Bending down, he examined the object. It was rubber. It had to be. Bluish in tone, it looked like a finger and emitted a ghastly smell. But it was a joke; any minute now someone would jump out on him and…

But then he saw it. The bone encased in skin, which told him it was all too real. Forcing himself to pick it up, a whimper escaped his lips. The nail varnish was pillar-box red, and the skin carried a faint white line where the wedding ring should have been. He could feel the blood drain from his face as the implications became clear. Dropping the finger back into the envelope, Phillip fumbled for his phone.

CHAPTER TWO

Scrolling through the updated list of incidents, Detective Ruby Preston tried to ignore her craving for a cigarette. Her inability to focus on her paperwork was the result of her conversation with her boss, DI Downes, just minutes before. The meeting was brief and intended to motivate but, for her, it failed to reach the desired effect. She was wasted as a sergeant according to her boss, and should be climbing the ranks of inspector by now. He would even give her a personal endorsement, on the proviso she kept her nose clean. It made her stomach clench to think about it. Becoming an inspector was something she had once hoped for in her career, but she had given up any designs on promotion now. The higher the rank, the bigger the fallout if her relationship with Nathan Crosby was discovered. Dating a known criminal was career suicide at the very least.

Her eyes fell on the droplets of rain still clinging to the outside of her office window. Spring was yet to make an appearance, and the dark and gloomy day had cast a shadow on her thoughts, as her life choices loomed up to greet her. She had opened her heart to a man who was known to the police for all the wrong reasons. But they were a family now, her, Nathan, and now Cathy. At the age of twenty, she had found them. Being traced by their daughter years after they gave her up for adoption had come as a shock to them both. They were still taking tentative steps, but Ruby could see a future for them all, if she could persuade Nathan to leave his old life behind. Pushing up her reading glasses, she returned her attention to the screen. Dare she hope that her job and her personal life could go hand in hand? She reined in her drifting thoughts. Right now, she needed to get to grips with the outstanding administrative tasks involved in supervising her team. Just as she prepared to switch back to the annual leave requests clogging her inbox, an incident caught her eye. She focused on the details updating live before her. Paperwork could wait.

There were many cases on the go within the Shoreditch Serious Crime Unit, all being dealt with by competent officers on her team. Each incident did not require her personal appearance at the scene. As sergeant, it was simply her job to oversee the team. Her superior, DI Downes, was on call Senior Investigating Officer this weekend. Ruby sighed. She should stay in her office, supervise proceedings as her officers visited the scene. But there was no way she could resist the lure of a high-profile kidnapping on her patch. She rose from her seat, pocketing the car keys from the hook on the wall.

'Have you seen the?—' Downes said, almost bumping into her as he exited his office. He pulled on his tweed jacket, quickly finger combing his hair. The pressures of the job had gifted him some extra grey hairs as well as some sleepless nights.

'I'm all over it, boss,' Ruby interrupted, not one to waste time. After updating control with their attendance, she had furnished her team with enough tasks to get the cogs of the investigation turning. Kidnappings were relatively rare these days, but Phillip Sherman was a prominent figure in the media. With no ransom note issued, Ruby was keeping an open mind. It was down to the call taker to decide how to classify the incident when it came in, and her team would listen to the recording to glean some extra clues. Phillip Sherman was known for his robust treatment of politicians while presenting his half hour nightly slot, *The Sherman Show*. It trended on social media with unfailing regularity and others had tried but failed to emulate his success. His wife, Melissa Sherman, was half his age and far more attractive. Having tried to break into acting, she appeared in a couple of low budget films before bagging herself a wealthy husband instead. DI Jack Downes filled Ruby in on all of these details as they sped to the scene.

When she woke up that morning, she had not expected to find herself in the company of a BBC celebrity, but at least she looked presentable. Ruby's new black suit offered a professional appearance, even if her personal life didn't. She'd even managed to pin her long dark hair into a bun. 'How come you know so much about Sherman?' Ruby threw her boss a sideways glance.

'An auld fella like me has to watch something of an evening. I'm not out dancing every night like you,' Downes quipped.

'Pfft,' Ruby said, 'my clubbing days are over.' Despite the fact she was almost thirty-nine, that wasn't strictly true. 'Try not to fan girl him too much. No Instagram selfies.' Ruby chuckled, knowing she may as well be speaking a different language as far as her boss was concerned.

As she weaved through traffic, her brain processed the information as it was relayed through her earpiece.

'Slow down, woman, this isn't a blue light run,' Downes chastised. 'Uniform's with him, he's not going anywhere.'

'And a speeding ticket won't help my chance of promotion, will it?' Ruby's lip arched in a smile.

CHAPTER THREE

Like all of the properties on that road, Phillip Sherman's house was opulence in its purest form. 'Here, put these on,' DI Downes said, handing her a pair of forensic overshoes that he had taken from the back of the car.

'Cheers,' Ruby replied, bending to slip them over her heels. They crossed the expensive marble flooring, wasting no time in getting to work.

'I'll lead, you listen,' DI Downes said, heading towards the open living room door. Their voices echoed upwards to the high ceilings as they spoke, and Ruby paused to take in the decorative embellishments lining the walls. From oil paintings to small marble statues, the property seemed more like a museum of fine art than somebody's home. The update from control had given her little to go on. From what she could see, they were dealing with a severed finger and nothing else.

For once, CSI had beaten her to the scene. The head of the team, aptly nicknamed Bones, was leaving just as Ruby walked in. His long black dreadlocks were tucked up in an elastic band, his large frame encased in a white forensics all-in-one.

'No time to talk, I need to get this back to the lab,' he replied, in response to Ruby's request for a catch-up. The finger was now in an evidence bag, soon to be booked in. After crime scene officers conducted their initial examination, it would be frozen to prevent further degradation. The parcel would be tested for fingerprints, fibres and residues, but given it had come through the Royal Mail system, Ruby did not hold out much hope.

'Just your initial thoughts,' Ruby said, keeping her voice low.

Bones checked for an audience before taking her to one side. 'I can't give you much at this stage. We have a very clean cut of the proximal phalanx – that's the bottom segment of the bone on the ring finger to you. Either the victim was dead, unconscious, or tightly restrained when the amputation was carried out. According to the postmark, it happened at least three days ago. The envelope is lined with plastic bubble wrap. There's no note.' Pushing up the sleeve of his paper suit, he checked his watch. 'Time waits for no man. Katie's about if you need to talk to her. She and the team will give the place the usual going over.'

Ruby thanked him before joining her DI in the lounge. She cast her eyes over Phillip Sherman, who was sipping from a crystal tumbler, his skin tone a pallid grey hue. His suit jacket discarded on the sofa, he sat with his legs spread wide, and his shirtsleeves rolled up his arms. A tall man of considerable bulk, he appeared fiercer in the flesh than on TV. Ruby reminded herself that people reacted in different ways. She waited until Downes had finished speaking before introducing herself, but Sherman barely looked her way.

'What makes you think this was a kidnapping?' Ruby asked.

'What else would it be, given my status in the media?' Phillip snapped, before downing the last of his drink. 'It's obvious they're after money. I just hope I've done the right thing by calling, instead of waiting for a ransom letter to come.'

'If they didn't want you to report the crime they would have been in touch by now. Have you checked your emails, texts, social media, post?' Downes's Northern Irish accent touched his words in an upward inflexion.

'No,' Phillip said, in a more respectful tone. 'But I left a pile of envelopes on the bedroom dressing table when I came in.'

After checking through his post and logging onto his emails, it seemed that whoever had sent the finger was in no hurry to get in touch.

'You mentioned you spoke to your wife three days ago,' Downes said. 'Any arguments? Anything that might cause her to leave without telling you where she's going?'

Phillip pursed his lips as if mulling it over. 'We had a minor tiff. It was nothing serious, just a petty disagreement over a credit card bill. She hung up on me after I gave her a telling off.' A frown crossed his face. 'We're meant to appear at an awards party next month. What's she going to look like now without a finger? It's repulsive, that's what it is.'

'Was this a common occurrence? Your arguments, I mean,' Ruby interjected. She had taken an instant dislike to him. No amount of gold cards would make her want to live with such a man.

Downes met her gaze, passing unspoken words. He was telling her to leave this to him. It was uncanny how they could communicate with each other through a single look. When attending scenes with members of the public, many of their exchanges were silent. They had been working together for years – long enough to communicate in such a way.

Sherman bristled. 'I don't see how it's any business of yours. It's obvious that Melissa couldn't have done this to herself. You should be out there looking for the person responsible instead of quizzing me.'

Ruby almost snorted at his presumption that he was exempt as a suspect.

Downes went on to explain their next steps and how they would progress with a search. 'It's important we gather some background knowledge of your home life. But rest assured, we have our best officers on the case.' His smooth, reassuring tone seemed to do the trick as Sherman's shoulders dropped half an inch.

Ruby smiled inwardly as she observed the conversation. It was her power that was winding this man up. He liked his women subservient, submissive. The total opposite of her.

'We haven't been married that long, just three years,' Sherman said. 'Melissa's spending was out of control. I had to establish some ground rules. She had the house, the car, she wanted for nothing.'

Except for your respect, Ruby thought, swallowing back her disgust.

'How much did she spend?' Downes said.

Sherman's lips visibly tightened before volunteering the information. 'Six thousand pounds – in one day. I don't see why you're making such a big deal out of this when you should be concentrating on where she's gone.'

'We'll have to seize her phone,' Ruby said, 'it may provide clues as to her whereabouts. Does she have a computer?'

'No, she's not into technology,' Phillip said. 'Her phone is upstairs.'

Ruby gave a slow nod. 'It's procedure to search the premises. Are you happy for officers to do so now?'

Phillip sighed. 'Very well, if you must. But I don't want any leaks to the press.'

Taking a deep breath, Ruby opened her mouth to speak but was quickly interrupted by Downes.

'My team are making enquiries as we speak. It's important you contact us if you receive any outside communications. Do you have any other postal or electronic addresses: work? Private?'

Sherman stretched to place his empty glass on the coffee table before him. 'Work, of course, but why send a random note there after posting a finger to my home? It makes no sense.'

'Perhaps not to us,' Ruby said, 'but I'd advise you check your work mail as a matter of urgency.'

'The Fields of Athenry' blasted out from Downes's pocket as his work phone burst into life. After mumbling his excuses, he departed the room, but not before shooting Ruby a warning look. Ruby would have felt mildly insulted, had she not known him so well.

'Is there anyone that may hold a grudge against you or your wife?'

'I thought I made my position clear, officer.' Phillip looked down his nose at her. 'Do you know who I am?'

'It's Sergeant Preston, and yes, I'm aware,' Ruby replied, curtly.

'Well, then you would know that my wife and I are not in the habit of mixing with the criminal element. I interview politicians. In fact, the last person I grilled was our very own prime minister. Are you suggesting our fine leader kidnapped my wife and chopped her finger off?'

'Of course not,' Ruby said. 'But I don't understand why you're so defensive. That is unless you've something to hide?'

'Why, I've never been so insulted…' Phillip said, his mouth gaping open as DI Downes walked back into the room. 'Who is your supervisor? I want to make a complaint.'

'I am,' Downes replied. 'Thank you for your time, Mr Sherman. I've just spoken to the family liaison officer, DC Ian Rutherford, who's on his way. In the meantime, I'll leave you in the capable hands of the uniformed officers. They'll take a formal statement before carrying out a quick search of the premises and making some local enquiries.' Plucking a business card from his back pocket, Downes passed it over. 'Here's my details, we'll be in touch in due course.'

Downes exercised less control in the car on the way to the station. 'Jesus, Ruby, why do you have to get people's back up all the time? The man's wife has gone missing. Is that any way to behave?'

'So he says,' Ruby replied. 'Did you see the way he looked at me? Sexist, misogynistic pig.'

The corners of Downes's eyes creased in mild amusement. 'Sexist or not he's still a victim… unless you think otherwise.'

'I'm not buying that Melissa didn't use a computer. Everyone has access to technology these days. Given her profession, she's bound to be active on social media at the very least.'

'Perhaps if I didn't have to pull you out of there to swerve a complaint, we could have asked him.'

Ruby braked hard as the traffic lights blared red. 'Perhaps if he weren't such a wanker his wife wouldn't have left.'

'Is that what you're thinking now?' Downes said, pressing his hand against the dashboard of the car as they came to a sudden halt.

'I'm just saying, is that finger really hers? Maybe that six grand spend was a pay-off for some elaborate fake kidnap attempt.'

'And what happens when he makes the payment?' Downes said, sighing heavily.

'She disappears with the cash. Reinvents herself. What has she got to hang around for? A failing career, a husband who sees her as nothing but a trophy wife. It's worth considering, don't you think?'

'Yes, except that finger was posted days ago. Why hasn't contact been made?'

'Well that,' Ruby said, pressing her foot on the accelerator as the light turned green, 'is what I intend to find out.'

CHAPTER FOUR

The team of detectives worked efficiently in Ruby's absence. Half a dozen of them were so absorbed in their computer screens and phone calls that they did not notice her walk in. The eggy smell of the last sandwich round still lingered in the air, and Ruby cast her eyes over the stained cups and mugs littering each desk. Housekeeping would have to wait. They had more important things on their minds.

'Any updates?' she asked as DI Downes strode past to his office. Having fought for ownership of the case, he was now preparing for the briefing that would soon be underway. A high-profile case such as Phillip Sherman's was a draw for officers wishing to make a name for themselves, but Downes knew from experience that it also had the potential to go horribly wrong.

DC Owen Ludgrove, more often known as 'Luddy', hung up the phone, his eyes alight. He had a boyish charm that came with an enthusiasm rarely present in his job-worn colleagues. A good-looking lad with short dark wavy hair, he still lived at home with his mum. 'That was DC Rutherford,' he said. 'He's driven Phillip Sherman to the television studio and checked his post.'

'Don't tell me the ransom note was delivered to his workplace?' Ruby said, trying to make sense of it all.

Luddy shook his head. 'No, but three separate photos were sent to his work address. Rutherford said Sherman near enough lost his head when he saw them. The victim in the images is gagged and bound – she looks dead, or close to it.'

'Where are they? I need to see them,' Ruby said, every muscle in her body tensing. She felt a shift in the air as the sense of urgency ramped up a notch.

'He's uploaded them to the system and pinged them over,' Luddy replied.

'In that case, brace yourselves,' she said to anyone who was listening. 'Looks like we're in for a long day.'

Thanks to technology, Ruby did not need to wait for hard copies of the photos to reach her. Within minutes, she was in her office, accessing her emails with a whole lot more fervour than she had that morning. The computer software dinged as the attachment came through. It was marked 'restricted access': available only to her eyes and a handful of senior officers on the case.

'Have you seen the photos?' DI Downes said, sliding in behind her. He seemed to spend more time in her office than he did his own, but Ruby didn't mind because their friendship extended beyond work. A tall man, with a kind face, Downes's presence was usually reassuring. She did not want to think about what she would do when he retired. Deep down, she knew he was priming her for his job. She pushed the thoughts aside, clicking on the first attachment. He was only in his fifties. Retirement wouldn't be for years yet. Who knows where she might be by then?

'Just getting them up now,' she said, knowing he was waiting for her thoughts. Ruby clicked onto the attachment saved as 'IR01' – the exhibit number that comprised the initials and order of the officer who saved them. She instantly recognised the woman in the picture as Melissa Sherman. Young and beautiful, with wavy blonde curls, she was dressed in black sequins; only her top half was visible due to the camera being in close proximity when the photo was taken. The presence of her hands suggested this wasn't a selfie, but the person taking the photo had backed away, with nothing but a glimpse of white shirt as they craned their head out of shot. A slight sheen of sweat on her brow, she appeared happy and relaxed.

'The second one's pretty grim,' Downes said, evidently impatient to move on.

'Hang on,' Ruby said, enlarging the first photo for a better view. 'Look at her pupils. They're like saucers.' It was true. They both knew that meant she was on drugs of some sort. Ruby scanned the edges of the photo. 'Looks like she's standing near a four-poster bed. I can't see too many people having one of those in their bedrooms, although they are in some hotels.'

Minimising the photo she moved on to the next offering. She would return to it later, and there would be many more eyes analysing the image today. She clicked on the second picture, 'IR02', which offered a far more disturbing scene. Ruby stiffened at the sight. Gone was the happy, carefree expression from before. Her eyes wide with fear, Melissa's nostrils flared as she appeared desperate for breath. A white scarf gagging her mouth, she lay on her side on the bed, her hands tied before her, her knees and ankles bound. 'God,' Ruby exhaled, unable to tear her eyes away. 'Her fingers are all there, and the photographer doesn't seem to care about us seeing the room.'

She enlarged the picture, scanning every area for clues. 'It's definitely a hotel room, probably not too far from where she lives, I bet.' She peered at the small round table graced with two chairs either side. A bucket of champagne lay placed next to two empty flutes. Deep emerald floor-length curtains framed the sash window that offered up a view of a building across the road. 'We should be able to get a trace on this.'

'The team are working on it now,' Downes said, 'but judging by the next photo, we may be too late.'

An invasion of thoughts galloping into her mind, Ruby clicked on the third image. Steeling herself, she dared not blink as it came into view. Melissa's eyes were open but devoid of life as she sat, her back against the headboard, her legs stretched out in front of her on the bed. Deep welts marked the skin on her throat, but Ruby's gaze was on the placard resting against the young woman's chest. Daubed in red the word 'SLUT' was emblazoned across the board.

'That wasn't written in marker, was it?' she said, horrified as she caught sight of Melissa's severed finger.

The room fell silent as the apparent loss of life brought a temporary pause. They should be used to it by now, having dealt with murders with sickening regularity, but the photos before her displayed a sequence of terror planned from the depths of a very dark mind.

'It's blood all right,' Downes said, 'and I very much doubt this young lass is still alive.'

Ruby nodded, summoning her professionalism to the forefront of her mind. 'OK, so there's no ransom demand that we know of. Domestic murder maybe? Melissa's been playing away, and her lover doesn't take kindly to being dumped? The finger, the photos, very much directed towards her husband, don't you think? Although…'

'Yes?' Downes said, resting on the swivel chair beside her. It creaked beneath his weight as he leant back and stretched his legs. He reminded Ruby of a big old tomcat. The world could be in flames around him, but he was taking it in his stride.

'Seems like an awful lot of trouble to go to, risking your neck like that,' Ruby mused. 'She must have been mixing in some dark circles to take up with someone like this. Maybe she was bored with her home life? She's young, she wanted to experiment, maybe meet someone different?'

'You're getting there,' Downes said.

'Do you know something I don't?' Ruby tilted her head to one side as she took in his knowing expression.

'I could be way off the mark here,' Downes replied, 'but I've seen something like this before. A case centred around infidelity. An illicit meeting that ends in murder, with the ring finger being sent to the other half.'

Ruby raised an eyebrow. 'Go on.'

'The killer takes a series of three photos. One before the crime, one during, and one after, usually a day apart. See those welts on her neck?'

'Yes,' Ruby said, 'strangulation marks?'

'Rope burns. In the case I dealt with, the killer hog-tied his victims, stretching the rope from their ankles to their necks. He pulled until they fell unconscious, but not before he'd had his fun. He'd pose them, play with them, and do all kinds of sick things before amputating their ring fingers. Then he'd pop it in the post to their loved ones before finishing them off.' Only a man of Downes's experience could describe such a scene as if he were talking about a programme on TV.

'God yes, I remember that case,' Ruby said, gathering her thoughts as she tapped her chin with her index finger. 'He's still in prison, isn't he? What did they call him?…'

'The Lonely Hearts Killer,' Downes said, his expression grim. 'He found his victims through newspaper dating ads. Listen, you need to keep the details of this crime close to your chest. A lot of that previous case was kept under wraps. If we do have a copycat, the scene will tell us how much they know.'

'This could still be a domestic murder, maybe borne out of revenge?'

'Doubtful,' Downes said. 'Too much of this seems similar. You'll find the hotel soon enough. Like I said, I'm betting this poor wee lass is dead. The biggest clue lies in if the wedding ring is found.'

Ruby frowned as she tried to remember details of the case from over ten years before. As a detective constable, it wasn't hers to access so her knowledge was gleaned only from newspaper and TV reports. 'Wedding ring?'

'The killer kept them as trophies. That little nugget of information was held back from the press. So if you don't find a wedding ring, we may have a serial killer on our hands.'

CHAPTER FIVE

Matthew chewed his nails as he waited for someone to answer. It was the first time in ages he'd had the place to himself and this phone call was long overdue. Why weren't they picking up? By the end of the fourth ring, he had bitten into his thumbnail and almost drawn blood.

'Hello, Sanity Line. I'm Laura. Would you like to tell me your name?' The voice was young and chirpy, irritating him even more.

'Matthew,' he snapped. 'Call me Matthew.'

'Matthew it is,' Laura said, apparently unaffected by his outburst. 'How are you feeling today?'

'I'm not suicidal, before you ask. Because you have to ask, don't you? You have to work that into every call. So here I am, getting it out of the way.' His words were delivered like a spray of bullets, without pause for breath. He reminded himself to calm down. This was about him. He was the one in control.

'We're here to listen,' Laura said. 'What's troubling you?'

'Relationships,' he said drily. 'The cause of so much pain.' Saying the words aloud reignited his anger. On days like these, his body trembled with the force of his vexation. He sloped into the kitchen, hoping a cup of coffee would help him calm down.

'Has your other half got a name?' Laura said inquisitively.

'I can think of a few.' He slammed his cup against the counter, waiting for the kettle to boil. Cocking his head to one side, another thought pecked his brain. Was she judging him? Wondering how many shades of messed up he was? 'Do you think it's odd, me ringing you, a stranger, about my personal relationships?'

'Not at all,' Laura said, the hint of an Essex accent on her lips. 'Some people find it hard to talk face-to-face.'

Matthew liked the sound of Laura. As she spoke about the benefit of talking to strangers, he felt his anger subside. She seemed nice. Pleasant. Someone who would never ordinarily spend time with him.

'I prefer the telephone too, more anonymity.' He fell silent as he carried his mug to the kitchen table and took a seat. A friendly ear created a pressure valve on the worst of days. If he closed his eyes, he could pretend that Laura was sitting across from him and he was having coffee with a friend. In these snatched moments he almost felt normal. He imagined Laura gently smiling as she asked him what was on his mind. He told her it was not what, but who. 'I met this woman online. Melissa. She was pretty, bubbly, sex on legs.' Matthew sighed, feeling the weight of the responsibility bear down. 'The thing is, she was married. Yet she met me for sex, even had the cheek to take off her wedding ring in front of me in the hotel room.'

'And that bothers you,' Laura said. It was more of a statement than a question.

'You could say that. But I found a way of making her see the error of her ways,' Matthew replied, his tone even. 'I know that some people would view my behaviour as… inappropriate. But I didn't drag her there. She made the decision to come, not me.'

Laura's voice lowered, almost conspiratorial in its tone. 'When you say inappropriate…'

Matthew imagined Laura raising her eyebrows as she deciphered the meaning of his words. He drew an intake of breath. 'Oh, nothing for you to worry about. Nothing bad.' He leaned on his elbow, basking in the warmth of Laura's attention. 'I like you. Are you new? Usually the call takers don't say a lot.'

'Technically we offer a listening service. We can't tell you what to do. Usually you'll find you hold the answers within,' Laura replied.

'It's a back and forth struggle in my mind,' Matthew said. 'Take Melissa, for instance. She was dying to jump into bed with me, a virtual stranger. Then later she went all funny on me, like I was the one in the wrong. I knew I should walk away, leave her to make her own mistakes…' He kneaded his shoulder. 'But she deserved to be punished. All of them do.'

'Have you told her how you feel?' Laura said, concern etching her words. 'When you say punished—'

'Our feelings extend way beyond words,' Matthew interrupted, enjoying the poetry of his phrase. 'We've bonded.' Entombed by his memories he recalled their last meeting. A scene that he could not relay aloud.

'Hello? Are you there?' Laura said, after too much silence had passed between them.

Matthew blinked, returning his focus to the call. 'Sorry. I was miles away. Every time I think about Melissa I feel like I'm in a dream.'

'Why do you think that is?'

'Maybe I'm crazy,' Matthew said calmly. 'But I'm determined to keep going with this. People like her… they need to be stopped.'

'I'm sorry, but I don't understand. You've spoken about punishing Melissa, can you elaborate?' Laura said, concern bringing an edge to her words.

'It's nothing more than she deserved.' Matthew shrugged, even though she could not see him. 'You know, when we met, she was much prettier than I imagined. Someone like me could never bed a stunner like that. I was tempted. A part of me wanted to forget my plans and have one night together. But then I saw her slipping off her wedding ring and I went cold inside. I told her to leave it on. You can't walk away from commitment like that. She was wrong to try.'

'What did you do?' Laura said, trying to draw out the answers.

'I told you, I taught her a lesson,' Matthew replied. 'Let her husband know what a slut he's married to.' Matthew tried to imagine the call taker's expression. Was she horrified? Shocked? Or maybe she was bored, having heard it all before.

Laura paused for breath, her exhalation ruffling the phone line. Matthew smiled. She had obviously thought that he had told Melissa's husband and left it at that. He swallowed back the chuckle that was rising in his throat.

'I'm not here to judge,' Laura said. But her words were constrained, and he heard her throat click as she swallowed.

Matthew felt a small surge of power. It was good to be the one in control.

'I like you,' he repeated, his smile carrying on his words. 'That's why I feel like I can tell you anything. I hope I get you the next time I call. I feel much better now.'

'Are you going to be OK?' was all Laura seemed able to think of to say.

'Yes,' Matthew whispered, his heart beating harder at the thought of the next delicious step of his plan.

CHAPTER SIX

It took less than an hour to find the hotel room. Briefing had been short due to the urgency of the case, and it had been a quick-fire round of everyone sharing what they had come up with so far. An online image search had produced three hotels in London with similar rooms housing four-poster beds and Ruby had managed to persuade Downes to allow her to drive him to the scene. The Grove appeared the stateliest of all the hotels she had visited. It was certainly a turn up from most of the crime scenes in which Ruby spent her time. To say the owner was disconcerted by the presence of a team of police officers would have been the understatement of the year. A tall reedy man, he gesticulated wildly at the officers invading the foyer of his luxury hotel.

'Who's in charge here? I need to speak to your commanding officer!' His eyes practically bulged as they searched out the plain clothes detectives in the room.

'That would be DI Ruby Preston,' Downes said with a grin. Sweeping past, he followed the trail of crime scene officers making their way to Room 114. But they were too late; officers on scene had already updated that a body had been found and declared void of life.

You sod, Ruby thought, at the sudden change of rank. It was not the first time Downes had shifted the responsibility and left her to deal with an irate hotelier.

'It's Detective Sergeant Preston,' she corrected, delivering her most patient expression. Dressed in an expensive black suit, the manager's gold-plated lapel gave his name as Mr Dines. A flowery fragrance rose when he moved, quite a feminine scent for a man. 'Given the seriousness of the crime, the disturbance can't be helped,' Ruby said. 'We're as keen as you to keep this out of the press, so I recommend you speak to your staff about this information going no further.'

'Then why do you have to march through my hotel in broad daylight? Can't you come in the back entrance?' he said, his head swivelling left and right as hotel guests craned their necks in their direction. As far as Ruby could see, he was the one stirring up attention.

'We'll bear it in mind,' she said tersely, her thoughts focused on catching her suspect rather than the hotel's reputation. 'Now if you excuse me, the quicker we can process the crime scene, the quicker we'll be out of your hair. My officers will need to speak to you about CCTV. We'll need everything you've got over the last couple of weeks.'

'We don't have CCTV,' Mr Dines sniffed, looking none too happy at being given the brush-off.

Ruby frowned. 'I'm sorry, what did you say?' she asked, as the chatter of nearby onlookers drowned his words. Surely she had not heard right? He must have CCTV.

'I said we don't have it. Our hotel is renowned for its discretion. Many of our clients spend endless hours in the limelight. They come here to get away from all that.'

They come to get their leg over more like, Ruby thought, sighing heavily at the hurdle being placed before her. 'We'll still need to speak to staff, see your duty roster for the last two weeks. My officers will be in touch with a list of enquiries.'

By the time she found the correct floor, Crime Scene Officers were taking measurements, working out angles, and instructing nobody enter the room until they were done.

Downes met Ruby on the landing, which had been shut off to the general public for now. A fingertip search of the vicinity would take place, but in such a public space, the value of any evidence gained would be significantly diminished.

'I've spoken to DCI Worrow,' Downes said, as Ruby zipped up her paper gown. 'She wants us to run this as a standalone for now, but we'll keep an open mind. This scene is too much like the Lonely Hearts Killer not to be connected.'

'I take it no wedding ring has been found?' Ruby said, annoyed her hold up with the manager had delayed her from getting inside the room. She knew how cagey Bones could be when it came to his crime scenes, and the most annoying thing was, he was right. Every officer's attendance disrupted the scene, potentially leaving forensic evidence as well as taking it away. Locard's exchanged principal was drummed into officers from their first day of training. With a murder as brutal as this, investigators had to make do with photos, video footage and their DI's vivid description. Not that Ruby needed it. She could not get the photographs of Melissa out of her mind. An unsolved crime scratched like an itch beneath her skin. Despite her training, she could not stay away.

Tentatively she entered the room, immediately greeted by the sweet stench of spilt blood.

'What part of no entry didn't you understand?' The face mask Bones was wearing failed to disguise the annoyance in his muffled voice.

Ruby shrugged, her forensics suit rustling as she moved. 'Give me two minutes. You won't even know I'm here.' She felt a chill descend as she took another step in. With the curtains closed and the air con on the coolest setting, the killer had done his best to preserve the body inside.

'Huh,' Bones grunted, sounding unconvinced. 'Don't touch anything, don't move anything; in fact, don't breathe.'

'And I won't stare for more than three seconds in case it affects the scene,' she said, her voice trailing away as she laid eyes on the four-poster bed.

The victim's black diamanté dress sparkled under the flash of the investigator's camera as her image was captured with careful precision. Ruby was grateful she had not yet eaten as another horrific image slotted itself into her memory bank. She swallowed, her breath momentarily stilling as she told herself to get a grip. Yet, she could not help but feel a sliver of the victim's pain. Legs splayed, Melissa's body was posed with her back against the headboard, her head lolling downwards, as if trying to read the cardboard sign propped up on her lap. Her bloodshot eyes were barely recognisable to those so full of life in the first photo that had been sent. Her tongue, now blue and engorged, protruded from between her lips, a small trickle of blood crusted over from when she had bitten down in her last moments of life. Red and jagged, deep welts were embedded in her neck from the rope that most likely ended her life. Ruby's eyes fell on the congealed puddles of blood that stained the plum satin bedcover and, on her left hand, she noticed the clean cut which had taken place just above the knucklebone. To go through all that and face the pain of an amputation was too much to comprehend. The air felt dense with the aftermath of such violence, and Ruby turned her head away. She headed for the bathroom that shone brightly from the spotlights overhead.

'Talk about déjà vu,' Downes said, his voice thick with emotion as he stood behind her. 'Everything's just like before. They won't find any wedding ring in there. What's the betting the fecker's wearing it on a chain around his neck?'

'So what do we do?' Ruby said. 'Open the collar of everyone in the hotel?'

'We go back to the source. Find out who Mason Gatley's been talking to. Because whoever's done this knows far too much.' He was talking about the Lonely Hearts Killer – the man who brutally murdered a string of women over ten years before.

'Did your original victim leave her knickers on the bathroom floor?' Ruby said, nodding towards the lacy black thong lodged next to the silver pedal bin.

Downes raised an eyebrow. 'Not that I recall, but I need to refamiliarise myself with this case. We have to be careful. I don't want this getting out to the press. If this is a copycat killer, he'll be feeding off the attention, so we need a contingency plan if he starts to leak the information himself. We'll need some extra resources. I'll put a call in, see if any can be spared.'

Ruby nodded in agreement. 'I'll gather the troops, see what they've got so far.' Taking one last look at the scene, they both headed for the door.

CHAPTER SEVEN

Twirling before the full-length mirror, Cheryl tried on her third outfit that day. Her breath quickened at the thoughts of what lay ahead. Out of all the profiles she had viewed on the *Debauchery* site, Matthew's was the most sexually adventurous. You could spot the fakes a mile off, the ones who were only interested in what they could get. But with Matthew, it was about what he could do for you. He didn't brag about good looks or extraordinary abs like most of the men featured there. He claimed to be a normal guy who blended with the crowd. But that suited her. She would have been too intimidated by anything more. One night was all he promised, and his lists of requests were full. As a flutter rose up inside her, she knew the boy-next-door type suited her just fine, even though her girl-next-door years were well behind her. At fifty-five, life was slipping by, and the looks she worked so hard to maintain were fading. Unfazed by the age difference, Matthew had promised a night she would never forget. To step back into a time when she wasn't somebody's mother, somebody's friend… somebody's wife.

The light chime of her doorbell broke into her thoughts. She cursed softly as her eyes lit on her Gucci watch and realised what time it was. Her best friend was typically early, no doubt unable to wait another second to hear all the juicy details of her future date. Slipping off the black backless dress, Cheryl placed it onto the hanger, having decided it would be her gown of choice for her date.

Quickly pulling on her capri pants and blouse she tiptoed barefooted down the stairs to answer the door.

'Hannah,' she said, composing herself.

Ten years her junior, her lifelong friend appeared as excited about her date as she was. After giving her a quick squeeze, Hannah invited herself inside, the scent of Marc Jacobs 'Decadence' trailing in her wake. An ex-model, with long blonde hair and excellent skin, Cheryl both loved and loathed her friend in equal measures. At five feet two and a size fourteen, she had spent half her life trying to emulate Hannah's glamour. She was fed up of being invisible when they walked into a wine bar together, and hearing of escapades she could only dream about. Tonight was all about her, and she was going to shine.

Hannah arranged a cushion before draping herself onto the living room sofa.

'Have you had your lips plumped?' Cheryl said, peering closer as she sat next to her friend.

'I've always had them done, darling, just got a little more filler this time. Stung like buggery but Tom adores them.'

'Which one is Tom?' Cheryl said. 'Is he the mechanic?'

'No, that's Mike. Tom's the chef. You know, the guy with the tattoos. Want me to get you up a picture?'

Cheryl snorted. 'From what I remember, not many of your pictures include faces. Besides, I don't think my ticker could take any more excitement right now.'

'I'm so excited for you too!' Hannah said, her voice dropping to a conspiratorial tone. 'Are you happy with your choice? This Matthew sounds a bit dull to me.'

'His bio is anything but.' Cheryl took a deep breath to calm her nerves. 'At least his sexual history isn't. But what about Gordon and the kids? I feel so guilty. If he knew what I was about to do…'

Hannah rolled her eyes dramatically. 'Oh, come on, are you telling me Gordon hasn't strayed during his weekends away with the lads? What about that time they went to Amsterdam? You think they went there to pick tulips?'

The Amsterdam trip was his brother's stag party, but Cheryl knew from his sheepish behaviour upon his return that Hannah was probably right. Lately his weekends away were becoming more frequent but she never had the heart to stop him. Despite everything, she still loved her husband. Working in the City was stressful; Gordon needed a release. Having never worked a day in her life, Cheryl could only imagine the pressure he was under. But these days it seemed like everyone was having fun except for her. 'You're right,' she said, with a twinkle in her eye. 'Besides, it would be a sin to waste the Brazilian.'

'You got it done!' Hannah said, a mischievous smile broadening her lips. 'Well done you!'

Cheryl clasped her friend's hand as she burst into an embarrassed giggle. 'I don't know how you do it. I've never been so mortified in all my life!'

'Sounds like Gordon's in for a treat. But not before you have your fun, eh?' Hannah said.

'You're right,' Cheryl said, feeling like a teenager again. 'It's just one night. What harm can it do?'

CHAPTER EIGHT

Another briefing brought a sense of urgency, as a second possible victim had been made known. Officers were crammed shoulder to shoulder into the airless space, both uniformed and specialist, as well as the detectives assigned to the case. DI Downes stood before the whiteboard looking restless; hands in his pockets, back out, rubbing his chin, hands in his pockets again. Ruby wondered just how much he would love a drink right now. She shuffled into the room, giving him a reassuring nod. The pressures of handling a high-profile case were making itself known. The thoughts of the suspect claiming another victim would crawl like ants beneath his skin. To Ruby, it just fuelled her determination to bring him in.

The door clicked closed as the last of the officers filed in. DI Downes's voice boomed as he clapped his hands together.

'Right! Let's get this show underway. Welcome to Operation Landslide. But first, a word of warning. It's been less than a day since the balloon has gone up and already we've had to instigate investigations into officers accessing restricted material.' He turned his head from left to right, his gaze taking in every person in the room. 'Just because this case involves a celebrity, it doesn't give officers the right to access sensitive material. Media liaison will deal with any enquiries from the press. Social media is a no no. In fact, I don't even want you on Facebook while you're investigating this case.'

The team nodded in agreement. Word had already spread in the force with regards to the investigation. Each of them left a digital footprint, and it cemented the necessity to keep their computers locked and password protected at all times. Although mobiles and computers were usually fiercely guarded, it was a common prank for declarations of love to be sent from their email address to their senior officers on the one occasion they forgot. It had been a favourite trick of DC Ash Baker's when he was around. Ruby sighed. His absence was sorely felt. One of the more popular members of the team, she wished he was still with them. His replacement could not be any more different. DC Richard Moss was early forties, wore sensible clothes, and was as boring as hell. But what he lacked for in personality he made up for in knowledge and Ruby was glad to have some stability in the team.

DC Owen Ludgrove was at the forefront, bringing them up to speed with his investigations to date. He'd had a haircut, his wavy black hair now trimmed in a short back and sides style. Ruby liked Luddy. He was a real asset to the team. She felt a pang of regret as she thought of the promotion opportunities that could become available to the young man so dedicated to the job. To someone who toed the line.

DCI Worrow listened intently, her black bobbed hair swaying as she gave an occasional nod of the head. Ruby pulled a pen from her own messy bun, before scribbling down the salient points. Luddy was still discussing the first victim, and the computer that was seized from her room.

'The laptop's been interrogated and we've come up with a list of websites. It seems she wasn't too bothered about deleting her Internet history, probably because she'd hidden the computer and didn't expect her husband to find it.' He held the list before him, picking out the most relevant sites. 'In the days leading up to her death, she's visited shopping websites, bought shoes and browsed Internet dating. Her last visit online was two days before she disappeared.'

'Two days before? What about the evening of her date? Could she have deleted her Internet history?' Downes said.

Luddy shook his head. 'No. The tech guys have interrogated her history and deleted files. There's no emails or private messaging either.'

'What worries me more is the thought of a copycat. One who won't be so easily stopped.' Downes's response elicited a series of mumbles around the room.

It was as if he had read Ruby's mind. She took a deep breath before airing her views. 'We need to speak to the original Lonely Hearts Killer, Mason Gatley. Find out who he's been talking to about the murders he committed.'

'It would be easier to get an audience with the fecking Pope than get in front of him,' Downes replied.

Ruby raised her eyebrows as if to say we'll see about that. She had an ace up her sleeve and contacts in the pipeline.

As Downes sped through the briefing, officers were told to extend their bail returns and cancel any annual leave. The message was clear. Their commanding officers demanded one hundred per cent commitment to this case.

CHAPTER NINE

'I wasn't expecting to see you here,' Ruby said, a smile flitting across her face as she pulled off her leather jacket and hung it on the hook on the wall. Unlike her previous abode, she loved going home to her Dalston flat, which was made all the more welcoming when Nathan dropped in. His home in Shoreditch was huge in comparison, but Ruby did not complain about the amount of time he was spending at hers.

'I had time to spare,' Nathan said, his head lowered over the bubbling pot on the hob. Dressed in black T-shirt and jeans, he looked more relaxed than she had seen him in years.

'And you're cooking too. Is it my birthday?' Standing behind him, Ruby slid her hands around his waist. She knew Nathan used cooking as therapy, a way of easing away the stresses of the day.

'Maybe, if you play your cards right,' Nathan said, turning from the pot and gently kissing her on the mouth. She could taste tomato and red wine on his lips and reluctantly allowed him to return his attention to the cooking pot.

'It's a bit late for pasta, mind,' she said, checking her watch. It was eleven o'clock, but she was used to eating at all hours of the day and night.

'Well somebody's got to look after you,' he said drily.

'Have you heard from Cathy today?' Ruby said. Her daughter was never far from her thoughts. It had been a shock when Cathy had found them. At the time, giving her up for adoption seemed like the right thing to do. She and Nathan were just teenagers back then. But it had broken Ruby's heart to learn that Cathy had not found the loving family Ruby had dreamed of. Things had been strained when she came back into their lives, but slowly the gap between them had narrowed.

'I've been thinking,' Ruby said. 'Maybe she should live with me. I don't like her being at your mum's. You never know who's going to turn up, and the police are no stranger to her door.'

'The place is like Fort Knox,' Nathan said, in a steady and reassuring tone. 'You don't have to worry on that score.'

'But I do,' Ruby said imploringly. 'Every time something nasty comes in I think about her and wonder if she's OK.'

'Ah, so that's it,' Nathan said. 'Something's rattled you at work.'

Normally Ruby didn't reveal too much about her job, given they were working on different sides of the law. The Crosby family had been known to police for generations, evolving from racketeering and bank robberies to supplying class A drugs to the élite. She knew Nathan had made a huge effort to clean up his act since they got back together but it would be a long time before he could resist the draw of the underworld in which he was so deeply entrenched – especially if his brother Lenny had anything to do with it. It was a constant tug of war between Ruby and Lenny for Nathan's attention. For all of her efforts in keeping Nathan on the right side of the law, Lenny worked twice as hard to drag him back into the sewers. Ruby sighed, her thoughts weighing heavy on her mind. She could not hold herself responsible for Nathan, not when she had so much to do. 'Have you ever heard of the Lonely Hearts Killer? He went to prison for murdering six women. Mason Gatley was his name.'

Nathan nodded in recognition before turning to switch off the hob. 'Lenny served time with him. Why?'

Ruby grimaced behind Nathan's back at the mention of his brother's name. 'It's a murder case I'm working on. It reflects that one from ten years ago.' She watched as Nathan plated up the food. She knew he was still listening to her because the subject matter guaranteed his attention. 'It's really grim,' she said, pouring them both a glass of red wine from the bottle he had left breathing on the side. 'Our victim's ring finger was amputated when she was murdered. If that's not bad enough, the killer took three photos of her over three consecutive days, then sent the picture, along with her finger, to her husband.'

'Nice guy,' Nathan said, carrying their plates to the table. Ruby knew he had seen worst things in his time. Nothing appeared to shock him anymore.

'Yes, but my boss is reluctant to spend too much time looking into the old case. I think there's a link and it's worth exploring. It would help if I could speak to Mason Gatley.' Ruby sighed, wishing Nathan would say something.

Nodding at the food, he signalled at her to eat. People that didn't know him perceived his silence as displeasure, but Ruby knew he only spoke when he had something valuable to say.

'This is good,' she said, after tasting her first mouthful. But she was keen to continue her discussion of the case. She was about to ask her lover for a favour and knew he might not necessarily approve. 'Mason Gatley met his victims through lonely hearts adverts in newspapers. Things have moved on since then. I've no proof, but I think our current killer is working online. Probably through one of these dating apps or Internet sites. God knows there's plenty of them around.'

'Probably,' Nathan said, pausing to sip his wine. His voice was deep and sexy, his physique bearing evidence of regular sessions in his private gym. Even now, he had the ability to make her blush when he fixed his gaze on her.

Ruby swallowed another bite before carrying on. 'While we've only had one victim, that's one death too many. It's too violent and vicious and I can't see the killer stopping there. Then again, maybe they're trying to make it appear like it's a copycat to divert the attention away from them. It could be a one-off contract killing but I need to be prepared in case this leads to more.'

To Ruby, the beginning of any investigation was like finding her way around in a darkened room. Each clue, no matter how small, could provide the tiniest chink of light. But Ruby didn't want to wait for spotlights in the blackness. She wanted to illuminate the room.

Nathan patted his mouth with a napkin before leaning back in the chair. 'Why don't you just come out and ask me?'

'Ask you what?' Ruby said, trying her best to look surprised.

'Oh, come on, you never talk to me about work, much less let me in on a case. You're after something. What do you need?'

Ruby took another forkful, chewing in silence as she played him at his own game. Eventually she swallowed, clearing her palette with a sip of wine. 'I want you to persuade Mason Gatley to see me in prison.'

CHAPTER TEN

'What's this I hear about you visiting Mason Gatley?' Heavy-footed, DI Downes barged into Ruby's office, completely oblivious to the fact she was on the phone. After some late-night phone calls and a few strings pulled, it seemed the prison visit had been arranged.

'What? Oh, that,' she said, ending her call to the tech department. Having just imparted the urgency of her request, her mind was racing forward to her next task.

'Yes, that,' Downes said, brushing away what appeared to be pastry flakes from his grey striped tie. 'At what point were you going to ask my permission? If it pertains to the investigation then you have got to get clearance from me.'

'I was waiting until it was agreed,' Ruby said, feeling her hackles rise. 'To be honest, I didn't think it would happen. He hasn't had a visitor in years and it's only thanks to my… connections that he's agreeing to meet.'

Downes frowned, apparently unwilling to drop the subject. 'Don't you think you should hold off and see how we progress with the investigation? You might not need to visit this guy.'

'I won't be there long,' Ruby said. 'It may just give us the answers we need.'

Downes raised his hands in protest. He had always been a gesticulator. From stomping around the office to waving his arms as he spoke, his body worked in unison to relay his passion for the job. 'Ach! He'll only play with you. Why should he help us? He's probably basking in the attention. You'll just be a way of passing the time.'

Ruby folded her arms, reminding herself she was talking to a senior officer. She wished she could make him see the bigger picture, but he was too long in the job to start taking advice now. 'Mason Gatley won't get much out of me. I know we're stretched, but we have competent officers who are working on finding our suspect online.' She pointed in the direction of the window that offered a view of their team. 'Any one of them is capable of the tasks we've set. But I'm the only one granted an audience with Gatley. If I turn this down, I may not get another chance. So as long as I'm progressing the investigation then it can only be a good thing.'

'As long as it's worthwhile,' Downes said, on the exhale. 'Like I said. You watch yourself with that one. What about if I come along? See if he'll meet both of us?'

'You're joking me, aren't you?' Ruby said incredulously. 'You handled the investigation that put him away. Besides, it's not as if I'm meeting him down some dark alleyway. He's safely tucked away behind bars.'

Downes gave her a look to say she should know better than to think she was safe because Mason was locked up. Sometimes prison did not stop the worst of offenders, it only provided them more thinking time to orchestrate their heinous crimes from afar. Of that, they were both well aware.

As Downes rose from his seat, Ruby squeezed his arm. She knew his concerns for her went way beyond a work relationship. He was her friend, her mentor and, briefly, her lover, less than a year before. Her voice was soft and warm as she imparted some reassurance. 'Hey, no need to worry. I just want to find out what he knows about Melissa Sherman, and who he's been talking to about his past. It could be fellow prisoners, family members... even journalists for all we know.' She tilted her head to one side as she caught his gaze. 'It's got to be worth a shot, hasn't it?'

Downes shook his head. 'According to prison liaison, he hasn't had visitors in years. His post is being monitored and there's been no details of his case.'

'I don't get why you're so worried,' Ruby said, searching his face for answers. 'I've dealt with people like Mason before.'

'The thing is, you haven't,' Downes replied, finally meeting her gaze. 'Sure, you've dealt with the sort of people that give ordinary decent folk nightmares. But they're pussycats compared to Mason Gatley. He is the most evil, soulless, psychopathic bastard you could ever be unfortunate enough to meet.'

'Don't hold back, boss, why don't you say what you really feel?' But Ruby's smile died on her lips as she took in the expression on Downes's face. Were there tears building up in his eyes? Just what was going on with him? She cleared her throat. She needed to wrap up this conversation and get on with the day. 'So, I suppose I should ask you officially. Can I go?'

'Well I'm hardly gonna say no to you now, am I?' Downes said. 'Not when your boyfriend has gone to so much trouble to put you in front of harm's way.' Downes was one of the few people to know about Ruby's connection with the Crosbys. He had kept her secret, but it did not stop him voicing his disapproval when they were alone.

Ruby opened her mouth to complain but Downes raised his hand.

'Keep your phone switched on in case of developments. If anything crops up, I'll pull you out of there, and I want no arguments. Agreed?'

'Agreed,' Ruby said.

Downes nodded sharply before leaving her to her thoughts. Something was eating him, that much was clear, and from what Ruby could tell, it was personal.

CHAPTER ELEVEN

Sliding into the church pew, Matthew enjoyed the firmness of the wood against his knees in the second row. Church was the one place he could think without fear of interruption. Holding his rosary beads, he crossed his hands together, his eyes turned up to the stained-glass display. Jesus on the crucifix, blood trailing down his face, hands and feet as he gasped his last breath. Above him, the sky was grey and thunderous, a signal of what was to come. That was how Matthew had felt when he had picked up Melissa. A storm had rumbled within him for so long, his displeasure of the world fuelling what was ahead.

He bowed his head as he whispered words he had memorised from Isaiah 47:10. He felt sure they would reach her, now she had passed on to the other side. 'And thou hast trusted in thy wickedness, and hast said: There is none that seeth me. Thy wisdom, and, thy knowledge, this hath deceived thee. And thou hast said in thy heart: I am, and besides me there is no other.' Pondering on his words, his fingers crept to the necklace beneath his shirt. He could feel the outline of Melissa's wedding ring nestled on his collarbone. It still carried a tiny streak of her blood. It had hardened now, clung to the metal band that meant so little to her. She did not deserve to wear such a sacred thing. But he did because he was carrying out the Lord's work. He took comfort in the fact that there would be many more to come.

A swell of love rose up inside him as he glanced at the stained-glass depiction. Sometimes you had to do terrible things to make the world a better place. It was his duty to spread the message to every corner of the globe. The world had become a depraved pit of iniquity. He would finish what other brave souls had started and soon his message would grow. There would be others like him. Ordinary people with God in their heart. He closed his eyes, emitting a contented breath. Peace and calm replaced his tumultuous rage, but he knew that it would return. A newspaper article, something said online. His anger was a gift, a tool in his armoury to propel him forward. Anybody that tried to stop him would soon become undone. He had greater powers than the law on his side.

His phone buzzed a silent notification. He knew without looking it would be another married woman requesting his presence for the night. There were so many to choose from. He could kill every day, if circumstances allowed. But no. He would follow the template that had been laid down before him. First a blonde, then a brunette, and then someone very special indeed. He would draw them in with promises of sex-fuelled private parties that would make their head explode. Class A drugs brought a welcome cocktail for those willing to experiment. All thoughts of Melissa behind him, his mind wandered forward to tonight's date. He would check in early this time and hide the rucksack in his room. It had not been easy, carrying out his plan, but sometimes when God wanted you to grow, he made you feel uncomfortable.

He threaded the rosary beads between his fingers, pressing down on each wooden ball as he drew strength. Now his first kill was complete, things would get easier from here. A tingle of excitement shot through his body at the thought of what was to come. His passion for God's work was a thrill like no other. He would do Him justice, inflict a wrath so terrible it would carry His message to the four corners of the earth.

Pocketing his beads, he stretched his hands out either side, tilting his head back as he opened his palms wide. Searching the murky passages of his mind, he tried to imagine himself nailed to the cross. He could almost hear the sound of steel on steel, feel the nails as they drove through his flesh. He squeezed his eyes tight, picturing the crown of thorns spearing his skin, rivulets of blood running down his face. 'Use me,' he whispered, his words echoing through the church. 'Use me as a vessel for your work.' He closed his eyes tightly, waiting for a response that only he could hear.

As a side door creaked open, a priest entered, his head bowed in prayer. Matthew dropped his hands to his side, rising from his knees. He'd received his answer. He knew what he had to do.

CHAPTER TWELVE

The computer screen reflected against Ruby's reading glasses as she absorbed the information to date. Briefing had been swift, and as their investigations had failed to reap answers, DCI Worrow had given the prison visit her blessing too. Now each detail of Mason Gatley's crimes were laid bare before her as Ruby refreshed herself with details of the case. The last thing she wanted was to encounter any nasty surprises when they met. The thought made her nerves jangle deep inside. Her DI's words had spooked her. Mason Gatley was quite clearly a psychopath, with no feelings or remorse for his crimes. But she had dealt with people like him in the past. Why was Downes so nervous about this meeting? Unlike some of their previous offenders, he was safely tucked away behind bars. But as she read details of each grizzly death, she felt her flesh creep. Reluctantly, her gaze returned to the photos and the chilling speed at which the subject's features changed from happiness to undiluted horror. With coy smiles, they posed for the first photo, their eyes carrying a hint of flirtation. How Ruby wished she could go back in time and warn these women before it was too late. Pretty yet understated, they did not appear to have a wide knowledge of the outside world. From their biographies, they were bored and lonely, but cheating was not a common practice in their lives. Their first foray into the world of adultery would tragically be their last. Ruby moved onto the second lot of scanned photos, their terror clear to see. The whites of their eyes flashed before the camera, their teeth bared as they drew back their lips from the gag in an effort to scream. It filled Ruby with both horror and searing anger. Why couldn't he have left it there? He got what he wanted, terrified these poor women. Why did he have to delay the agony by killing them the next day? She nibbled on her bottom lip, chewing away the Ruby Woo red lipstick she had applied an hour before. Would an insight into Mason Gatley's mind provide answers in relation to this modern-day killer? The responsibility felt like a physical weight being placed on her shoulders. Sure, she was part of a greater team, but it would be her staring into Gatley's eyes, her face in his thoughts as he slept. Was he instructing the new killer? Was she putting herself directly in the line of fire?

She clicked through the last of the photos, snapped mercilessly after death had claimed its victims. Molly, aged just twenty-three, the top button of her blouse undone. Blood seeped into the crumpled white material as it trickled down from the wound where the rope had bitten into her throat. Her head slumped to one side, she sat against the headboard of the four-poster bed. A sign was propped against her chest, the word 'SLUT' emblazoned in jagged red letters. Just like Melissa, the ring finger of her left hand was missing with nothing but a bloodied stump in its wake. A red trail of blood had seeped into the bed linen and turned it a Merlot red.

Tina, aged fifty, was featured in the third lot of photos, and Ruby shuddered as she took in her dead-eyed stare. Another placard was propped against her, the word 'WHORE' bleeding red across its surface. On and on the photos went, each victim treated the same as the one before. Each profanity voiced the killer's thoughts as the camera clicked for his satisfaction. How they had managed to keep them out of the press during the investigation she didn't know. Perhaps it had been easier back then, without the aid of camera phones and grizzly online sites too keen to share. It made her all the more assured that whoever the killer was, they must have had eyes on these pictures, or at least know someone who could provide a vivid description capable of invoking a chilling re-enactment in the present day.

Ruby clicked, unblinking, through the remainder of the photographs, hoping the families had been spared from seeing the brutality inflicted upon their loved ones. How torn they must have felt, coming to terms with their infidelity as well as their murders. Had they gotten on with their lives? Married again? Such vile acts touched everyone involved, putting each family member through their own life sentence as they carried their loss for the rest of their days. Broken husbands, damaged children, and then the parents who had buried their young. Ruby had seen it all before, but this crime seemed to go that one step further, involving the loved ones by inflicting further pain. Why else would he send their amputated finger in the post? Is that what he got off on? The ripple effect of such monstrosities? Knowing he had stained their souls with evil so dark that it would never be removed?

She worked through the evidence, switching her focus to the officer statements and interviews that followed. Pleading guilty, Mason showed no remorse, but the families were spared the stresses of trial. She read through the file, searching for the conclusion. Mason Gatley had been caught in the act after murdering his sixth victim. Ruby's eyes flicked from left to right while she digested the text. Mason had killed just the week before, but believing he was unstoppable, was already en route to another hotel as part of his murderous spree. It was thanks to a quick-thinking officer that he was stopped at the scene. His final victim had been a decoy police officer, and she had gleaned enough information to discover his whereabouts that day. Such was the ferocity of his attacks that the blood was barely dry on his hands before he plotted his next kill. Even then, he had plenty women to choose from, and an array of letters were later found at his house.

Ruby continued to read, relieved to discover that the decoy police officer had been unharmed. Spotted by a plain clothes officer in the hotel corridor, Mason Gatley was followed as he got wind of the police and abandoned his date. The tiny red stain on the cuff of his shirtsleeve could have passed for any number of things, but it gave the observant officer enough concerns to follow the man to the roof. It was there that Mason picked up the rucksack containing the rope he had used to murder one of his victims earlier that week. So Mason was caught – all because he could not bear to leave without the precious rope that meant so much to him. Exhaling a long, slow sigh, Ruby felt a little bit better. It was easy to identify with the killer as some inhuman monster, impervious to their efforts to stop him in his tracks. But killers were people. And people made mistakes.

CHAPTER THIRTEEN

Mason Gatley used every inch of his six feet six frame as he walked into the room. Unlike many of his fellow inmates, he had not allowed the system to grind him down. His hair, now shoulder length, was slightly kinked but clean, the mousy brown streaked with wavy rivers of grey. The tip of his beard ended below his chin, but it was all lost on Ruby because she was hooked into his gaze. Gatley was not a handsome man, yet he held a presence that was hard to escape.

'Detective Sergeant Preston, I presume,' Mason said, his chair screeching against the tiled floor. There were no barriers between them in the sterile interview room, but a nearby member of staff was keeping a close eye on them both. Like several other rooms around them, the top half of the walls comprised see-through protective glass. Such transparency was welcome when dealing with a serial killer with a thirst for blood.

'Thank you for agreeing to see me,' Ruby replied in a formal tone, seeing little point in wasting time. When it came to murder cases, every second, every word, every syllable of conversation was precious. She could not help but think that some terrible fate awaited some poor soul as she sat here. She was not going to make small talk.

'I can't tell you how nice it is to have some female company.' Mason settled into his chair, voicing his thoughts in an almost theatrical manner. 'I get fan mail and pen pal requests from women all over the world, even a proposal or two. But they're just ghouls, you know? They look at me with morbid curiosity. They don't see me for who I am.'

'And I do?' Ruby finished his sentence, keen to move on.

Mason delivered a slow nod of the head, the corners of his mouth turning upwards in a smile. He seemed pleased with her, although she was yet to figure out why.

'Mason…' Ruby said, wondering if the man ever blinked. 'Is it OK if I call you by your first name?'

'Of course,' Mason replied, 'as long as I can call you Ruby.'

'Sure,' Ruby said, figuring she needed to build up rapport. 'Do you know why I'm visiting you today?'

Mason began to stroke his beard. 'You want my advice on a murder which has all the hallmarks of mine.'

Ruby did not disagree. 'I can't disclose too many details but it's similar to the murders you committed ten years ago. Do you know why anyone would want to copy you?'

'I know lots of things,' Mason said, 'and I can see you're in a great hurry to find out what. But this is a two-way deal. I don't sell my soul to just anyone.'

'What do you want from me?' Ruby asked. 'Because if you're unhappy with your living conditions I'm not sure there's much I can do.'

'I came to terms with my surroundings a long time ago,' Mason said. He pointed to his temple. 'It's what's in here that needs stimulating.'

'I'm no shrink,' Ruby said.

'I don't need you to be.' Calmly he assessed her, allowing precious seconds to pass before continuing. 'Try to imagine living in a room the size of a shoebox with no communication from the outside world. Every day is Groundhog Day, and the people you do come in contact with don't exactly provide scintillating conversation. I'm in need of a change, and you are that change.'

'I'm a police officer,' Ruby said. 'I think it's important we don't lose sight of that, don't you?'

Mason chuckled, giving her a look that said he knew better. 'From what I've heard, you've lost sight of your position more than once. I served time with Lenny, you know. Now he was an interesting sort. I don't think I've met anyone who hated the world as much as him.'

Ruby folded her arms and leaned back in her chair. 'Don't believe everything you hear. Look, as much as I'd like to chat, there's also an issue that's a matter of urgency I need to talk to you about. Do you know anything about the murder of Melissa Sherman?'

Tutting, Mason shook his head. 'Just when we were getting along so well. I'm afraid if you want information from me you're going to have to wait for it.'

Ruby set her jaw in frustration. She could almost hear a clock ticking backwards in her head. 'I don't have time. My visit is on work hours. If you can't help me then I'll go.'

Inhaling deeply through his nostrils, Mason leaned forward. 'I didn't say I couldn't help you. I only said you have to wait. You haven't asked me yet.'

'I've asked you twice,' Ruby said, her frown growing as her patience ran thin.

'No, you haven't asked me the question. The one everyone wants to know.' Mason craned his neck, his veins bulging as he whispered his words. 'Why did I kill?'

Ruby exhaled tersely, her tone flat. If such antics were meant to intimidate she was not playing along. 'Let me guess. You had a bad childhood. You were dumped by your ex. Some sad story along those lines. Life was hard. You got angry. Need I go on?'

'So you think I killed those women out of a thirst for revenge?' Mason said, leaning back in his seat.

Ruby nodded in response, having heard it all before.

Jabbing the table with his finger, Mason spoke with ill-concealed disgust. 'That's what gets me. People read the news reports, watched me in court and they made their own opinions, just like you. But they're wrong. You want to know why I did it?'

Ruby inhaled a deep breath, refusing to leave his gaze. 'Enlighten me.'

A salacious smile widened Mason's face. 'Because I enjoyed it, of course.'

Ruby fought to keep her expression neutral. She felt the heat of his glare and it made her squirm in her chair. She uncrossed her legs, making preparations to go. She would not allow pond scum like Mason Gatley to make a chink in the defence of the wall she had carefully built around her. 'This visit isn't about you, it's about your opportunity to do something good in your life. You said you know something. I've been here ten minutes and I'm no further on. So how about you stop wasting my time and give me something to go on?'

'You've got guts. I like that,' Mason said. 'Have you ever heard of the butterfly effect?'

'Sure. It's cause and effect. A metaphor on how the smallest natural causes – such as the beating wings of a butterfly can have a profound effect.'

'Eloquently put. Think of me as the butterfly. They may have plucked my wings but I'm still able to whip up a storm.'

'So you're saying that you've orchestrated these murders?' Ruby said, her eyebrow involuntarily arching.

'Inadvertently. Someone has been inspired by my acts, wouldn't you say?'

'I can't disagree with you there,' Ruby said. 'The question is, who?'

Mason threaded his fingers together and leaned forward on his hands. 'Will you come back to visit me?'

'Are you saying I'll need to?'

Mason bared his teeth in a smile. 'I'd like you to. I'll tell you what, how about I give you something to go on, at least until our next visit?'

'Go ahead,' Ruby said.

'Examine the details of my past kills with a fine-tooth comb. Compare what's been said to the press, and what the cops kept back. Then examine the recent murder and see what your killer knows.'

'You're saying that our killer knows intimate details of the case.' Ruby's eyes narrowed. 'And that there'll be more murders to come. Am I right?'

Mason nodded, his eyes never leaving Ruby's. 'You're a very attractive woman, but I don't get why you're mixing with criminals. Surely someone with your intelligence should be higher in the ranks by now?'

'It's my job. I mix with criminals all the time,' Ruby said drily. 'And the information you've given isn't anything more than I already know.'

'Oh, it's early days,' Mason replied. 'I hope when you return we'll get to hear a little more about your background. Let's see if I can dissect you better than you attempted to with me.'

'I won't be coming back,' Ruby said. 'We're going to catch this killer and that will be the end of it. Perhaps the pair of you can share a cell.'

'Humour too, I like it. Have you ever been tied up, Ruby? Had a rope around your neck so tight that you couldn't breathe?'

'Goodbye, Mr Gatley,' Ruby said, rising from her chair.

'See you next time,' Mason replied.

CHAPTER FOURTEEN

Shoving her bag beneath her chair, Ann gave her colleague, Jean, a knowing smile. Today had been hectic and she was looking forward to sitting down for a few hours. With the kids tucked up asleep in bed, and her husband Karl watching the footie, she was free to forget her own world for the rest of her shift. 'Busy?' she said, keeping her voice low so as not to disturb the other call takers.

'It's not been too bad,' Jean said, masking a cough with the back of a liver-spotted hand. 'No suicides. Although this cough will be the death of me. I'll be glad to get home.'

'More like those cigarettes,' Ann said, smoothing down her rain-drenched cropped blonde hair. 'Have a good evening, take care.' Jean had been volunteering at Sanity Line for what felt like for ever, but Ann had a feeling that ill health would bring her stint to an end. There was more to that cough than she was letting on. There was little time to dwell on it, as the telephone rang for her attention. Unwinding the scarf from around her neck, she rested it on the back of the chair before taking a seat.

'Hello, Sanity Line, can I help you?'

Silence followed, so Ann waited patiently for a response. In the background, a television blared, and from the sound of it, the same football match her husband was ensconced in front of was on at the other end of the line as well. A low voice broke into her thoughts.

'Oh, hi… I don't have to give you my name, do I?' A male voice replied.

'Not if you don't want to,' Ann said, crossing her legs beneath her chair.

'I was wondering if it's OK for me to be calling you like this? I'm not suicidal or anything. I feel a bit guilty about taking up your time when you could be dealing with needier cases.'

Ann nodded into the phone. It was a common misconception that you had to be suicidal to contact them. 'We value all our calls. How are you feeling today?'

The caller sighed. 'Disjointed. Tied up in knots. I've nobody to talk to. Well, nobody that would understand.'

'You can talk to me,' Ann said. 'It might help.'

A slight hesitation ensued, followed by a deep exhalation of breath. 'Would you though? Are you married? Have you ever cheated on your other half?'

Ann shuffled in her chair as she made herself comfortable. She thought of Karl and hoped he wouldn't drink too much tonight, not while he was minding the kids. She returned her focus to the call. 'Is that what happened to you? Why don't you tell me about it?'

A sudden cheer erupted from the football game in the background, and Ann guessed that someone must have scored a goal. She hoped it was West Ham. Karl would be in a pig of a mood if they lost. 'Hello? Are you there?' she said, presuming her caller was watching the game too.

'Sorry,' they replied. 'I was looking for the remote. Here, let me turn this down.' Muting the background calamity, he continued. 'I met someone, you see. Well, when I say met, we've spoken a few times online. Her name is Cheryl. But she's married.' A short, exasperated sigh followed. 'Which is why she shouldn't be talking to me. Do you think I'm crazy? Getting all het up over someone I've not even met?'

Ann smiled. How sweet, her caller was in love. But it was not up to her to give an opinion, only listen to what they had to say. 'You say they haven't met you yet?'

The response was instant. 'Not in that way, but they will. I've been getting ready, making sure everything's just right for our date. I suppose you could call me an old-fashioned soul. I want it to be perfect, you know? That takes time. Planning.'

Ann nodded into the phone. Her days of being wooed ended as soon as Karl pushed an engagement ring on her finger: a hasty response to their first unplanned pregnancy. Her caller was still talking, and she murmured encouraging noises to show she was listening to them.

'I'm going to give her the night of her life, then I'm going to make her wish she never strayed.'

'Really?' Ann said, her initial friendliness fading away.

'It wasn't easy, choosing just one when there were so many offers. But I had a template to follow – from someone who's inspired me. Someone who's been there before.'

A frown furrowed Ann's brow. Her voice was reassuring and non-judgemental but her facial expressions were her own. 'I'm sorry, I don't understand. Can you explain a little more?' she said, gently probing.

'No, other than to say I have it all planned.' A smile carried on the caller's voice. 'I don't expect them to understand right away. Sometimes people just don't know the difference between right and wrong. It's up to me to show them the way.'

Tiny alarm bells began ringing in Ann's mind. She reminded herself that she was not one to judge. 'Is there something concerning you about your feelings towards Cheryl? I'm guessing you rang me for a reason. Perhaps it would be good to talk things through?' She waited for their response, hoping she had not crossed the line. They were there to listen, not pick things apart. She did not have to wait long for an answer.

'I'm worried they won't make it easy for me. People… they don't always get me to begin with. I guess I'm calling because you've helped me in the past. I couldn't sleep. I still had your number so I thought I'd give you a ring.'

There were so many questions rising in Ann's mind. Who was their caller? What were their intentions? All this talk about templates and punishment – what were they planning to do? 'You've rung us before?' she said, knowing she should stick to the rules, ask them how they're feeling and leave it at that. Not all her callers made sense. It could be down to drugs or mental health issues, even making up stories for an excuse to talk. A feeling of helplessness tempered her thoughts. There was something about her caller that felt off-kilter.

'I've rung in the past.' The sense of happiness that imbued the caller's voice now evaporated. 'It was a very dark time for me then. But things are better now. How are you? Are you having a busy night?'

Ann checked her watch. 'We don't get as many calls after midnight. Is there anything else you'd like to talk about?'

'No.' He yawned. 'I feel a bit silly now. I just needed to talk. It will all work out. I'm prepared.'

As the caller hung up, Ann gently placed the phone handset back on the receiver. She had taken far worse calls, from people in deep despair, but this caller had set her on edge. She imagined a watcher following their intended victim, their final words ringing in her ears. I'm prepared.

CHAPTER FIFTEEN

'That Mason Gatley's a piece of work,' Ruby said, throwing the car keys onto her desk. DI Downes had followed her in, looking slightly harried as the team raced to complete their tasks. 'Any developments?' she asked, eyeing him as he opened a Tesco bag and unwrapped a tuna and sweetcorn sandwich.

'That's what I was going to ask you,' he said, offering her half.

Ruby took it gratefully, catching Luddy's eye through the window and making the tea sign with her hands. She did not always treat him as the tea boy, but today she felt like she was running on empty. She watched him delegate the task to Richard, the newest member of the crew. Ruby smiled. He was learning.

'Sorry,' she replied. 'It was an interesting visit but it didn't bear fruit.' She took a seat, glad to slip off her heels and take the weight off her feet. She had dressed sharp today, a show of empowerment in her crisp white shirt, black suit and matching black heels. She could still see Mason Gatley in her mind's eye, his face difficult to eradicate from her thoughts. 'He was watching me like I was his next meal. He has a real big opinion of himself too. I think he gets a kick out of frightening people, making them see how monstrous he is.'

'He *is* a monster,' Downes said, pushing his empty sandwich wrapper back into his Tesco bag. 'And you'd do well to remember that. Be careful what you say to him, especially about your private life. He's still got contacts on the outside, I wouldn't put it past him if he was controlling all of this.'

'Like a puppet master?' Ruby said. 'I got that impression too. He mentioned it at one point but then quickly backtracked. He hints that he knows things to reel you in, but then he laughs it off when you want to know more. He's definitely enjoying playing the game.'

'He'll squeeze more information out of you than you'll get from him,' Downes said, his voice edged with a warning. 'I remember him in interview, only the most experienced officers were allowed in. He's very manipulative. I guarantee he'll be planning your next visit already.' He eyed Ruby with concern. 'Don't get sucked in. If you've got nothing useful it's not worth going back there.'

'We'll see,' Ruby said, taking another bite of a sandwich. 'Perhaps we'll get this wrapped up quickly and I won't have to.'

'With our resources?' Downes gave her a wry grin. 'See out that window?'

Ruby followed his gaze out to the streets below. 'Yes, why?'

'You're more likely to see a herd of pigs come flying past.'

Ruby withdrew her gaze with a snort. 'You're pessimistic today.'

'I'm being realistic. There's staff shortages all over at the moment. People are overworked and dropping like flies. Keep an eye on the team. We can't afford for anyone to go off with stress, not with DCI Worrow breathing down my neck.'

Ruby sighed. The existing team were buried under a mountain of work due to staff shortages, which in turn caused people to go off sick as they buckled under the pressure. She was not into politics, but under the current government, things had never been so bad. It was less 'strong and stable' and more 'stressed and struggling'.

'Have you looked over his old case files?' she said. 'I've read a fair extent. Six murders. It's amazing just how far he got.'

Downes nodded in agreement. 'Shocking more like. And it wasn't due to lack of effort on our part. He's a clever bastard. He'd been planning his campaign for over a year. He had all these different scenarios worked out. But in the end, it was his own arrogance that got him caught out. He thought he was untouchable.'

'I think he still does, despite him being on the inside. He mentioned Lenny, you know.' Ruby lowered her voice as she spoke. 'I think that's half the reason he allowed me in. He knows about me and Nathan. I think he's curious as to how it all works.'

'Then it's all the more reason not to go back there. You've far too much to lose.' Downes's face hardened at the mention of her lover's name. He was one of the few people Ruby trusted with the details of her love life. She knew how bad it sounded, dating a man known for underworld crime, but her friendship with Downes ran deeper than their association in the police. Their brief fling while she was on a break from Nathan had served to cement their bond even more.

'The victims have plenty to lose too,' Ruby said, 'so we'll play it by ear.' Mason Gatley was responsible for the deaths of six women. That sort of bloodthirst did not end overnight. He would relive the horror in any way he could, whether it be talking about it or encouraging somebody else to do the same.

'How's the investigation going?' Ruby asked. 'Did you explain to Worrow why I wasn't at the briefing?'

'Aye, she already knew. She gave me the glare. The one where she looks like she's crawled out of her own backside.'

Ruby blurted a laugh at Downes's disdain. 'I have no idea what that even means but it sounds foul.'

Downes shrugged. 'She's panicking about keeping this on a need-to-know basis. All the same, we need to be ready in case it hits the press. It's Phillip bloody Sherman for God's sake.'

'How has he been coping?' Ruby said, briefly opening the door to take two cups of watery looking tea from Richard. She tried not to frown as she thanked him, making a mental note to relay her preferences later.

'Better than expected,' Downes replied, taking a cup from Ruby's extended hand as she closed the door with her foot. 'That laptop they found hidden in Melissa's bedroom, Phillip said he knows nothing about it but I'm still keeping my eye on him. For all we know this could be some elaborate set-up. He's recovering well from her death – a bit too well if you ask me.'

Ruby nodded. She knew that Downes had personal knowledge of grief, having lost his wife to cancer over a year before. But people grieved in different ways. 'Maybe the fairy-tale marriage wasn't such a fairy tale after all?' she said. 'Perhaps he wanted to get rid of her, but she wouldn't leave because of the prenup?' Ruby thought of the photographs and the crime scene she had viewed. Surely the expression of horror on Melissa's face could not have been extracted by somebody she knew? 'Have you shared the old case files in briefing? They could be relevant.'

'God, what kind of piss water is this?' Downes replied, making a face as he knocked back a mouthful of tea. Placing the cup on the table, he carried on. 'I want investigators to go into this with an open mind. It's enough that we know about it. We don't have the luxury of delegating this to anyone else.'

'What was his motivation?' Ruby said, a question that the old case files failed to cover. 'He got pissed off when I said it was down to an abusive past.'

'He had a decent childhood, no worse than most. He seemed to do it just for kicks. There was no remorse. He's just a vicious, calculating bastard. That's all there is to say.'

Ruby watched as her detective inspector's jaw clenched from the power of his words. It was obviously a case that still stirred up a lot of anger, even after all these years. In a way, it was reassuring to know he had not become desensitised to other people's pain.

'You mentioned the laptop that was found at Melissa's address. Anything of interest on it?' Ruby said.

'One thing I've gathered is that she willingly met a mystery man. It seems that our victim was playing away.'

CHAPTER SIXTEEN

'How are you feeling now?' Matthew said, handing Cheryl a glass of water as she perched on the side of the four-poster bed. She seemed in a haze, her breath reeking of the alcohol she had consumed.

'Woozy,' she replied, swiping for her glass and missing. 'Goodness. I shouldn't have taken that tablet. Does it always affect people like this? My voice feels really far away, like it's not coming from me.' She slowly waved her open hand in front of her face and giggled. 'My hand, it feels weird. I don't know what to make of it.' Another giggle erupted and she put her fingers to her mouth. 'Oh my goodness, I'm so sorry, I've come over all funny.'

'You're fighting it,' Matthew said, pressing the glass of water against her lips until she took a sip. 'It's been so long since you've had fun you don't know how to let go.'

After placing the glass on the bedside table, he removed her shoes and lifted her legs onto the bed. Seconds later, he was lying beside her, watching her intently. He smiled as he watched the drug take effect. Cheryl had not been as easy to convince as his previous date. Thankfully, she had a trusting nature and – after a few more drinks – had caved in. 'Relax,' he said, cupping her cheek, his palm warm against her flesh. 'Breathe nice and slow, give into the feeling. Now isn't that better?' Leaning forward, he kissed her gently on the lips.

'Yes, that is kind of nice,' she said, her giggles abating.

Swiftly, Matthew slid his phone from his trouser pocket and flicked the camera app into life. Tilting his head out of shot, he knew he could crop any of his distinguishing features. As long as it was enough to make Cheryl appear she was happy to be here, in bed, with someone other than her husband.

'What was that?' Cheryl said, as Matthew slid his phone back into his pocket.

'Just the air con controller,' Matthew said lightly. He had already set the air conditioning to low. Things started to smell when the room got too warm. He exhaled a breath of relief as Cheryl slowly closed her eyes. He didn't want to have to kiss her again. In truth, he didn't find her attractive. But then this wasn't a sexual encounter. That was what differentiated him from Mason Gatley. The promise of sex was just a means to a bigger end.

Snorting, Cheryl took a breath and opened her eyes. 'I almost dozed off there. What must you think of me?' Lifting her wrist to her face, she squinted at her watch. 'How long have we got left?'

Matthew rolled his eyes before plastering on a smile. 'Enough to do what we came here for. I was just letting you catch your breath.'

Bouncing onto his knees, he took her left and right hand, pinning them above her head as he straddled her. Clamping his legs around her body, he held on tight, getting a feel for the strength she had left. 'Why don't we play a game?' he said, a wicked grin spreading on his face. 'Something to really get you in the mood.'

Cheryl bit her bottom lip, flushed at the sudden physical contact. 'I don't know, this feels all wrong.' Trying to raise her head, a flicker of concern crossed her features as Matthew held her down. 'I'm sorry,' she said, 'can you let me go? You can keep the money. I don't think this is such a good idea after all.'

But each time she tried to rise from the bed, Matthew forced her back down. He hadn't come this far for her to change her mind now. Not that it would matter. Her black intentions were set when she came here. It was too late for forgiveness now. Licking his lips, he lowered his body on top of her, inhaling her perfume as he nuzzled the crook of her neck.

'I shouldn't,' she moaned, her breath growing heavy.

Releasing her hands, Matthew silenced her words with another lingering kiss.

'Good girl,' he said, reaching for his bag at the side of the bed. 'Remember what I said about letting go. Close your eyes, you're going to get everything you deserve and more.'

His words did not concern Cheryl as she had fallen into unconsciousness, her head lolling to the side. Matthew knew he had very little time until she awoke again.

Working swiftly, he bound her wrists and ankles, just as he had the woman before. He was becoming quite adept at knot tying. He smiled. His years as a scoutmaster had served him well.

'What's going on?' Cheryl murmured, her eyelids fluttering as she awoke.

'Just a bit of fun,' Matthew said. 'Just close your eyes and let me do all the work.'

CHAPTER SEVENTEEN

Clutching the cordless phone, Matthew dialled the number that was his lifeline. At three in the morning, the remnants of a storm still rumbled outside, driving the wind down his bedroom fireplace in a ghostly howl. He had plugged the gap with newspapers, but much like his emotions, the gale came with a force too strong to be halted. He hated his bedroom: the cold unforgiving floor, the old-fashioned furniture and the joyless view.

'Hello, Sanity Line.' The tone was deep, spoken from an accent he did not recognise.

Matthew blinked as he returned to reality, having taught himself how to switch between two worlds with ease.

'It's Matthew. I was hoping to speak to Laura. Is she there?' He spoke abruptly. He was in no mood to be courteous today.

'I'm a good listener, if you'd like to talk,' the man on the other side said.

Matthew's natural distrust came to the surface. 'What's your name? I'd feel better if I knew what to call you.'

'I'm Joseph,' the call taker responded. 'Why don't you tell me what's been bothering you?'

Matthew frowned. He had left Cheryl drugged and unconscious in the hotel. But now that he was away from her, contradictory thoughts were making themselves known. They whispered words of forgiveness, passages of the Bible preaching about the sanctity of life. He took a deep breath, preparing to bare his soul. 'Lately… it's been like swimming against the tide. I want to do the right thing, but I keep getting conflicted feelings.' He exhaled a resigned sigh. 'Have you ever been in love? Do you know the pain that it brings?'

Joseph was quick to respond. 'I'm sure it will help to talk it through. How tough have things gotten for you? Are you feeling suicidal?'

Matthew replied with a grunt. 'You know, I usually answer no to that question but today I'm not so sure. I don't want to hurt myself, but sometimes I feel like it might take the edge off my frustrations.' He thought about what he did to Cheryl in the hotel, how his blind anger had taken over. That other side of him that he could not stop. Was this really part of God's plan? His head felt foggy and out of sync. He exhaled, his voice groggy. He hated having to recap on what was previously said. 'The last time I called, it was for advice about Cheryl – a married woman I was seeing. I wanted to make her see that what she was doing was wrong – meeting me for sex behind her husband's back.'

'And did you? Tell her?' Joseph said.

'Oh yes, I left her in no doubt that what she was doing was wrong. I'd planned it down to every last detail. It strengthened me, knowing I was doing the right thing.'

'What happens now?' Joseph said, and Matthew could feel his call taker's interest growing.

'My head is buzzing with conflicting thoughts. One side of me says what I'm doing is wrong. That's the side that's talking to you now. But when I'm with them and I think about what they've done, I'm compelled to carry out my plan.'

'How does that make you feel?' Joseph said, his voice soft and calming.

'Right now? Lost. I feel lost,' Matthew replied, his words loaded with emotion. 'And it's not as if I can talk to anyone else about it. They wouldn't understand. I feel like I'm on the precipice of something big but I'm not quite ready to let go.'

'You mentioned "they" as in plural. Are you talking about more than one person?' Joseph said.

'Perhaps,' Matthew said. 'You wouldn't believe how many people are willing to cheat on their other halves.' He had calmed now, his emotions like the ebb and flow of the tide. Silence fell as he examined his mind for answers. He knew he was being vague – purposely so. But it still felt good to talk to another living soul. Not one with clipboards or prescriptions, but someone normal, just a regular guy you could meet down the pub. Not that Joseph was chatty. He just kept repeating the same questions in that monotone voice.

'How does that make you feel?' Joseph said, his response ill-timed.

'How the fuck do you think it makes me feel?' Matthew shouted down the phone. 'Is that all you can think of to say? If I didn't know better I'd think I was on to an automated line. It just goes to show that you don't care. Nobody does.'

'Sorry.' Joseph cleared his throat, 'I'm just trying to help you express your feelings. So many people go through their day saying that they're fine.'

Matthew nodded into the phone, agreeing, at least with his sentiments. 'No, I'm sorry. It's my moods. One minute I'm fine, the next…' He sighed. 'I went to church today. I wanted to confess. Sometimes I feel like I'm losing my mind. I try to act normal… but on the inside all I can think about is the betrayal. It drives me to do desperate things. I have… compulsions.'

'What sort of things?' Joseph said, filling the silence that fell between them. 'You talked about your plans and how you're compelled to carry them out. What are you referring to?'

'Trust me, you don't want to know,' Matthew said in a low voice.

'It might help to talk,' Joseph replied.

Matthew smiled. He was not so robotic now. A nervous giggle speared the line and he realised it was coming from him. 'Sometimes I feel like I'm losing control. I think I'm doing the right thing, but then I'll hear this voice from deep inside telling me it's wrong. That's what tortures me. How do I know which voice to listen to? What do you do when you've more than one speaking in your head?' His words died in his throat and the only sound was Matthew's breathing on the line. 'It's just not fair,' he said, wrapped up in his annoyance. 'Those women… they drive me to it, filling up my inbox with their lurid suggestions. The flirting and teasing. Someone's got to stop them.'

Matthew wiped a sweaty palm on the leg of his jeans after he switched the phone handset to the other hand. 'They're like a drug to me. I'm addicted, that's what it is. I can't get them out of my head, and one is never enough. Do you know what a mammoth task it is, trying to stop them all? Sometimes I feel so overwhelmed.'

'How can you move forward from here?' Yet another textbook question.

Matthew rubbed his mouth, as if trying to contain his words. *What are you doing?* A voice whispered from within. *You've already said too much.* Closing his eyes, he inhaled deeply through his nostrils, holding the air in his lungs as he made his choice. He exhaled, calm now. This time his voice was firm. Resolute. 'I keep doing what I'm doing. Stay focused. They're the wicked ones, not me. My intentions are good.' Another deep breath, as if to strengthen himself for what lay ahead. 'Thanks for the chat. But I have to go. I've got some unfinished business to take care of.'

CHAPTER EIGHTEEN

It was still dark when Ruby went to work. There was nothing she would have loved more than to stay snuggled up in bed with Nathan. As always, there were more pressing matters at hand. She barely noticed the dim light in the corner of the office and jumped when she saw a figure hunched over their computer. It was Richard, his wide-rimmed glasses shoved down the bridge of his nose as he analysed the data on his screen.

'What time did you get in?' Ruby said, composing herself.

'I never left,' he said, unsmiling as he continued to peer at his monitor.

Ruby walked around to his side of the desk. There were times when she had felt like pulling an all-nighter, but her DI had rightly sent her home for a few hours' sleep. Burnout was commonplace when working under such pressure. Tiredness slowed you down and fogged your thoughts. 'Well in that case you need to go home for a few hours' kip,' she said. 'There's no point in being dead on your feet.'

'I got sleep,' he said, turning his swivel chair to point to a bag in the corner. A rolled-up sleeping bag was tied with some string next to a grey rucksack.

Ruby smiled as she shook her head. 'Where did that come from?'

'I keep it in my locker in case of emergencies,' Richard replied, as if it were the most normal thing in the world. 'It's just as well as we've had another missing person's report.'

'Already?' Ruby said, feeling crestfallen. 'When did this come in?'

'An hour ago, but the call takers didn't think to make us aware. I found it when I was trawling through the CAD reports.' Richard examined his paperwork, pulling out a printout of the incident. 'Here's the latest update.'

Ruby took the paperwork and, whipping out her reading glasses, poured over the details. Informant Gordon Barber had called at 6.55 a.m. to report that his wife had failed to return home. After calling friends and family to check her whereabouts, he called police and mentioned the discovery of an envelope that had been posted through his front door just prior to midnight the night before. Contained in the envelope was a photograph of his wife, which appeared to have been taken recently. A tag had been placed on the report for uniformed officers to visit his address. A further update had gone on the incident to say that DC Richard Moss had arranged for Gordon to attend the station at eight o'clock, where he would speak to a member of the team.

'It was the earliest I could get him in here,' Richard said. 'His sons don't know and he wanted to wait until they'd left for work.'

'It might not be connected to our case. I know there's a photo but it's not a given at this stage. If she went missing last night then her kidnapper would have had to work very fast to take her photo and deliver it to Gordon's house before midnight.' Ruby placed the paper printout back on Richard's desk.

'I'm afraid it's looking like it is,' Richard said grimly. 'I've made some background checks. They're a fairly wealthy couple and they mix in the same circles as victim number one. These aren't random incidents.'

'That's very commendable,' Ruby said. 'What have you found?'

Richard pushed his glasses back up the bridge of his nose. 'They both socialise at the same golf club once a week. It seems to be a "ladies who lunch" type of thing, for well-to-do women who have never worked a day in their lives.'

'Sounds like I'd fit right in,' Ruby winked, then remembered she was not talking to Ash, his predecessor. The ghost of his presence still lingered here, and despite everything that had happened, she still missed the silly sod. The loss of a colleague was hard to bear, but Ash's death had hit Ruby hard. Even now, she felt like she had blood on her hands. She cleared her throat. 'We need to speak to these women after we've dealt with Gordon. Do we know when the next meeting takes place?'

'Well that's the thing, I looked at their online Facebook group and it's today at 11 a.m. Apparently, it's to talk about Melissa. Maybe they're scared the same thing is going to happen to them.'

'Good. It's in Coleman Street,' Ruby said, reading the address from his notes. 'Shouldn't take us long. They'll probably panic when they hear Cheryl is missing too.'

'Us?' he said, looking mildly horrified at the prospect of leaving the office.

'Yes, us. If we leave here around 10:30, we should get there in plenty of time. See what you can find out about this group of women before then. Anything outstanding, criminal records, bad debts. Pop in to the divisional intelligence unit. See if they can dig anything up. I know you don't have their dates of birth—'

'That's no problem,' Richard interrupted. 'I've got most of that from Facebook.'

Ruby smiled. A computer whizz with an analytical mind was exactly what they needed on their team. 'Good. Tell DIU we need it pronto. Perhaps Melissa and Cheryl had been mixing with some shady characters. You know how the well-heeled like a bit of rough sometimes.' And Ruby did know this first hand, given who she had woken up with that morning. She thought of Cathy, her daughter: a gangster for a father and police officer for a mother. No wonder she was mixed up. She swallowed, her throat dry. Right now, she needed a strong cup of tea. She opened her mouth to ask Richard, then sighed as her conscience told her to make it her bloody self.

'Can I get you a drink? Coffee, tea? I'll even stretch to a bar of chocolate from the vending machine, seeing as you've worked so hard.'

Richard grimaced, barely affording her a glance as he clicked from site to site. 'No thanks, I don't eat chocolate or drink caffeine.'

Ruby blinked, wondering how he could function without them. How had she not noticed up to now? 'Do you go to the pub? I was thinking, we're long overdue some team drinks. Maybe next weekend we can head next door after work. You up for that?'

'I partake in an occasional beverage or two,' Richard said, offering up a polite smile before returning his attention to his work.

'Good. I'll arrange it with the team. Call it a belated welcome. Drinks are on me.'

Richard nodded in approval as Ruby collected up the dirty cups and mugs littering the surrounding desks. The cleaners were due in any minute, but given the state of the office, they had enough work to do. She cringed as she caught sight of the remnants of an egg sandwich that had been ground into the carpet. She would have to have a word with the team.

An announcement on the tannoy requesting Richard's presence at the front desk notified them that Gordon was there.

'I'll take a statement,' Richard said, rising from his desk.

Ruby raised her hand to stall his movements. 'Let me have five minutes with him first. Do us a favour, give DC Rutherford the heads-up, will you? I've got a feeling we'll need a FLO involved.' They would need to put a family liaison officer in place in case anything further was pushed through the door. She would also request eyes on the property; although with budget cuts, they could probably only spare an hour or two.

Richard sighed as he sat back in his chair. 'I hope we find Cheryl before it's too late. I can't imagine getting a finger in the post like that, much less photographs of a loved one being treated that way.'

Ruby wanted to ask if he had anyone special at home, but Richard seemed the private type and such questions were better asked in the pub. 'The killer seems to get off on hurting as many people as he can,' she said instead.

Richard stretched out his arms, his muscles cracking as he moved.

'Time you took a break,' Ruby said. 'Stretch your legs first. Grab some fresh air.'

Richard nodded wearily, locking his computer as he stood.

'And Richard?' Ruby said, giving him a backward glance as she pulled the door open. 'Well bloody done.'

CHAPTER NINETEEN

Gordon Barber was a portly but not unattractive man, with broad shoulders and striking blue eyes. His face filled with angst, he immediately rose as Ruby entered the small interview room.

'Thanks for coming in,' Ruby said, pulling a chair from beneath the functional wooden table and sitting down. After formally introducing herself, Ruby waited for Gordon to speak.

'As I told the call taker, it's my wife,' he said, perching on the edge of his chair. 'She didn't come home last night. Then this morning I found this photo in an envelope shoved under my door. I wasn't sure if the police could help, but Hannah told me to call.'

'And Hannah is?' Ruby said, taking the photo from his grasp.

'Her best friend. She hasn't heard from her since yesterday. I'm worried. It's not like her to take off like this. The officer on the phone… he told me to come in.'

'We thought it best to speak to you sooner rather than later, given your concerns,' Ruby said, trying to inject some normality into her voice. 'Given this is out of character, we'll put some feelers out right away. We'll also take a statement covering her last movements. Is that OK?'

'Sure,' Gordon said, looking a bit bewildered. 'How serious is this?'

Ruby's throat tightened as she glanced at the photograph of the middle-aged woman lying on what looked like a bed. She offered the camera a woozy smile, her eyes half closed as she blinked, her mouth open as if caught mid-sentence. Just like with Melissa, she appeared happy and relaxed, but Ruby had a horrible feeling that it would not last for long. 'It's too early to say. Has she packed a bag? Any of her belongings missing?'

'Her handbag and phone are gone. The dress she's wearing in the photo – it's missing from the wardrobe. So are her shoes. And the picture – at first, I thought it was Cheryl mucking around. But it's not, is it? And if she hasn't sent the photo then who has?'

Ruby stiffened, his words a chilling re-enactment of the previous murder victim's case. Unlike Melissa's husband, Gordon had not jumped to the conclusion that this was a kidnap attempt. But then again, he had not yet received her severed finger in the post. Ruby suppressed her growing turmoil. There may still be time to save this woman. They could start by putting a trace on her phone. Keeping her thoughts to herself, Ruby tried to offer as much reassurance as she could. 'I'm afraid I can't tell you anything until I've more to go on, which is why we need to take a statement while you're here.'

A knock on the door signalled Richard's arrival. *He's keen*, Ruby thought, before making a quick introduction to them both. 'DC Moss is going to take your statement, and we'll hold on to the photograph for now. Can I have Hannah's contact details?'

Gordon frowned. 'Is there something you're not telling me? You must get people reported missing all the time. Wouldn't a uniformed officer deal with this or am I watching too many cop shows on TV?'

'We're just covering all bases,' Ruby lied. 'Do you have any CCTV surrounding your home? The photo was hand delivered, wasn't it?'

'It's live streaming only, it doesn't record. I've been meaning to upgrade for ages…' his words trailed away. 'Something's wrong, isn't it? Please. You can be straight with me.'

Ruby sighed. Imparting information to family members was tricky at best. Say nothing and she could risk him being exposed to the most horrific news. Reveal details of the previous case and she was opening a can of worms. 'We've had a similar case of a missing woman, but there's nothing to say this is linked to your wife's disappearance. Having said that, we may need to monitor your post. I know it's intrusive but it may be of evidence forensically…'

'This similar case. How did it end up?' Gordon said, interrupting her flow.

'I'm not at liberty to say,' Ruby replied. 'And it may have no bearing on your wife. Did Cheryl have access to a computer?'

'Yes, she has a Dell laptop at home. Why?'

'We'll need to seize it, and any other electronic devices, in order to track her last movements. One of our officers will accompany you home when you're done here. I'm sure I don't need to tell you to keep your phone on at all times, and call us if you hear from her. We'll give you a reference number in case you need to ring.' She turned to Richard and, in a low voice, spoke in his ear. 'Leave a copy of that statement on my desk as soon as it's taken, then request to triangulate Cheryl's phone.'

Richard nodded, his face pensive.

After taking Hannah's number, Ruby made a swift exit. She could not face any more questions because she had barely been able to look the poor man in the eye. The close-up of Cheryl's face offered no clues, just as with the previous victim the first time around. They would come later, when the killer's work was done. Cheryl was playing away, she had to be. But would she meet the same fate as Melissa? Why was this envelope delivered by hand? She would ask her boss for a unit to have eyeballs on the property, but it all came down to their budget in the end. Their last big case involved 'the fairy-tale killer' and the resources needed had almost bled them dry. Ruby took a breath, stalling her racing thoughts. *Steady. Calm down. You might just be jumping the gun here. If there's one person who might know what's going on, it's Cheryl's best friend.*

As she strode down the corridor to her office, she paused at the chocolate machine to buy a Twix bar.

By the time she closed her office door, she had eaten one finger of chocolate and briefly quietened her grumbling stomach.

'Hello, am I speaking to Hannah Cowen?' Ruby said, swallowing back the last mouthful of chocolate. 'My name is DS Ruby Preston. I'd like to speak to you about Cheryl.'

The voice on the other end was well spoken but hesitant, as if unaccustomed to speaking to the law. 'Oh,' she said, as if gathering her thoughts. 'Yes, I'm Hannah. I take it Gordon's been in to see you then? Any news?'

'We're taking his report now. He said you're good friends...' She paused, allowing the gravity of the situation to sink in. 'Have you any idea where she could be?'

No response. Ruby was beginning to wish she had made it a personal visit. 'Hannah,' she spoke firmly, 'if you know something then now is the time to tell us.'

'Is Gordon with you?' Hannah said, an edge of caution to her voice.

'No, I'm alone in my office,' Ruby said, pulling open her desk drawer to search for a pen. 'Did Cheryl mention where she was going, who she was meeting?'

'She did... but, if Gordon finds out he'll be so upset. And then there's the kids. Well, when I say kids they're grown up now but—'

'Please,' Ruby interrupted. 'This could be serious. Cheryl's not the only woman to have gone missing in similar circumstances. Did she give you a location? A name? I can assure discretion if that's what you're worried about.' She wanted to ask if Cheryl had been having an affair but could not afford to put words in Hannah's mouth.

'To be honest, I'm worried. Cheryl shares everything with me. It's not like her not to call. She stressed that she'd be back before Gordon got home but he said their bed's not been slept in. I'm scared something's happened to her, but I asked Gordon to report it so he wouldn't get suspicious about where she's gone. If he sees me getting into a flap, he'll know there's something wrong.'

'And that something is?…' Ruby said, finding a piece of scrap paper and wishing she'd get to the point.

'She was using a dating website for married men and women. It's called *Debauchery*. Only you won't find it online, at least not straight away. You have to go in through some online back door. I don't know; I'm not very technical. Anyway, it's by introduction only. I asked Cheryl if she could let me have a peek but she was very insistent that I couldn't. I'm single, you see, but even so, I was a bit miffed. My money's as good as everyone else's.'

'Details,' Ruby said, making room on the desk and scribbling the name 'Debauchery' on a scrap of A4. She was not interested in Hannah's bruised ego. 'I need details.'

'All I can tell you is that she was getting all dressed up to meet this guy for what was promised to be the night of her life. She didn't have his profile picture but he had lots of five star reviews. And… gosh, I don't know if I should be telling you this. The last thing I want is to have her arrested.'

'As far as I'm concerned Cheryl is a high-risk victim,' Ruby reiterated. 'I just want to keep her safe.'

'OK.' Hannah gulped, her footsteps echoing down the phone line as she paced the floor. 'There were possibly drugs involved during this date too. Now don't get me wrong, Cheryl's never taken a drug in her life. When I asked if she was going to use them she said she didn't know. It's a very high-class affair by all accounts. Probably ecstasy or coke.'

'And she was meeting him where?' Ruby demanded, her fingers curling tighter around her pen.

'Somewhere in London. That's all I know. She didn't use public transport so she may have ordered a cab. It's very cloak and dagger though. I don't know why she couldn't have confided in me. It's like she was scared by what might happen if it got out.'

Ruby's pen dug into the paper as she continued to take notes. Her sense of urgency fuelled her actions and she felt every muscle in her body tense. 'So let me get this right. You said it was a dating agency, but what you're describing sounds more like an escort service. I don't know of any dating agency that involves the promise of drugs and then reviews the date afterwards.'

'It's a bit of both from what I gather. Lots of men and women cheating on their partners. But some dates are bought and paid for by people who want discretion guaranteed. After all, if you're only going to be unfaithful once in your marriage, you'll want to get it right. I think it was two thousand pounds for the top reviewed men. That includes a night on the town, a meal and the hotel room: a five star, of course. If your date doesn't measure up, you can apply for a refund afterwards.'

Ruby balked at the mention of such an extortionate amount. Two grand for a shag? Such a price tag would surely limit their potential victims to the very wealthy. 'Did she tell you anything about this man, a name? Skin colour even?'

'She said he goes by Matthew but it's not his real name. He had a basic description of trim, white, average build young man. She said she'd be home by two or three in the morning at the latest. I told her I'd stay up so she could ring me with all the juicy details, but when she didn't call, I figured she was having too much fun. Then Gordon came back from a camping trip with his sons this morning and rang to say Cheryl wasn't at home.'

'What did he say about the photo?'

'Photo? What photo?' Hannah said.

Ruby rested her pen and brought her hand to her forehead, leaning on her elbow as she spoke. She knew she was not going to get anything more of value from Hannah from this phone call. 'Gordon found a picture of Cheryl through his letterbox last night. Didn't he mention it?'

'No. I'd just woken up when he called me this morning… I was groggy. Was she… OK? It wasn't one of those explicit ones, was it?'

'No, she looked fine. Look, Hannah, I'm going to be frank with you. There's something not quite right about this. I'm going to send an officer around to take a full statement. I need you to tell them everything you know, no matter how insignificant it may seem.' Ruby interrupted as Hannah took an intake of breath to speak. 'We'll be discreet; Gordon won't have access to our statements. But if you see or hear anything suspicious, you've got to let me know.'

'Very well,' Hannah said, a tinge of fear creeping into her voice. 'She's going to be OK though, isn't she?'

'I honestly don't know,' Ruby said truthfully, a feeling of foreboding consuming her thoughts.

After saying her goodbyes, she hung up the phone. The cases were connected. Everything pointed to that fact. She imagined Cheryl, terrified out of her wits as she was bound and gagged in a London hotel. They had to find her before photo two, when unspeakable things would be inflicted upon her. But where in this vast city was she?

Ruby pushed open her office window, staring out at the streets below. If Mason Gatley murdered six women before being caught, then what hope did she have this time around? She briefly closed her eyes as a welcome breeze from outside kissed her skin. With good officers behind her and advances in forensics she had to believe she was on the winning team. If she wasn't… God help them all.

CHAPTER TWENTY

Cheryl shifted her head to the left, her eyes blurred with tears. Pleading with her captor had been fruitless. He had regarded her with a blank expression as she cried silent tears, turning up the television to drown out the sniffles that followed. At first, she thought it was some kind of kinky game, and had been too spaced out to put up a fight. She even giggled as he pushed her onto her stomach before binding her knees and ankles behind her back. Was this what he had meant about having fun? There was nothing about masochism in his profile. She thought back. She had barely returned from the toilet before he gave her something sweet to drink. Just what was in that cocktail? And what else was in the rucksack that he pulled from the wardrobe that night? Once she was tied, Matthew had stepped back from the bed, wiped his hands on the back of his trousers and turned on the TV. In stunned amazement, Cheryl had lain there, wondering what on earth was taking place. All of a sudden, she didn't like this game anymore. She half expected him to put on the porn channel to get them in the mood. But instead, some old Mel Gibson movie played out, while Cheryl lolled in and out of consciousness, waiting for the drug-induced fog to clear.

'Let me go,' she said, arching her back as the ropes cut into her wrists and ankles. Deftly he had tied his knots, and as fresh fear drove its way into her thoughts, she realised he had done this sort of thing before. 'Do you hear me?' she said, her voice splintering as it raised an octave. 'The game's over. Set me free.'

But Matthew just laughed at the television, a comedic moment in which the actor was dressing up as a woman to get a job. It was as if Cheryl was not there at all.

This morning she was awoken as he drew the blinds and light flooded the hotel room. Panic gripped her as she realised just how much time had passed. Calmly, her captor drank a bottle of water from the minibar, barely acknowledging her presence in the room. It wasn't until she threatened to scream that he glanced in her direction. Tutting, he, reached for his rucksack on the floor. It clanked as he placed it on the table, and her stomach clenched in fear as she realised there were heavy tools inside.

'In that case,' Matthew said, reaching for a black ball-shaped object, 'you'll have to wear the gag.'

Cheryl knew that this was no game. This man was here to hurt her. A ransom demand, or something worse. But why keep her overnight? Surely if he were going to sexually assault her, he would have done it by now. If anything, he went to great care not to touch her intimately as he bound her arms and legs.

'No,' she spat, wrenching her head from left to right to avoid the hard rubber ball gag. But Matthew had immobilised her within seconds, tying the attached bindings to the back of her head.

'Now for another photo,' he said, pulling his iPhone from his back pocket. 'But we just need to get the right look.'

What did he mean, another? Cheryl's heart was hammering so hard she felt it was going to tear its way out of her chest. A vague recollection crept in of Matthew snapping their picture before. He had said it was an air con remote but she was too woozy to challenge him at the time. With fear-driven clarity, she realised the danger she had walked into. All for the sake of a bit of fun. What was her husband doing now she had not come home? Had he called the police? Had Hannah? Would they be too late?

Matthew scrunched up his face as he held the camera phone aloft. 'No, you're not quite there yet.'

The mattress bounced as he sat on the bed. She flinched as he touched her hair, but he continued as if he were petting his favourite dog.

'Do you know what I'm going to do with you?' His words crawled from his mouth like black legged beetles, a terrifying contrast to his actions. 'I'm going to chop off your ring finger and send it to your husband, along with a photograph of you lying on this bed. There will be three pictures for him to pour over. This one's photo number two. Tomorrow we're going to take a very special one, but you won't be alive for that.' Thin laughter escaped his lips. 'Shame; I'd love you to see it.'

Consumed with terror, Cheryl's eyes bulged as she tried to scream. But her panicked expulsion came out as a garbled moan, blocked by the gag fastened over her mouth.

'Shh shh,' there's no point in fighting it.' Matthew rose from the bed. 'You put this in motion when you became a whore. You broke one of God's commandments. It's all you deserve.'

He smiled, holding his camera phone aloft once more. 'I'm going to wrap the rope around your throat and pull until you stop breathing.' A chuckle laced his words. 'Bet you wished you were faithful now.'

Cheryl's eyes rolled to the back of her head, the whites flashing in the morning light. As she squirmed and fought against her bindings, they only served to numb her limbs even more. She was vaguely aware of the flash of a camera before Matthew returned to her side.

'There. All done. Sorry to frighten you, but the photo would have been a bit dull otherwise.' He leaned closer still, his breath hot on her ear as he whispered his final threat. 'If I were you I'd start praying, because you've earned yourself a place in Hell.'

Cheryl felt as if she were about to implode. Tightly bound, she was unable to move, the scream building in her throat searching for release. Adrenalin pumped through her veins as she tried to work out how to escape. The look in Matthew's eyes told her death was near. He leaned forward to stroke her hair one last time, the top button of his shirt undone. The small jingle of jewellery caught her attention and she focused to see a gold band dangling in front of her nose. It was a wedding ring, just like hers. As he tugged at her ring finger, cold fear sliced through to her bones. He palmed her wedding ring before stepping away and undoing the chain around his neck.

'Another one for my collection,' he murmured, threading Cheryl's ring onto the chain.

Unable to stop trembling, Cheryl tried to comprehend his words. She needed to focus. Try to negotiate. Find a way out of here. But what did he mean, *his collection*? And who owned the ring before? She thought of the person who gave her the referral. Just what had she gotten herself caught up in? She was an ordinary housewife, nothing special. Her heart drumming in her ears, she tried to slow her breath. He would remove her gag. She would offer him money, agree to his demands. But as Matthew rooted in his rucksack, she caught sight of a glint of steel. And all at once she knew he was not going to let her go.

CHAPTER TWENTY-ONE

'Are you OK to drive?' Ruby threw Richard the car keys from across the desk. She felt bad for judging him for being boring. Unlike his predecessor, Richard actually cared about the people he dealt with. Job-weary Ash had failed to see outside his own problems when it came to ownership of the cases on his hands. To him they had just been the means to an end, making light of the tragedies to get through the day. Richard may not be the most talkative of people, but he held a quiet dignity that carried to every aspect of his work. Regardless, Ruby knew that it took time to build up a level of trust and having a new member on the team could be unsettling at first. It had also occurred to her that he could be a mole. Such people rarely formed friendships because it made their betrayal much harder later on. The professional standards department regularly placed people into various departments, and she would not have put it past them to give Richard such a role. Had someone reported her for her criminal associations? Her connection with the Crosbys that made her feel paranoid. A team was only as good as its leader; had Richard been sent in to keep an eye on them all?

She gave Richard a curious glance. He drove as he worked: slow and steady with careful consideration. She wondered what the ladies down the golf club would make of his old-fashioned side burns and his M&S suit. She took a slow, soothing breath, her thoughts solemn. It felt strange not to be racing around like when she was at the wheel. The mood in the office was at fever pitch as they investigated the latest leads. A courier had been sent to the home of Gordon Barber with a small padded package from an unknown source. The arrival of the second photo and what was believed to be Cheryl's amputated ring finger had confirmed her worst fears. This case was connected to the last. And given the previous photo had arrived the night before, they were now on day two. Thankfully, it was intercepted before it reached Cheryl's husband's letterbox. If they didn't catch the killer, there would be one more photo to come. It brought with it a chilling conclusion. They had less than twenty-four hours to save Cheryl's life.

She had known before she saw the photo that it would be grim. Just like the previous victim, Cheryl was tied up in submission, the rope connected behind her back to her ankles and wrists. Could it be the same rope used to murder the previous victim? Was he playing with the police, teasing them with similarities known only to very few? Cheryl's face still haunted Ruby's memory. Streaked with tears, her eyes were puffy from crying, her screams contained in what looked like a ball gag stuffed into her mouth. But just like before, the photo offered few clues of her location. They would come in the next photo, when it was far too late. It gave Ruby scant relief to see Cheryl's fingers still intact, but there was a damning sense of inevitability that she had tried hard to shake off.

A flash of her police warrant card gained them access to the golf club. According to Facebook, the ladies in Cheryl's circle of friends were allowed special out-of-hours entry. This was no doubt facilitated by their hefty membership fees, as well as the sponsorship provided by their spouses' companies for the various tournaments that took place over the year. Highfield Country Club catered to many people, and judging by the glitzy decor, they were all well above Ruby's pay grade. Heads turned as she strode to the function room that overlooked the course. The damp and drizzly morning brought few golfers out today. But despite the early hour, the bar was open for business. It was also manned by a barman who would not look out of place on the cover of *Esquire* magazine. *No wonder these old lushes come here at this hour with talent like this serving them*, Ruby thought, as their eyes briefly met.

'They're over there in the corner, near the back door,' Richard said, pointing to the group of women he recognised from social media.

Sipping their gin and tonics, the women did not appear to notice Ruby until she was halfway across the room. Dressed in a mixture of linen trousers, floaty dresses and butterfly print chiffon tops, they turned to greet her with curious glances as she approached their table. After introducing herself, Ruby allowed the flutter of excitement to die down before taking a seat. Her nose twitched as the cloud of expensive perfume enveloping them threatened to make her sneeze.

'Are you here about Cheryl and Melissa?' a petite auburn-haired woman enquired. Her face was tight and worried, as she clasped her glass in both hands.

'Yes,' Ruby confirmed, shocked that news of Cheryl's disappearance had spread so quickly. 'I was wondering if any of you can shed any light on their whereabouts?'

But questioning seemed fruitless as the six women gathered stated they knew nothing of the plans of either woman on the day of their disappearances. 'Friends' seemed to be a loose term as they preferred to gossip over Melissa and Cheryl's financial status rather than show empathy and genuine concern.

'How did you come to know each other?' Ruby said, aware of their eyes raking over her as they made their own mental calculations. *Designer suit, expensive watch, and ooh a pair of Jimmy Choo suede ankle boots*: Ruby could almost hear their thoughts. But such items had been gifted by Nathan, and were not as a result of her mediocre sergeant's wage.

'We're the golf widows,' a woman named Amelia replied with a smile. 'We meet up once a week as our husbands are often away on business. Gordon rang us this morning to ask if we knew where Cheryl was. We've not known poor Melissa for very long. She was very quiet. Didn't seem very interested in what we had to say.'

'She's a good twenty years younger than us, Amelia,' a dark-haired woman named Shirley piped up in a cynical tone. 'Of course she wasn't interested. But we were all shocked to hear of the kidnapping. That's what it was, wasn't it? A ransom gone wrong?'

'I'm afraid I can't say,' Ruby said, sensing their hunger for the truth. Richard had excused himself to use the bathroom and seemed to be taking an incredibly long time. Ruby wondered how an introvert such as Richard could be attracted to a role in the police.

'But what about Cheryl?' Amelia said, pausing to sip her G & T. 'Has she been kidnapped too?'

'I was hoping you might be able to help me with that. Do you know of any other social groups? Meeting places? Social events she could have attended recently?'

The women shook their heads, all delivering a blank stare.

Ruby inhaled a deep breath as she took the decision to share some information on the case. 'What about clubs? Nightlife? Any of you go out on the town while your husbands are away?'

Shirley's eyes flickered momentarily before she swiftly shook her head, staring into her empty glass. 'I'm going to get another round,' she said. 'Can I tempt any of you ladies? It's been quite a shocking week…'

'I'll come with you,' Ruby said, quickly recognising the appeal for privacy.

They were barely at the bar before Ruby swooped in. Richard would not be too pleased at being left to deal with the gaggle of women upon his return, but there was no fear of them getting very much out of him.

'You know, don't you?' Ruby said firmly, as Shirley placed her order from the Adonis at the bar. 'You know where Melissa and Cheryl went.'

Shirley paled, clearly shaken. 'If they find out I've told you…'

'If you don't cooperate then Cheryl could die. Is that what you want?'

'You can't tell my husband…' She hesitated, checking over her shoulder before lowering her voice. 'I know I'm getting on, but there's life in this old girl yet.'

'Nobody will know. I'll put you down as an anonymous source. Please, Shirley, Melissa's dead and Cheryl might not have long left.'

Plucking a card from the back pocket of her trousers, Shirley slid it across the bar. Ruby cupped it with her hand. 'I'm never recommending that place again,' Shirley said. 'If Melissa died because of me…'

'Melissa died because a psychopath strangled the life out of her.' She ran her thumb over the velvety black embossed card, the words *Debauchery* styled in red. Underneath was an unusual-looking web address and beside it what looked like a password. 'Who gave you this? What else do you know?'

'That's as much as I can tell you,' Shirley said, smiling sweetly at the barman as he approached to take payment for her drinks. She seemed reluctant to speak until he turned away, then looked at Ruby as if to ask what she was still doing there.

'You're hiding something. Who's your source?' Ruby said, pocketing the card.

'I don't remember,' Shirley said, glancing over her shoulder at her group of friends. 'Someone slipped me some cards at a party. I don't know who they were.'

'A woman's life is at stake,' Ruby said, gripping Shirley's wrist as she reached for the tray of drinks.

'You think I want this?' Shirley jerked back her arm, her eyes wide. 'Cheryl was my friend. If I could help you I would, but I've told you all I know.'

Ruby took the hint, leaning over to deliver one last piece of advice. 'Don't even think about using them again, and not a word of this to anyone.'

'You don't need to worry on that score. From now on it's monogamy all the way,' Shirley said, fixing a stiff smile as the barman returned with her change.

The urgent buzz of Ruby's phone cut into her thoughts as she and Richard returned to the car. It was the ringtone of a person sure to gain her immediate attention. But Cathy knew better than to contact her at work. A call from her meant something was wrong. Ruby clicked in her seatbelt, preparing to ring back as a text popped up on her screen.

Help me, I'm being kept a prisoner. Come quick.

Ruby balked as she stared at the screen. She had hated her daughter living with the head of the Crosby family, and now it seemed that her worst fears were coming true. There was nothing in briefing this morning about a raid on their home address. It led to a far more frightening conclusion. Had the Crosby's underworld connections turned upon them? If so, just what kind of danger was her daughter in? Her heart hammering, Ruby's hands trembled as she tried to call Cathy's number. The dead ringtone that ensued made her blood run cold.

CHAPTER TWENTY-TWO

'What's all the fuss about?'

Nathan's mum, Frances Crosby, answered the door. Despite her diminutive stature, her expression was fierce, and in any other given situation, Ruby would not be approaching her home in such an aggressive manner. But there was no point in her feigning surprise, given the CCTV had captured Ruby's car upon entering the drive.

It had been difficult to tear herself away from work now a new development had come in. After a hurried phone call to DI Downes, he had agreed to cover for her while she found out what was going on with Cathy. Any normal parent would have called the police and allowed them to deal with the situation, but Ruby knew that the presence of any other member of law enforcement could serve to make things a whole lot worse. She would deal with this alone. That's if she got out of here in one piece. Regardless of her relationship with Nathan, when at Frances Crosby's home address, Ruby never felt like she was on safe ground. Today anxiety dictated her movements and she needed to know what was going on.

'Why have I received a text from my daughter saying she's being kept a prisoner in her own home?'

Frances snorted, her hands on her hips as she spoke. 'You wot? That girl wants for nothing.' As always, she was immaculately turned out. Dressed in a pink satin blouse and cream-coloured skirt, her clothing gave no clues of her background, at least not until she opened her mouth and her East End accent spilled out.

Ruby approached the wide stairwell, her voice echoing upwards as she spoke. 'Then call her down here so I can see for myself.' She strained her neck as she called her daughter's name, hoping Lenny would not appear. 'Cathy, are you up there? Come here and explain yourself.' Ruby knew it would take time to heal the rift between her and the daughter she gave up for adoption. She was ill-acquainted with motherhood, and Cathy had insisted she stayed with the Crosbys after tracking them down online. But today Ruby's heart burst with protectiveness, the memory of Melissa's death still fresh in her mind.

'Oh,' Cathy said, a smile touching her face. 'What are you doing here?' Dressed in faded dungarees and a striped crop top beneath, Cathy leaned over the top of the bannisters, her dark hair trailing down her face.

Ruby frowned at the sight of her daughter greeting her so nonchalantly; particularly given she had broken the speed limit to get there. She looked at her incredulously. 'What am I doing here? You said you were in trouble. I tried calling you back but the phone went dead.'

Cathy descended the stairs in her stocking feet, two pink spots creeping onto her cheeks. 'Sorry, my battery died. I didn't expect you to come racing over.'

'Well I have,' Ruby said, feeling foolish as she caught the smug grin on Frances's face. She returned her glance to Cathy, thinking she would never live this down. 'So would you mind telling me what this is all about?'

'Best we bring this into the living room,' Frances said, instructing Carla, her maid, to bring refreshments.

Ruby sighed, feeling all the anger evaporate like steam. She had forgotten what a hot-head she herself had been in her youth, how one minute it was the end of the world, and seconds later peace had been restored. Now she realised why it always seemed to take everyone else a bit longer to catch up with her emotions. 'Look,' she said, 'I didn't come to start a fight. I've taken time off work to get here. I just want to know what's going on.'

'That makes two of us. Would you care to elaborate why you've been texting your mother while she's at work, Cathy?'

Ruby raised an eyebrow, temporarily stilled by Frances's supportive words. It was the first time she had referred to her as Cathy's mother. Was she mellowing now that her relationship with Nathan was working out? Or had she given in to the inevitability that Ruby wasn't going away?

'I'm sorry,' Cathy said ruefully. 'But you're bang out of order, Nan. I'm in my twenties, a grown woman. I should be allowed to see who I want.'

'And you are, just not him,' Frances said, her face growing taut. 'You'll thank me one day.'

Ruby frowned as she took a seat in the living room. Dust motes danced in the generous shafts of sunlight beaming through the large sash windows. It was a beautiful space, complemented with expensive artwork and tasteful furnishings. Ruby glared at Cathy, unable to believe her ears. She was in a relationship? This was news to her. 'Who?' she said, expecting the name of some underworld gangster to roll off her tongue.

'Darren. You know, from the block of flats where you used to live?'

'Oh,' Ruby said. She was aware of their friendship from when Cathy had visited her in the past. 'I didn't realise you were an item.'

'Not any more,' Cathy sulked, her mouth turned downwards into a childish frown. 'Which is why I'm moving out. Sorry, Frances, but I've made up my mind.'

'Hold up a minute,' Ruby said. 'What's the problem with her seeing Darren? He's a nice kid; he works hard. He's a bit tied down looking after his mum but…'

'His mum's dead and buried,' Frances said. 'Silly bitch overdosed on smack last month.' She raised a hand as in self-defence. 'And before you say anything, she didn't get that shit off my boys. We don't sell gear to the likes of her.'

Ruby's mouth dropped open as she turned to her daughter, now perched on the sofa across the way. 'I didn't know any of this... why didn't you tell me? I would have gone to the funeral at the very least.' It wasn't that Ruby was particularly friendly with Darren's mum, but she had a lot of time for the young man who worked so hard to make something of his life. Gang violence was rife in the estate where he lived, yet he had grabbed the chance of an apprenticeship when Nathan called in some favours from the owners of an up-and-coming Shoreditch hotel.

Cathy shrugged. 'Because I thought you'd kick up a stink too. So you don't mind me seeing him?'

'Of course not.' Ruby frowned. 'Why would I? He's not a user. It's not his fault he had such a rough start in life.'

Cathy glared at Frances for the answer. 'Tell her, Nana. Tell her why you don't want me seeing him.'

Looking distinctly uncomfortable, Frances placed her cup on the table after taking a delicate sip. The contrast in her actions made for an amusing picture as the working-class woman in her fought for dominance. 'Oh, for Gawd's sake,' she said, reverting back to her true self. 'I don't mind Darren, he seems a nice enough lad, but he's just not good enough for a Crosby girl.'

Ruby winced as she realised where this was going. She pursed her lips as she tried to contain her disgust, reminding herself whose home she was in. But Frances was still talking, trying desperately to dig herself out of the hole she had just found herself in.

'There's lots of nice lads interested in Cathy. I just want her mixing with the same sort.' She appealed to Ruby, her face falling as she caught her look of disdain.

Ruby took a deep breath as she tried to calm her response. 'Are you saying you don't want him seeing Cathy because he's black?' she said, placing her cup on the coffee table and pushing it away.

'Wot?' Frances said, looking from Ruby to Cathy. 'No! Of course not. What do you take me for?'

Cathy interjected. 'It's because of his mum. Can you believe the hypocrisy? She thinks Darren's not good enough because he's got no money and his mum took drugs.' She folded her arms, scowling at Frances. 'I'm not saying we're getting married or anything, but I'm old enough to make my own decisions about who I see.'

'I see.' Ruby nodded in understanding, trying to voice her opinion as diplomatically as she could. Sure Frances was as sweet as pie now, but she had seen her turn without warning in the past, and the last thing Ruby wanted was to be thrown out by her goons – the hired help who were never very far away. 'Cathy's right. What's more, we're very fortunate to have her in our lives. As she said, she's a grown woman. She's managed to get by in life so far without us. We don't have any right to tell her what to do, much less inflict our personal… beliefs on her.'

'I disagree,' Frances said, her temper rising as the two women shot her down. 'Just because you don't care about what she gets up to, doesn't mean I can't have a say.'

'A say which is very outdated and not helping in the slightest,' Ruby cut in. 'Do you want to lose your granddaughter, is that it? Because that's what's going to happen. How do you think Nathan's going to react to this?'

'It was Lenny that said it was a bad idea,' Frances said. 'He told me I had to intervene.'

Ruby's frown grew at the mention of his name. She knew Lenny could never resist the opportunity to stick the knife in. 'And what does Lenny know about parenting for that matter? What do any of us?' she said. 'Cathy's not twelve. The family dynamics are different and we're all just settling into it. Don't you remember what happened when Nathan and I got together? How you tried to split us up? What was the result of that?'

Frances paled, unable to reply.

'Yes, that's right. We gave Cathy up for adoption. Because we couldn't see a way we could stay together.'

'I didn't know about the pregnancy,' Frances said. 'Things would have been different if you'd told me.'

'We were too scared to approach you, terrified of what Jimmy might do,' Ruby said, the mention of Nathan's father releasing a sense of oppression into the room. 'You go laying down the law with Cathy then history is going to repeat itself. And if she ever has kids, you'll never get to see them. Is having your own way really that important to you?'

Frances sighed. 'Of course not. I just want what's best for Cathy. For all of us. Look, Ruby, I know I've been hard on you. It's taken me a long time to get over you joining the filth. But you and Nathan… well, it seems to be working, and I don't want to come between you.' She looked at her hands, now clasped on her lap, her fingers glistening from the diamond-encrusted rings bought from the proceeds of crime. 'I'm not getting any younger. I just want us to be a family. Is that too much to ask?'

Ruby's voice softened. 'Of course it's not. But you're not a dictator. You can't impose your views on others, no matter how strongly you feel.' She turned to Cathy. 'What is it you want?'

Cathy smiled, regarding her mother with new-found respect. 'I want to see Darren. To be able to make my own choices. I've had my own way for a long time. Coming here… it's been nice to be around people who care but I need my freedom too.'

'Which is?' Frances said.

'I'd like a place of my own. Somewhere Darren can come and visit. I have a job now, and I'm applying for a better one once I finish my college course. I can't afford all the rent but Dad won't mind helping me out until I can.'

Ruby bit back her smile. She still couldn't get used to Nathan being referred to as Dad. 'I'm sure he will, but he's still very protective of you. I'll broach the subject with him if you like? I know you've had a tough time. I think Nathan likes the idea of you being looked after for once.' Ruby sighed, the memory of her flat in the tower block still fresh in her memory. 'Living on your own isn't all it's cracked up to be, believe me. And this house is huge enough that you can have your privacy… as long as there's no limitations on who you can see.' She looked at Frances pointedly.

'Very well,' Frances said. 'You can see who you want. But I don't want you bringing back fellas here. Not while Lenny's around anyway. It's not worth the grief I'm going to get.'

'Why don't we compromise?' Ruby said. 'Cathy stays with me Saturdays and Sundays and lives here during the week. My flat's virtually empty at weekends as they're my busiest times at work. You can see Darren at my place and be close to work here.'

'OK,' Cathy said. 'But I'd still like a place of my own soon.'

'All in good time.' Ruby smiled. 'Just let us mollycoddle you a bit longer. What do you say, Frances?'

Frances gave her a grateful smile. 'Sounds good to me. I'm sorry about our… misunderstanding. Let's hear no more about it.'

'Good,' Ruby said, checking her mobile phone for any missed calls. A sense of relief filtered through when she saw there were none. Why was she here, sorting out her domestics when she should have been supporting her team? A sense of guilt rose from within as the urgency of her case hit home. 'I have to get back to work. I've got a double murder case on the go.'

'Sorry about the dramatics,' Cathy said, following her to the door. 'I'll think before I text next time.'

'Make sure you do,' Ruby said, giving her daughter a quick hug before saying goodbye.

*

Speeding back to the police station, she was grateful to have made progress in her home life at the very least. Perhaps there was hope for their family after all. Her fingers tightened around the steering wheel as she took the shortcuts destined to cut time off her journey. Cathy's problems were dwarfed by what lay before her, and she admonished herself for her knee-jerk reaction that took her away from the case. The ring of her phone broke through her thoughts as it flashed up on the car hands-free display. Ruby stiffened. It was DCI Worrow. As she answered her call, she prepared her excuses about where she had been.

'I'm glad I caught you,' Worrow said, as Ruby answered the phone.

'I'm just heading back to the station now, Ma'am,' Ruby said, flicking on her windscreen wipers as a sudden shower blurred her vision of the road ahead.

'Then make a diversion,' Worrow said, her voice clipped. 'They're expecting you at the prison. I want you to pay another visit to Mason Gatley. Don't leave until you have answers. Time's running out and the command team are asking questions. We've got just hours to save Cheryl Barber's life.'

CHAPTER TWENTY-THREE

It was not the best of starts to an informal interview, feeling like you were on the back foot. DI Worrow's sudden insistence of a prison visit had left Ruby feeling unsettled. She was obviously pulling strings for her, desperate for a new lead. Unlike DI Downes, DCI Worrow was keen for Ruby to make her next move. It felt odd to have her DCI's approval and be at odds with Downes, who always had her back. Sitting in the prison, she tapped her nails on the table. She had ensured her shirt was buttoned up to the neck. Her hair was straightened, scraped back into a ponytail and she had even wiped off her red lipstick for a natural look. Everything about her visit today was about putting on a professional front. She shuddered at the thought of being under Mason's control. He was the one locked away, she reminded herself, but deep down, she knew he held the key. He would feed from her emotions, enjoy watching her beg for a crumb of information that might catch the killer inspired by his evil acts. Nathan's words from the night before echoed in her mind. If he was worried about Mason's behaviour, then she had a right to be on her guard.

She stiffened as he entered the room. Just as before, he was clean and tidy, his wavy hair brushed back from his face. His grey sweatshirt fit snugly over a well-defined chest, and Ruby guessed he took advantage of the prison gym.

'Welcome back,' he said, a smug smile touching his lips. But like before, the emotions etched on his face never quite reached his eyes. Ice blue, they reflected a coldness that emanated from his very soul.

Ruby met his gaze, unflinching as he pulled in his chair to be nearer to her. 'You were right about the evidence,' she said, happy to stroke his ego to get him onside. 'Our killer has gone to great lengths to copy your previous MO.'

'Which was?' Mason said, looking pleased that someone had copied his pattern of procedure.

'It's confidential,' Ruby replied. 'But similar enough to make me realise that you've spoken to someone in detail about it.'

'Is that so?' Mason said. 'You surprise me, officer, I would have thought that an intelligent woman like you was capable of thinking outside the box.'

Ruby shook her head. 'It's not one of our own, if that's what you're hinting at.'

'Oh, come on.' Mason emitted a thin laugh. 'Your team aren't loyal to you, they're loyal to the idea of you. When their desires change, so does their loyalty. Now I…' He leaned forward, his fingers intertwined as he pushed his face closer to hers. 'I'd be loyal to you all day long.' His words silenced as he tested her limits, his eyes cold and unyielding, waiting for her to flinch.

'Those who don't know the value of loyalty can never appreciate it,' Ruby said, unwavering in her glare. 'How have you managed to keep your American accent after all these years?' It was a good way of changing the subject, as well as turning things back onto him.

'I'm a British citizen,' he said defensively.

'But you spent most of your childhood over there, living with your mother in a trailer park. I suppose some things aren't as easy to shake off, no matter how hard you try.' She was referring to their last conversation, when she tried to work out his childhood and the motives behind his murders. 'But I'm not here to play an armchair psychologist. We have another victim. Her husband has received two photos as well as an amputated finger in the post. I won't try to appeal to your better nature because I know you don't have one. So what do I have to do to find out where she's being held?'

Mason grinned, leaning back in his chair and clasping his fingers behind his head. 'A phone number.'

'Whose?'

'Yours.'

Ruby frowned. 'What for?'

'Don't be coy; so I can talk to you, of course.'

'I'll see that my office number is left for you,' she replied, knowing that was not what he meant.

Mason glanced around the room before lowering his tone. 'I'm not talking about ringing during office hours. Come on, Ruby, you know we have access to phones in here. I've been serving enough time in here to gain some privilege from the screws.'

'I don't do sex talk with strangers,' Ruby said drily. 'Besides, there are phone lines that offer a much better service than I could.'

'You think that's all I want you for? Don't put yourself down, detective. You're an intelligent red-blooded woman. I just want to hear the sound of your voice.'

'I'll think about it,' Ruby said, knowing Nathan would never allow it.

'And in the meantime your victim is languishing in some shoddy hotel room, bleeding out as the rope bites into her neck. Do you know how long I left my victims to die? Tightening and loosening, bringing them back to life only to cut off their air supply. It was a bit like orgasm, the delicious build up, only to feel the release at the end.'

'Tell me where Cheryl is,' she said, cupping her clenched fist with her other hand.

'I don't know where she is but I can hazard a good guess. Text me from your new phone number. I expect you'll buy a pay as you go.'

'I don't know your number,' Ruby said.

'Turns out I'm not the only one that enjoys playing a game. Lenny has it. He'll pass it on when you give him a call.'

'Why are you doing this?' Ruby said, the mention of Nathan's brother adding another sting to the tail. 'Are you just stringing me along?'

'A man has to find amusement where he can.' Mason grinned.

'This better be worthwhile,' Ruby said. 'I need something to go on in the meantime.'

Mason shrugged. 'In my case, the press reported the victims were bound and gagged. But they didn't know that the rope had been taken away and reused. I suppose you could call me the sentimental type. I tied the bottom of each victim's finger with a piece of string to stem the bleeding then cauterised it to seal the skin. It smelt like a barbecue in that room, but the general public don't like to hear of such things and it never made the press.'

'How can you tell me where the victim is being kept if you're not responsible for the current murders?' Ruby asked, refusing to join in as he raked over the embers of his crimes. She could have arranged for an official line of questioning, but in this informal setting, there was more information to be gained.

He arched an eyebrow. 'I know London has changed somewhat in the last ten years, but I've no doubt that the information I can give you will bring you to their door.'

'Then tell me now. Please. Do you want me to beg? Is that it?'

Mason smiled, looking pleased to have Ruby eating out of the palm of his hand. 'I'd like you to do lots of things but I don't think the guard would approve. In which case, I will have to make do with your phone number instead.'

As if on cue, Ruby's phone buzzed in her pocket, providing a much-needed break in conversation. The text was short but to the point. It was Downes, and Ruby's heart faltered at the sight of his text.

We've got him. On our way around there now.

CHAPTER TWENTY-FOUR

Leaving the prison, Ruby recalled her conversation with Mason, having turned down his request to speak to him on a mobile phone. She should report it, have his cell searched at the very least, but the offer was an ace she was pocketing for now. DI Downes was right, he had been toying with her, reeling her in for his own amusement. Was this whole scenario created just because he was bored? The way he looked at her when he spoke about having a rope around her neck… she shuddered. The man made her skin crawl.

She turned over the engine of the Ford Focus, allowing it to sync with her phone. 'Hello? Ruby? Where are you?' Downes's voice boomed in her airspace, a sense of urgency lacing his tone.

She turned the volume to a more tolerable level, her car crawling through the car park as she awaited further instructions. She needed time to gather her thoughts, make notes on her conversation with Mason, but time was a luxury in sparse supply. Everything about this day felt like a clock ticking backwards, and Ruby clenched the steering wheel tightly as she spoke.

'I'm just leaving the prison. Tell me where to go and I'll meet you there.'

'Thanks to that passcode you got, we were able to access the dating site straight away.'

Ruby's heart fluttered in her chest. She would ask him how later on. Right now, they had a life to save. She prayed they weren't too late. 'Give me the address,' she said, shoving the car into gear. She flipped on the wipers as a sprinkle of rain dappled the windscreen of her car.

Downes relayed the address of a flat on a quiet street ten minutes away. 'Matthew Johnson's his name,' he said. 'Softly, softly approach, we don't want to spook him. Don't go in, do you hear me? Not until backup arrives. There's a unit on its way.'

Clicking her seatbelt into place, Ruby pressed down on the indicator before turning left. It was rare to find answers so quickly, and her heart pounded at the prospect of bringing the killer's reign of terror to an end. Mason Gatley had killed six women before he was caught. Would the present-day killer have left a breadcrumb trail of clues? Surely if he was colluding with Mason then he would have ensured he covered his tracks? Or was the Internet and its workings beyond his control? Ruby shifted uneasily as her car weaved through traffic, alarm bells signalling in her mind. A sudden thought injected a cold chill down her spine. Perhaps it was a trap. She recalled the last big case she dealt with and how horrifically that had ended for them all. She turned right, Matthew's street address looming into view. Adrenalin pumped through her body, her left leg shaking as it flooded her veins. She inched down the accelerator, keeping a watchful eye on her speed. At least traffic was reasonable. She would take the bus lane if she had to.

Turning into the address, she bumped against the kerb, slamming the brakes of her car. So much for the softly, softly approach. She peered up at the block of flats, the rain dampening her hair as she stepped onto the pavement. Was Matthew looking down at her right now? She imagined a silver chain gracing his neck, dipped from the weight of his victim's wedding ring. Was there one? Two? Maybe more? Each one representative of a life lost. Did he smile as he felt them shift from his movement? Take comfort from their presence while he plunged their loved ones into a world full of betrayal and pain?

Traffic whooshed past on the main road and she listened for a siren cutting through the backdrop of city noise she had grown accustomed to. Downes would have instructed her colleagues to make a silent approach. A rustling noise caught her attention and she walked around the corner to find a dirty-looking Staffordshire Terrier rooting through a pile of bin bags. Snuffling through the leftovers, he clamped his teeth around the carcass of a cooked chicken and regarded her for all of two seconds before giving her a look that suggested he was not in the mood to share.

'Rockkkky!' A shrill voice sent the dog running, its tail clamped between his legs.

'Catch him, will ya?' the woman yelled, as the dog skirted past Ruby's legs.

She gave an apologetic smile to who she presumed was its owner, as she did not fancy getting bitten today. A middle-aged woman, with wet black hair, she was wearing a dressing gown that was struggling to close around her expansive waist.

'Sorry,' Ruby said, approaching her as she held open the door. 'Do you live here?'

'Of course I bleeding live here,' the woman replied, lifting a slippered foot for good measure. 'I hardly go out dressed like this, now do I? Why didn't ya catch me dog? She's been giving me the slip all day.'

'Because I've better things to do,' Ruby said, lifting her warrant card and peering at the names listed beside the buzzer system on the front door. 'Do you know a man named Matthew Johnson?'

'It's just me and me dog, if I can catch the little bugger,' she said, pulling a lighter and a crumpled pack of cigarettes from the pocket of her dressing gown. 'I don't pay no attention to what anyone else gets up to around here.' She flicked the lighter into life against the bent up cigarette hanging from her mouth. 'Why? What's he done?'

Ruby smiled at her contradiction. 'Probably nothing, but it's best you go indoors until this is dealt with.' She was itching, really itching to speak to him. But rushing in without adequate cover meant risking his escape. According to the buzzer system, Matthew was on the second floor. She took a few steps back to stare up at the windows.

'It's the one with no nets,' the woman said, exhaling a long wisp of smoke. 'Not exactly 'ouse proud that one.'

Blinking against the fine mist of drizzle, Ruby frowned as she saw the telltale signs that something was very wrong. Even from here, where she was standing, she could see the unwanted guests that occupied their suspect's window. At first, she thought the dark shadow on the window was a trick of the light when it began to move from left to right. Shielding her eyes with her hand, she drew a sharp breath as she figured it out. 'No,' she whispered. Her heart plummeting at the small cloud of blowflies tapping the window for escape. It could only mean one thing. As the police cars drew up behind her, she quickly pointed out what she had found. There was something festering in that room. She only hoped that it was not Cheryl. Had they come too late?

Ruby followed them up to the second floor, DI Downes by her side. 'What kept you?' she rasped, the sound of heavy boots against stairs almost drowning out her words.

'Strategy meeting,' Downes said irritably. 'How come you weren't at the rendezvous point?'

'It was quicker to come here.' Ruby agreed that officers should be kept safe and pre-empting their arrival made sense. It did not stop her from wanting to rush head first into danger, if it meant saving their victim's life.

'What's going on?' a thin-faced elderly man half opened his door as officers banged on Matthew's flat.

'Why don't you get yourself back inside?' Ruby said, steering him back in. 'We'll come and talk to you shortly.'

In the absence of a response, officers wasted no time in forcing open the door. It flew off its hinges almost immediately; two swift raps of the enforcer against the hinges was enough to bring the cheap plywood door crashing down. The stench hit them instantly, making Ruby lift the back of her hand to her face. She gave DI Downes a look which said she did not hold out much hope. A few stray flies zipped past her as she followed the officers inside. Death had paid a visit. The question was, whose body were they going to find?

CHAPTER TWENTY-FIVE

Ruby slowly accustomed herself to the humidity in the room, swatting away the flies that had been feasting on the body that lay unmoving on the threadbare bedroom carpet. A uniformed police officer reached out his hand to open the window, battling through the swarm of insects as he choked a cough.

'Leave it,' Ruby said, knowing that Bones, the crime scene investigator, would want the scene untouched. The presence of blowflies, or blue bottles as Ruby liked to call them, could be useful to the investigation. Even the tiniest bit of trace evidence could be gleaned from the unlikeliest of places. Their corpse was not going anywhere any time soon. With the rooms secured, DI Downes wasted no time in dispersing the officers who had already updated control with their find. It was imperative they move quickly. Establishing the time of death would be a priority for crime scene officers as they tried to work out if the deceased could have been involved in Melissa's death.

Lying in a pool of congealed blood with a bath towel around his waist, the man's bloated body was barely recognisable from the picture on the wall. Livor mortis was evident beneath his skin, the dark discolouration of blood often mistaken for bruising by inexperienced officers at the scene. To Ruby, it was merely the blood pooling in one area, no longer being pumped by the heart. Tearing her eyes away from the corpse, she dipped her hand into the pocket of a leather jacket hanging from the wardrobe door. Sliding out the driver's licence with a gloved hand, she confirmed her suspicions. This was the body of Matthew Johnson. But was it the same Matthew Johnson responsible for killing Melissa and kidnapping Cheryl? She checked the date of birth, calculating he was in his early thirties. No doubt there would be lots more clues as to his occupation on the scene. But that was as far as Ruby was willing to go until the CSI arrived. She took a shallow breath, feeling the contents of her last meal make itself known. It was hard to bear the meaty smell that would cling to her clothes long after she was gone. Putrefaction was well underway and a rough time of death would be identified by the pathologist later on.

She stepped aside as Bones, the head CSI, entered the room. His eyes flicked from left to right over his white face mask, making note of the numerous insects buzzing around in the room.

'We thought we were coming to arrest our suspect,' Ruby said, as means of explanation for her presence in the room.

'I heard the update. So I guess you're going to ask me how long he's been here. You know that's a job for the pathologist, don't you?'

'We've requested their attendance but nobody can spare the time,' Downes replied.

Bones peered at the body as his colleagues set up their equipment to record the scene. 'Let me give you a quick lesson on entomology,' he said, nodding towards the glass pane which was still vacated with flies. 'When a body is left exposed like this, it's only natural for blowflies to appear. After being laid in a nice moist spot, maggots can hatch within hours if undisturbed. It takes about twelve days for an adult fly to emerge. Then you're talking between eighteen to twenty-two days before the whole cycle begins again.'

'So he's been dead at least two and a half weeks?' Ruby said.

'At least,' Bones replied, 'but Vera will give you a better idea after the post-mortem. Can't say I envy her there.'

Ruby exchanged glances with DI Downes. If he expected her to attend that, he had another think coming.

She withdrew from the room, retracing her steps in order not to disturb the scene. Taking one last glance, she took in the minor details that suggested that Matthew most likely lived alone. It was sad that nobody had discovered his body until now. From the living room a television hummed, a programme providing cheerful background chatter at odds with the violent scene. The double bed was unmade, a pizza takeaway box on the floor. A pair of cufflinks lay on the dresser table under the glow of a bedside light. The fact it was switched on suggested that Matthew could have died during the hours of darkness. That, or the killer had switched it on to divert them from the truth. Another thought sparked in Ruby's mind. Could the person that killed Matthew be responsible for Melissa Sherman's murder too? Perhaps Phillip Sherman had decided to get his own revenge after his wife's death. Or had he hired Matthew to murder his wife then killed Matthew to cover himself? Ruby would get no rest from such theories until firm progress was made.

Back at the station, a briefing was quickly assembled as they brought the investigation up to date. Ruby stood with her shirtsleeves rolled up, having left her jacket on the hook in her office. It was another item of clothing that would need a dry clean. For now, such annoyances were minor compared to the thoughts weighing heavy on her mind. After already seeing his driving licence, Ruby was not surprised to hear that the corpse had been identified as the same Matthew Johnson who had used the *Debauchery* site.

Gratefully she lifted a mug of tea from the tray being passed around. She was still playing catch up and it felt like she was running up an escalator that was going the wrong way. Scene of crime officers had worked diligently to try and glean some clues as to Cheryl's current whereabouts, but there was little forthcoming so far. With evening closing in on day two of Cheryl's kidnapping, they were only too aware of her fate if they failed to locate her tonight.

'How did you track down Matthew's address?' she asked, trying to piece together the clues that had led them to his flat.

Downes lumbered in beside her, spilling his coffee as he sat. Swearing under his breath, he mopped up the spillage seeping into the paperwork he had just put down. In the absence of DCI Worrow, briefing was in his hands. 'That site you gave us wasn't as difficult to infiltrate as we first thought. Once we had the passcode, the tech department was able to access the online profiles. They found Matthew's username that then linked to a user who seems to be Melissa. Turns out this poor sod had been active on other dating sites too.' He glanced around the room. 'He's used his credit card to pay a subscription fee. Thanks to Luddy's smooth-talking, we were able to secure his bank details and address.'

Ruby acknowledged Luddy's good work with a nod of the head.

He flicked through the pages of his notes. 'He mainly advertised on high-class shag sites. *Debauchery* is by invitation and they're very particular about who they allow in. Given they know each other, I think that Cheryl and Melissa got in the same way.'

Ruby nodded, glad that they were both on the same page. 'But what about Matthew's flat? Didn't look very high-class to me.'

'I spoke to his landlord,' Luddy said. 'He was due to move out at the end of the month; apparently he'd got this posh pad in Knightsbridge.'

Most likely paid for by a benefactor for a bit of fun on the side, Ruby thought. The press only spoke about mistresses, but Ruby knew there were plenty of powerful women who liked to play away too. She returned her thoughts to the case, her mind buzzing with activity. 'OK,' Ruby said, delivering an apologetic smile to her DI for hijacking the briefing. 'So, usernames aside, have we any other evidence to suggest that Cheryl and Melissa used *Debauchery*?'

'Stationery supplies,' Richard piped up, looking mildly embarrassed as all heads turned in his direction. Clearing his throat, he explained his outburst. 'Both Cheryl and Melissa made purchases on their husband's credit cards. The transaction shows up as stationery. I did some digging. It's a fake company used to take payments which eventually end up in *Debauchery*'s account.'

'The cheek of it,' Ruby said, shocked for the second time that day. 'Not just playing away but letting their husbands pay for it.'

'It's hiding the lie in plain sight,' Richard said, stony-faced. 'The last place they would expect to look is right under their very own nose.'

Ruby leaned back in her chair leaving Downes to take centre stage.

'So we're pretty clear on one thing. Matthew Johnson has been murdered, and evidence points to him owning the profile that was visited by Melissa Sherman and most likely Cheryl Barber too. But according to Bones, Matthew's been dead for more than two weeks.'

A rumble of chatter filtered around the room. Downes silenced it as he raised his hand. 'Our records show that Matthew's profile has been and still is active, which means that somebody is logged in and using it for their own motives. It's my belief that we have an imposter. Someone who's posing as Matthew to lure these women in.' Pushing back his chair, he walked to the whiteboard.

'We've got to pre-empt this killer's movements,' Downes said, tapping the photos of Melissa's crime scene, which were pinned to the board. 'Are they using only high-class hotels without CCTV? Three days that poor lass was in that hotel room while people walked past in the corridor outside. During that time, our killer casually ordered room service and watched cable TV. Can you imagine that?' His eyes wide, he glanced around the room. 'Even after he killed her, he was in no hurry to leave. He took his time cleaning up after himself, wiping away every trace. The involvement of such a cold-hearted killer means there's less chance of them leaving evidence at the scene.'

'But surely that must have aroused suspicion?' DC Ludgrove piped up.

'Staff are vague on details. But then again, they're known for being discreet. Their reputation will mean more to them than helping us out.'

He's right, Ruby thought, the only thing that staff would confirm was that the room had been booked by a man. At last, they were getting somewhere, as the results of their investigations began to filter in. But her optimism was tinged with sadness as she knew, deep down, that for Cheryl they would now probably be too late.

CHAPTER TWENTY-SIX

Matthew sat on the floor, legs spread amongst the remnants of things he had collected. To the right of him was a lock of Melissa's hair and a sequin that had fallen from her dress. To the left was Cheryl's false fingernail and a tangle of hairs he had plucked from her head. His bedroom rug was adorned with his trinkets. But none were as precious as the wedding rings nestled against his collarbone on the chain beneath his shirt. He clutched the cordless phone in his hand. His calls to Sanity Line helped maintain balance in the world. Nobody knew why he was suffering, only that he needed help.

Sleep evaded him since he had murdered Melissa. He had lain in his bed, silent prayers crossing his lips as he stared at the crucifix over his door. He hoped it would be easier the second time around. Each encounter brought its own risks, and after the first one, he considered walking away. But these women… these sluts. They just kept contacting him. Why wouldn't they leave him alone? He had told himself to stay offline. What these women did wasn't his business. But the truth would gnaw on him like a hungry rat on a bone. His mind would not rest as it conjured up images of their despicable acts. He clenched his teeth. Something had to be done. Shoving away their belongings, he rose to his feet. He caught his reflection in the mirror, stepping closer for a better look. Was he changing? Was his anger visible on the outside now? He was taking a risk having their belongings here. What if he got caught? Who would carry on his good work then? With shaking fingers, he dialled the number of the only people who understood.

'Hello, Sanity Line,' the call taker answered.

Relief swept over Matthew as he recognised their voice. It was Laura. He imagined her, sitting behind her desk, playing with her hair as she took his call. He was so relieved to talk to her that he found himself babbling as he delivered a diluted tale of his recent encounter with Cheryl. Laura waited patiently while he brought her up to speed. He glossed over the ending, his ramblings focused on wondering why people stray. The sudden sense of confusion he had felt when things had ended so abruptly between them. After days of online flirting, it was over. Soon she would be over. She would never stray again. So why wasn't he satisfied? Why did he feel the need to carry on with someone else? Following in Mason Gatley's footsteps was often unappealing because a voice deep inside told him it was wrong.

'First Melissa and now Cheryl,' he sniffled, his words ragged and disjointed. 'I must be a glutton for punishment.'

'It's normal to feel like that when a relationship comes to an end,' Laura said. 'Perhaps you need to look at why you're attracted to married women.'

'As in rake over my childhood memories?' Matthew asked. 'Believe me, you don't want to go there.' His stomach tightened as the humiliation of his youth came back to haunt him. He never envisioned life would take him to this place. 'I confronted Cheryl and Melissa about their behaviour. They said they were sorry, that they only wanted a bit of fun. They were sorry by the time they met me.'

'Really?' Laura said, hesitant now. 'What happened?'

Matthew's fingers curled over the telephone receiver, his anger resurfacing. 'Let's just say they won't be cheating again.'

'What are you going to do now?' Laura said.

Matthew shrugged, even though she could not see his reactions down the phone. 'I've barely touched the surface. I had three more emails today from women asking to hook up. The world is buried in filth and degradation. I shouldn't fight it. It's time for change.'

'So what are you planning?' Laura said.

Matthew exhaled an anguished moan. 'Either I do something about it or I allow it to eat me up inside. In the old days, I found comfort in the church. But so much of the Bible contradicts itself. Sometimes it feels like there's only one way out. I wish I had the courage to…'

'Go on,' Laura said, her voice soft and warm.

'To kill myself and take them with me,' he continued.

'But religion states it's a sin to take another person's life, as well as your own, doesn't it?' Laura said.

He ungraciously snuffled into the phone, gulping back his deep sense of shame. 'I suppose so. But there's no way I can bear to sit by and allow others to suffer as I have. I can't allow that to happen. I won't.'

'What are you going to do?' Laura said.

Matthew's sobs dissolved, his moods swinging like a pendulum. 'I'm going to bring the world around to my way of thinking. I don't care what it takes. Those bitches are going to pay.'

Silence passed, and Matthew's glance was drawn to the window. He rubbed his arms as an errant breeze brought goosebumps to his skin.

'Have you thought about getting help?' Laura said, falling back on the words that call takers used when they didn't know what else to say.

'Me get help? You think their behaviour is OK? Have you ever been unfaithful? Whoring yourself out for some mindless fun?'

'I-I,' she stuttered, taking a breath before finally responding. 'I think we should focus on you.'

A flame of hope lit in the pit of Matthew's stomach. At least he was being listened to; he could draw strength from her support.

He inhaled deeply, his words floating down the line. 'I'm going to keep going, spread the word until I close them all down. There are websites – there for immoral use. I should get a medal. I'm doing this to spare others my pain.'

'Would you like to talk about that?' Laura said.

Matthew's response was instant because it was a question he had asked himself many times already. 'There's no point in going backwards. We can only look to the future now.'

Laura sighed before breaking free from the pro forma questions that were getting her nowhere. 'Do you really think this is for the best? You don't sound very happy living like this. When you said you'll make them pay?…'

Matthew snorted. There was no getting through to Laura, not when she had such blinkered vision. 'I'm not the first person to do this, you know. Only unlike my predecessor, I'm not going to get caught.'

'Do you think that's a normal way to react, lashing out at others because of how you've been treated in the past? Shouldn't you distance yourself from toxic relationships and get some peace in your life?'

Matthew raised an eyebrow, picking up the note of disbelief in her voice. How dare she patronise him like that. 'Huh!' he spat, clutching the phone tightly to his ear. 'You don't understand me. You haven't got a clue.'

'Matthew, wait…' Laura said, as the call came to an end.

He checked his watch. In just a few hours it would be midnight. It was time to get back to the hotel. Cheryl would be waiting, and it would be a shame to let her spend her last few hours alone.

CHAPTER TWENTY-SEVEN

It seemed only fitting that Ruby make a personal visit to Sergeant Jimmy Patterson of the high-tech crime unit servicing their area. It was late, but he was still working and she knew she would not sleep tonight. A wiry middle-aged man with a salt-and-pepper beard, he wore the expression of someone who was permanently hounded. Given the rising levels of cybercrime, Ruby knew that there would never be enough money in the budget to stretch to the demands being placed upon their team.

'Got time for a quick word?' she said, taking a seat in the open-plan office. She knew Jimmy preferred to work amongst his colleagues rather than on his own. For her, the office was the only place she was afforded any peace.

'And if I say no?' he replied, minimizing a programme on his computer.

'Please,' she said, leaning forward. 'Just two minutes. I need to ask you about *Debauchery*.'

'It's all in my report which will be uploaded to HOLMES by the morning,' Jimmy replied.

Ruby rubbed her eyes, staining her fingers with mascara that she'd forgotten she had applied. She could not go off duty until she found answers to the questions running around in her head. She glanced up wearily, rubbing her hands on her black trousers. 'We're on a time limit, and for one of our victims, it's running out. Can you at least tell me who's set up the site?'

Jimmy sighed, a glimmer of pity in his eyes. 'It's a big money spinner from what I can see. They have thousands of subscribers from all over the globe. So, if you're asking me if the head of this organisation is the killer then I doubt it. They're making too much money to ruin it with such bad press.'

'"Thousands"?' Ruby said. 'But it's on the dark web. How are all these people gaining access?'

'Any idiot who downloads a programme to their computer and follows the instructions can find their way in. The site appears to originate from Russia. I can't narrow it down any more than that.'

'"Russia"?' Ruby replied, realising she had repeated his words for the second time.

Jimmy nodded. 'Hence why I don't think the creator of this site is connected to your killer. Most of its users portray themselves as wealthy businessmen or women. *Debauchery* is heavily geared towards women meeting men, and they seemed to have tapped into a good market. Sometimes I feel like I'm in the wrong job, you know?…'

Ruby smiled. You didn't join the police to be rich or successful. 'But if there's more women than men, who are they dating?'

'The theme is all about being sexually adventurous. You know, the "you only live once" and "try before you die" attitude, encouraging its users to be sexually promiscuous. There are women meeting women, threesomes, and all sorts of kinky fetishes. But for women who just want an illicit shag, they're encouraged to use what's called the professional daters. Men who are clean, discreet and recommended.'

'Male prostitutes, in other words.'

'To us, yes. But they're sold on the site as ordinary men who are good at what they do. They're selling you the fantasy – their words not mine.'

'Hmm,' Ruby said. 'Some fantasies are best left in people's heads. So what can you tell me about this Matthew guy?'

'All in my report,' Jimmy said. 'But he appeared to be kept in regular work. The professional daters are sold by their reviews and he is – or should I say was – well rated.' He smiled. 'Makes me shudder to think of having your sexual prowess reviewed online. God knows what our exes would say about us over the years, eh Ruby?' He followed up with a sly wink.

'Speak for yourself; I've had no complaints,' Ruby grinned. Truth was, she'd only ever had two serious relationships. One with Downes and the other with Nathan. True, there had been advances from others, but Ruby's main love had always been her job. She leaned back in her chair, bringing their attention back to the task in hand.

'If I was the killer and wanted to take Matthew's identity, how would I go about it? I mean, how would I know where he lived if I wanted to kill him off?'

'Easy enough. He or she could arrange a date with Mr Lover Lover here, do a no-show, then follow him home. They would have paid up front so it was no great loss to Matthew when his date didn't turn up.'

Ruby shook her head in disbelief. 'That's so dangerous though, isn't it?'

'No more dangerous than our local toms selling themselves on the streets every night. The only difference is, these dating sites charge a hell of a lot more. They also allude to drug use, so they cream off extra money selling it on the side.'

Ruby frowned, the investigation becoming more tangled by the hour. 'We can't rule out a dealer's involvement in all of this either. We need to have a closer look at this site, find out what's going on. Why do you think they're on the dark web? Surely they'd make more money if they were more visible online like some of the other sites?'

'Remember the scandal when hackers downloaded member details from that famous marital dating site and posted them online? A hidden site is more appealing to people who want their details kept private.'

'But you hacked in easily enough.'

'Ms Preston, *I* am an expert in the field. Of course I got in.' He gave her a look of mock disgust. 'Doesn't mean any Tom, Dick or Harry would be able to.'

'You know what I mean,' Ruby chortled, aware of his earlier contraction that anyone with a brain could find the site. 'Surely other highly qualified people can hack it too?'

Jimmy responded with a left shoulder shrug. 'To be honest, I was surprised at how easy it was. It's a false sense of security, which comes with a high premium. Until now, it seemed to work pretty well.'

'But we're not talking about details being leaked, are we? We're talking about people losing their lives. Is there any way we can shut this site down?'

'Even if I could get in touch with the owner, I can't see them agreeing to close down such a lucrative site. I won't go into the technical jargon but they have their own servers and it's not as if we could override the systems to shut it off. Even if they did, I don't think it's going to stop your killer. These sites are ten a penny – they'd just move on to another one. Besides, you can privately message people here too. Matthew had a waiting list as long as your arm. He can contact any one of these people off the site and meet them in confidence. Well, rather his impersonator can.'

'So what will stop him? Isn't there anything you can tell me? I've got a potential victim in a hotel room, minutes away from death.'

'Site users are very careful about meeting locations, for obvious reasons. From what I gather there's a long list of discreet hotels that they use throughout the UK. But Cheryl wouldn't have known where she was going until hours before, when she paid her fee. She paid the agency and they booked the hotel so it doesn't show up on her credit card. The agency shows up as something mundane, a retail outlet, something like that.'

'Stationery,' Ruby said, remembering Richard's words. 'So how am I going to catch my killer if we can't locate him online?' she asked.

Jimmy scratched his chin, giving it some thought. 'Despite the membership numbers, you're dealing with a small circle of people locally, who appear to have links in high society. Take that code, for example. It leads directly to Matthew's page.'

'Wait a minute,' Ruby said, straightening in her seat. 'Did you say it led to Matthew's page? They're not all like that, are they?'

'Sorry, I thought you knew. Each member is assigned a code. It's a password you can use to invite people to view your page. And get this – the code refreshes every two weeks, so new cards would have had to be printed off and made.'

Ruby paled as Jimmy's words sank in. 'You need to focus on the source of these invites. Because chances are, whoever's giving them out will lead you right to our killer's door.'

CHAPTER TWENTY-EIGHT

'You don't really need me, you're just winding me up,' Ruby said, digging her hands into her jacket pockets. Her heels felt glued to the ground as DI Downes gently tugged on her arm, dragging her across the police station car park. A playful smile briefly crossed his face as he lowered his head to the shower of drizzle which penetrated the night air.

'I'm serious. Vera's good enough to slot us in. We can't keep her waiting.'

'At this hour of the night? Seriously?' She double-checked her watch to ensure she wasn't imagining it. Twelve thirty and they were about to go to a post-mortem? Having exhausted their enquiries surrounding Cheryl, she had instructed her team to go home.

'Are yous coming or do I have to tell her you've chickened out?' Downes said, releasing her arm.

'I'm coming,' Ruby huffed. Her dislike of the forensic autopsy was no secret. It wasn't being in the presence of dead bodies that bothered her, it was watching them being sliced open that made her stomach churn. She wished she could become hardened to it, but no matter how many she attended, she could not stop her stomach from rolling over at the sounds and smells that it produced. Still, if the pathologist, Vera, was diligent enough to work late, then the least she could do was to show willing and attend.

Melissa's body had been stripped, photographed, measured, weighed and X-rayed by the time they arrived. Ruby suppressed a shudder as she entered the cold and sterile room, tightening her blazer across her chest. To Vera, the corpse was just a vessel, but to Ruby, it was Melissa, a young woman whose life had been cut short in the most brutal way. Her beauty had been taken along with her life, and the bloated face was unrecognisable to the ones featured in the tabloids and magazines alongside her famous husband. Protruding from between her teeth, her tongue appeared like a thick grey slab. Her body, now dull and lifeless, carried the scars of a vicious attack.

Vera smiled broadly at their arrival, perhaps glad of the company during this late hour of the night. But Ruby's attention was on the young woman's body laid out on the cold unforgiving mortuary table. Her tongue clicked against the roof of her mouth as she swallowed. She did not want to think about how they had straightened her into such a position after rigor mortis had taken hold. White blonde in colour, Melissa's curly hair was drawn away from her face, her eyes mercifully closed.

'We've already searched the body for trace evidence and sent fibres to the crime lab for examination,' Vera said. 'Her fingernails appear to have been scrubbed and the body cleaned prior to being posed.'

'Just like the previous killer,' Downes mumbled under his breath.

'But unlike the previous case, there's no evidence of sexual intercourse this time around.' Vera gave Downes a smug grin. 'I read up on the case. Only what's printed in *True Detective* magazine mind. The killer left the sheets on the bed though, just like before. Hopefully we'll get something back from them.'

'What about the amputated finger?' Ruby asked.

Downes sighed, his shoulders drooping from working all day without a break. 'The test results have come back positive. It belongs to this poor wee soul.'

Ruby's eyes trailed to the mangled hand and a pang of sorrow took hold.

'And you're sure there was no sexual intercourse?' Downes said to Vera.

'Absolutely. I conducted both vaginal and anal swabs for semen and latex residue, in case a condom was used. There's nothing to say she didn't have sex voluntarily and the evidence has been washed away, but there's no sign of force being used.'

'Just like before, the killer was in no hurry to leave,' Downes mused, speaking his thoughts aloud. 'But Mason's murders were sexually motivated. What does this say about our man?'

'He could have masturbated, disposed of the evidence…' Ruby said. 'Or he could have had other reasons for wanting to kill.'

'Aye,' Downes said sadly, his eyes roaming over the face of the deceased. 'But where does that leave Cheryl?'

CHAPTER TWENTY-NINE

'Do you want me to stay?' Nathan said, turning up the collar of his coat. After sharing a meal, he seemed all set to go home. He had business to attend to and Ruby knew better than to ask what it was.

'Am I that transparent?' she said, dreading the thought of being on her own. Left alone with her thoughts she knew that guilt would plague her. Given their lack of leads, DI Downes had sent her home to get some sleep. But what right did she have to relax in bed when Cheryl Barber could be losing her life?

'Tough case?' he said, taking off his jacket and hanging it back on the hook.

'You don't have to stay,' Ruby sighed wearily. 'We can talk about it tomorrow. Honestly, I'll be fine.'

Nathan seemed to consider this for a moment before plucking his mobile phone from his pocket. He swiftly tapped out a text before following her back inside. 'It's nothing that can't wait.' Kicking off his shoes, he sat back on the sofa that he had vacated moments before. 'It's not Mason Gatley, is it? Because if it is…'

'Relax, it's not Mason. I'm just frustrated that we've not been able to find the killer. It's been three days now, and we're no further on.'

'Can I help with anything?' Nathan said. His fingers elicited a shiver as they trailed down the side of her neck.

'You've done more than enough,' Ruby replied, leaning into his chest. Beneath his shirt his heart beat strong and steady and she was exactly where she needed to be. 'If it weren't for you I wouldn't even have got in to see Mason Gatley,' she said, feeling her body relax as he rhythmically stroked her hair. 'He's not given me any definite leads, but he's hinted he knows what's going on.'

'Doesn't surprise me in the least,' Nathan said, his voice deep and full of knowing. 'That's why I want you to be careful around him.'

'You sound like Downes,' Ruby said, wishing she could take back the words as they left her mouth. She briefly gazed up at him to see his face darken. He knew about their past relationship and was not the biggest fan of her boss.

'Yeah, well if anyone's going to watch out for you it'll be me,' Nathan said.

Ruby exhaled, a wave of tiredness inflaming her irritation. 'I'm a big girl, I can look out for myself.' Untangling herself from his embrace, she straightened her posture and drove her fingers through her hair. 'I should have let you leave. I'm too tired for all of this crap.'

'Why don't you tell me what's really bothering you?' Nathan said, ignoring her annoyance. In the old days, he would have stormed out. The pair of them used to argue more than they got on. But these last few months, things had changed between them. The friction that had infiltrated their relationship was now replaced by a new sense of calm.

She sighed, feeling guilty for her outburst when he was only trying to help. 'I just feel so helpless, you know? Cheryl's out there somewhere trussed up in some hotel. Her three days are up, which means we've failed her. I guarantee we'll find a third photo tomorrow which gives us the identity of the hotel.'

'That's good, though, isn't it? If you can find her…'

'No, because by then she'll be dead. If he mimics Mason, he kills them on the third day. He's probably moved on already, set his sights on someone else.'

Nathan rubbed his stubbled chin. 'You're no good to anyone if you're wound up. The best thing you can do is get some kip.'

'You don't run any online dating sites, do you, or provide coke to them?' Ruby said, referring to the company firm.

'You pointing the finger at me now?' Nathan said. 'Seriously, Ruby, are you trying to pick a fight or what?'

'No, of course not,' Ruby said, taking him by the hands. 'I know you'd never be willingly involved in that sort of thing.'

Nathan's once calm exterior dissolved; he shook his head. 'The only part of the business we ran online was the escort service and you know I shut that down ages ago. Look it up if you don't believe me. Those murders have nothing to do with me.'

'Jeez, Nathan, I'm not accusing you of being a murderer…'

'Why not?' Nathan said, 'Mud sticks, doesn't it? Any other unsolved crimes you'd like to put me down for?'

Leaning forward, Ruby slouched over the seat, her head hung low. 'I'm sorry,' she said, 'I'm grasping at straws. I know you'd never be involved in anything like that.' She rubbed her face. 'If you'd seen those photos… they were awful. I mean I'm usually hardened to crime scenes but the look on their faces. It was as if they were pleading with me to save them. I don't think I'll ever get them out of my head.' Her chin trembled under the weight of her emotions, a lump rising to her throat.

'Babe, come here,' Nathan said, pulling her towards him and hugging her close to his chest. 'I know it's hard, but you've got a good team and you're doing everything you can.'

'Come to bed with me?' Ruby sniffed, taking comfort wherever she could.

Cupping her face in his hands, Nathan silenced her tears with a kiss.

CHAPTER THIRTY

'Firstly, can I say that I don't normally do this sort of thing,' Thomas said, his fingers tracing the outline of his wedding ring. 'It's just that lately life is passing me by, you know? And it's not as if I can talk to my wife. She'd be disgusted if she knew what I was about to do.' He took another swig of his whiskey, one of several he had downed before reaching the hotel. A spot of Dutch courage for what lay ahead. But then this was supposed to be fun, wasn't it? So why did he feel so nervous? A sense of exhilaration raced through his veins. Could he really go through with something he had fantasised about since his teens?

'Relax,' Matthew said. 'You can call a halt to this anytime you like.' His voice was warm and soothing as he dipped his hand beneath the table and rested it on Thomas's knee. 'But I don't think you want that, do you?'

The question hung in the air as Matthew stroked his companion's thigh. Both dressed in business suits, they looked like many other men in the bar that day. Thomas had wanted to skip dinner, but asked for formalwear. There was something about a man in a suit that turned him on. Something forbidden.

Thomas swallowed, wiping his mouth with the back of his hand. His breath was coming faster now as his arousal grew. He wasn't gay, not really. He was a married man with children and had a job as an airline pilot. It didn't get any more respectable than that. But the problem with getting older was that you attended funerals instead of weddings. You became invisible. He was all too aware of his own mortality. He could deny his sexuality all he wanted, but there was another side of him buried deep that was desperate for a bite of the poisoned apple. The two thousand pound investment he had spent on his fantasy declared he had a curious interest at the very least. It was an itch, he told himself, something that needed to be scratched. But despite his excitement, he had been carrying a feeling of foreboding all day. Nervousness, he guessed, but part of him wanted to drop everything and run away.

'Want to go upstairs?' Matthew said, leaning forward to whisper in his ear. 'You've got quite a hard-on there.'

'Best you walk in front of me then,' Thomas joked, his throat feeling constricted, his heart pounding hard.

Matthew threw him a wicked grin before getting up and leading the way. The hotel he had chosen was one that Thomas had never used before. A pang of guilt made itself known. His wife would have loved staying in such a luxurious hotel. But he could not fulfil his fantasy in some seedy back alley. If he was going to do this it would be a lasting and memorable experience, something that would not come back to his wife. He pushed the memory of her face from his mind. She was the last person he wanted to think about now. He followed Matthew into the lift, his stomach lurching as it rose to the fifth floor. Justifications rebounded inside his mind as he tried to extinguish his ever-increasing guilt. It was not as if he was being unfaithful. Matthew was a man. He was simply being paid to deliver a service his wife wasn't equipped to do. Thomas had poured over his many reviews from satisfied customers and they had written how wonderful he had made them feel. Yet there was a coldness behind his eyes when he spoke. He hesitated at the door as Matthew opened it. Yet again he touched him, checking the corridor was empty before leaning in to give him a kiss. He had never experienced the roughness of another man's face pressed against his. Thomas caught his breath as Matthew pulled away, his reservations dissipating in the aftermath of their intimacy. Closing the door behind them, Thomas followed him into the room.

CHAPTER THIRTY-ONE

'This parenting lark isn't easy, is it, Mum?' Ruby said, after spending a restless night thinking about her daughter. With no further news on the case, her first stop that morning was Oakwood Care Home, and she was now experiencing the never-ending cycle of guilt for not being able to visit her mother more often. Joy's mobility was fading, as was her mind. Her periods of lucidity made less of an appearance these days, but it was better that than the upset she experienced when she first moved in, veering from being happy and content to crying and begging to go home.

'Let's face it, Gertie, you're not exactly mother of the year,' Joy said, holding Ruby's hand as it was offered.

Ruby smiled. Gertie was an old friend of her mother's, but there was truth in her words just the same. It felt strange coming into motherhood so late. Joy had forced Ruby into giving Cathy up for adoption, but Ruby held no grudges, as life was so unsettled back then. She was just a teenager herself, having run away with Nathan due to the violence he encountered at home. With no money and no prospects, Joy had been quick to point out that giving up her daughter would result in her having a better life. A selfless act, she had said. Yet it had not turned out that way. Ruby had caught a glimpse of the scars her daughter carried, and she was living rough when she found her again. It broke her heart to know she had made the wrong decision. But it was too late now. All she could do was be there for her as best she could. She voiced her concerns to her mother, whose head was tilted towards the sun. Her mother was an early riser and she loved sitting near the garden after dawn broke. The open door brought in the sweet smells of honeysuckle and the sounds of the thrushes setting the air alight with their tune. Spring was her favourite time of the year. Ruby fell silent. It was no longer her mother's job to be her sounding board.

'Just be there,' Joy said, giving her hand a squeeze. 'That's all you can do.'

As with many of her mother's mumblings, Ruby did not know what context the words came from, but she took the crumb of comfort where she could find it. 'The problem is that we barely know each other,' Ruby said, forgetting her earlier thought to leave her mother in peace. Ruby consoled herself that such was her short-term memory, she would forget what she had said just minutes before. 'You've always been there for Frances, haven't you, Mum?' she said, smiling at the memory. The best way of prolonging a conversation was to talk about times long past. Joy's friendship with Nathan's mum had spanned decades. Ruby had grown up next door to Nathan, their friendship blossoming to love. It was a relationship her mother did not approve of, despite the ties that bound them.

Joy turned her face from the sun, blinking away the light from her vision before settling on Ruby's face. 'For all the good it did, that husband of hers beating her every time he got drunk.' She took a breath, her features furrowed. 'And those boys… what hope have they got, growing up in the shadow of violence like that?'

Ruby nodded. Lenny, Nathan's brother, had inherited his father's mean streak, but despite Nathan's tough exterior, Ruby knew he housed a softer side. Their relationship had been on and off more often than a light bulb, but the return of their daughter had brought peace where there was turbulence. They were beginning to feel like a proper little family at last. It was strange, feeling so settled. Ruby's chaotic party lifestyle had now calmed to a once weekly blow out at Nathan's club. She gazed into her mother's kind face, vacant of so much of the personality she once held. It served only to remind her just how fleeting time was.

A sing-song tune carried in the hall as Harmony, her mother's nurse, came to greet them. The generously proportioned Jamaican lady was aptly named, and Ruby warmed at the sight of her as she arrived to take her mother to the dining hall. Visiting times were flexible as far as Ruby was concerned, but breakfast loomed and she had to get to work.

'Well if it isn't my favourite police officer,' Harmony said, her Jamaican accent adding an exotic flavour to her words. 'I must say, you've been looking a lot brighter these days. Your cheeks are carrying a fine rosy glow. That man of yours, he be looking after ya right well.'

Ruby smiled. She had only recently discovered that Nathan was a shareholder in Oakwood Care Home. He had bought into the business behind her back during their year-long separation, to ensure her fees were kept low. Such an act of love had been difficult to argue with when her mother's welfare was at stake. She knew that Harmony was aware of their relationship, but discretion was assured and she seemed to be genuinely fond of them both.

'He's been looking after me a little too well,' Ruby said. 'How's things been with Mum? Sorry I've not been able to come any sooner, work's been…'

Harmony laid a hand on her shoulder, cutting off her sentence with several tuts. 'Don't you say another word. Your mum's not short of visitors. Don't go beating yourself up when you're out there trying to keep the streets safe for the likes of me.' She took Joy's hand, encouraging her to link arms before turning back to Ruby. 'Your mum… well, she's as good as can be expected. She needs help to eat her food, and she's not so quick on her feet.' The last statement was evident as Joy took baby steps beside her, the act of walking proving to be more effort than it should. 'We've tried to keep her mobile for as long as we can, but it'll be easier on her joints if she starts using a wheelchair to get about.'

Ruby nodded, swallowing back the tightness in her throat. She couldn't bear to think of her mum becoming immobile, her body failing as well as her mind.

'Don't look so sad,' Harmony said, 'she's in no pain. Now you get to work, show that team of yours who's boss.'

'I will,' Ruby said, knowing any attempt to kiss her mother would result in her being swatted away. 'See you next time, Mum, love you.'

Tears blurred Ruby's eyes as she searched for her car in the car park. She swallowed them down as she tried to focus on her job. Work was a much-needed distraction, giving her focus when her thoughts ganged up on her, replacing guilt and sorrow with determination and resolve.

CHAPTER THIRTY-TWO

Sitting in a visitation room with Mason Gatley was the last place on earth Ruby wanted to be. It had come as a surprise to hear of his transfer to the secure psychiatric unit in Manor Lodge. The sprawling pale brick building could be mistaken for a leisure centre from the outside. With gentle piped music floating through the corridors and innocuous pastel-coloured walls, it had a completely different vibe to the cold and sterile prison visiting rooms. Most prisons had their own psych units but Mason's transfer was deemed appropriate, given the escalation of his recently perceived mental health issues and his threat of self-harm. All kinds of strings had to be pulled to visit him. Ruby had thought long and hard about his request for her phone number, but as much as she wanted to bring in the suspect, such intimacy was taking things a step too far. The thoughts of Mason's voice whispering in her ear while she sat at home with her daughter made her skin crawl. She was also in no doubt that Nathan would go through the roof – it was why his brother Lenny had suggested it. Another way to tear down the family she and Nathan were building. But Ruby had more than one trick up her sleeve when it came to the likes of Mason Gatley.

Baring his teeth in a smile, he slid into the wooden chair. The room was light and airy, with sunlight flooding in through the secure meshed window that provided a view of the car park outside. Here, Mason was deemed a 'service user' instead of a prisoner, and with all high-risk cases, a member of staff was present to supervise their visit in case things went wrong. The unsmiling man was dressed in a badly ironed uniform, his short hair combed in an unflattering side parting. Standing by the door, he clasped his hands behind his back and stared blankly ahead.

Ruby's focus was on Mason. He was wearing an arrogant smile, his eyes crawling over her.

'Nice to see you again,' he said. 'Did you miss me?'

'What do you think?' Ruby replied wearily. She was guarded, tetchy. Fed up of playing his games.

'Oh dear,' Mason said. 'Things not going very well for you then? Didn't you find your victim in time? You've done a wonderful job of keeping it out of the news. I thought it would have hit the TV by now. Or are journalists somewhat slow on the uptake?'

'They've got more important things to cover,' Ruby said; a recent terrorist plot had gripped the nation in the last week. Besides, Phillip Sherman commanded respect in their world, and such unsubstantiated information was dangerous to print. But still, it felt like defeat, having to come crawling back to Mason Gatley. Sometimes Ruby felt she was swimming in a tsunami, and it was all she could do to keep her head above the tide. 'I'm at the end of the line here, Mason. I'm not going to beg but enough with these cryptic clues. Can you give me something concrete or not?'

'Perhaps…' Mason said, licking the dryness from his lips. 'If you ask me real nice.'

'This is me asking nice,' Ruby said, deadpan.

'I'd love to help but, as you see, I'm in the psychiatric ward so who knows what I'd say? It's much nicer here than my prison cell mind, although the company could be improved upon.' He gave a nod of the head at the member of staff keeping watch in the room. 'His name's Norman,' Mason said in mock whisper. 'He's not exactly a laugh a minute.'

Ruby barely afforded him a glance. 'Well you may have time to sit around all day and ponder but I don't. Now are you going to tell me who's responsible or not?'

Mason wagged a finger in mock retribution. 'I told you, ask me nicely.'

'And what would that consist of?' Ruby said, her patience wearing thin.

Mason pointed to his cheek. 'How about we start with a kiss, and then see what you can do with this?' He nodded towards his groin. 'I'm sure Norman wouldn't mind, as long as you put on a good show.'

'I've had enough of this,' Ruby said, rising from her chair. Her jaw clenched, she pushed her knuckles against the table as she rose.

Mason laughed. 'Calm down, I was only kidding; a guy's got to pass the time somehow.'

But Ruby was in no mood to be anyone's plaything. 'I should never have come here,' she said, turning to leave.

'I've already given you the answer,' Mason said, the mirth evaporating from his voice. 'And I've gone to a lot of trouble to do so, so a little appreciation would be nice.'

Ruby's eyes narrowed as she took a step towards him. 'What do you mean?'

'Just what I said. The answers are staring you straight in the face.'

'Why do you have to be so bloody cryptic all the time?' Ruby exhaled sharply. Was he delaying her from getting back to work or providing an actual clue?

Mason grinned, his eyes alight with amusement. 'You're a detective. Are you saying you're not up to the job?'

'I'm saying I don't have time for this. Why can't you just tell me straight?'

'So much communication is granted without words,' he teased. 'You find that when you're incarcerated. You would be amazed at what you'd learn if you just clear your mind of the endless stream of thought.'

His words rang in Ruby's ears as she sat in her office later that day with the doors closed. She had asked not to be disturbed and was trying to clear her mind just as Mason had suggested. But as she stared blankly at the wall, the answers would not come. All she could hear was that damned ticking clock in her brain as precious seconds slipped away. Never had there been such a sense of urgency, because she knew he was telling the truth. The answer probably was staring her in the face. She took a deep breath, briefly closing her eyes as she willed it to come. It was clear he knew someone, he had leaked the information, no, surely encouraged them to kill on his behalf. What did he mean, he had gone to great trouble? He was no different now from the last time she saw him… her thoughts broke away as in the midst of all the gloom and despair a tiny light bulb flickered in her brain. There was a difference. He was in the psychiatric ward. She had the list of prison visitors and acquaintances. Why hadn't she thought of other facilities too? Was that where his contacts lay? But who would he talk to in such depth? She thought of Norman, standing in the corner, silently taking it all in.

Maybe he was joking about him not being much of a conversationalist. Perhaps Mason had been the one keeping conversation all along. Even so, would he have the nerve to stand there if he was a suspect in a murder case? Ruby grabbed a pen and began to scribble a list. Psychiatrists, fellow patients, doctors, nurses, visitors. She sighed. This was going to take ages to investigate and they could ill afford the time.

Opening the door, she strode out into the office gathering up her team. 'Right everyone, for the next hour I want you to focus on this list of all the people who could have visited or spent time with Mason…'

'We're working through the list now, sarge, with no leads so far,' Richard said. 'We're trying to track down his son, but from what we can see he's cut off all ties.'

'Let me finish,' Ruby said. 'I want you to investigate all the people who visited, dealt with or spent time with Mason in the psychiatric unit where he's currently being held.' She glanced around the room. 'I visited him this morning. He told me the answer was staring me in the face. He's laughing at us. Don't let him treat us like fools.'

CHAPTER THIRTY-THREE

'How are we doing?' Ruby said, cracking open a can of diet Coke she had bought from the snack machine in the corridor.

'No big breakthroughs so far,' Luddy said, the effects of such long working hours evident on his face. 'We've managed to locate CCTV of our first victim, Melissa Sherman, on the street outside the hotel where we found her, but she's alone. There were plenty of people staying there that day. Our suspect could have gone there anytime to meet her. There are quite a few people with umbrellas up too, so the view is obscured.'

'Bloody rain,' Ruby muttered. 'But good work for tracking it down. Don't be afraid to ask uniform for a dig out if you need help with viewing. I know we're all up against it but they might have someone on restricted duties who can help us out. What about the rope?'

'They're measuring the victim's neck wounds for depth, width and fibres,' Luddy replied. 'Nothing concrete back yet.'

'Forensics have found fingerprints on some of the exhibits seized from Melissa's hotel room,' DI Downes said, making Ruby jump as he spoke behind her. His gait seemed determined by his moods. Some days he was heavy-footed, others, he seemed to hover rather than walk. She turned to greet him, disappointed by the lack of enthusiasm in his voice. 'I take it there's no match on our systems?'

'No,' Downes said. 'And given its location it could be anyone. Cleaners, concierge, previous guests, with no match it doesn't narrow things down.'

'Unless we get our suspect into custody and then it can be used against them,' Ruby replied, trying to remain positive.

'Have you turned any corners so far?' Downes asked.

She relayed her conversation with Jimmy from tech the night before. 'I think we should pressure Shirley, the woman I spoke to at the golf club, and find out where she got the invite from.'

'Didn't she say she couldn't remember?' Downes replied.

'That's what she told the statement taker when they went back to speak to her, but I'm not buying it. She said some random person gave it to her at a party when she'd had a few drinks. But in a club that exclusive people don't just dole out cards. She's hinted that she's no angel. This has got to be connected, all of it.'

'What about Mason Gatley? You think he had a hand in it too?'

'Yes,' Ruby said. 'You said yourself, the killer has an in-depth knowledge of the case. We need a list of anyone who could have spoken to him, including police.'

'You may as well put me on that list, in that case,' Downes answered.

'You know what I mean,' Ruby replied. 'We need his visitor list to double-check that he didn't have any pen pals. He said he gets lots of requests. There's got to be someone squeezing him for details. If we find out where the inside information is coming from then we may just find our suspect.'

'I agree,' Downes said. 'This isn't a case of Chinese whispers. Our victims are linked by two things – the original case and this dating site. Keep digging but be smart with your time. Every minute counts.'

Ruby nodded slowly as thoughts ran around her head. 'Can I borrow Luddy for half an hour, boss? There's someone I need to talk to.'

'Is it connected with the case?' Downes said.

'Of course. I want to make a quick visit to one of Cheryl's friends.'

'And is it worthwhile?'

'I believe so. I wouldn't be dragging him away otherwise.'

'In that case, yes. But be quick about it. We're due another briefing at two.' He turned on his heel and walked to his office while Ruby took another swill of her drink. Luddy was already switching off his computer, and grabbing his police harness from the chair.

'You really should move about every hour,' Ruby said, as Luddy complained of stiff shoulders. 'It's not good for you, hunched over a computer screen all day.'

'Is that where we're going? Pilates?' Luddy offered her a boyish grin.

Ruby's heart warmed. He really was a cute little sod when the mood took him. The office had been so solemn since Ash's departure. She reminded herself to organise a works' drink night when this investigation was complete. 'Yeah,' she said, pocketing the keys of the unmarked Ford from the hook on the wall. 'Thought I'd put you through your paces. Do us a favour, give your hair a quick comb, will you? Where's your tie?'

'In my drawer,' Luddy said, ruefully. 'Sorry, I meant to put it on.'

'Got any aftershave in there too?' Ruby said.

'I've got a washbag for emergencies. Sarge, where exactly are we going?' His face paled. 'You're not using me as a decoy, are you?'

Ruby snorted as the colour drained from his face. For a moment, she was tempted to play along. But time was a luxury and she needed to get to the point. 'No, you silly sod. But we are meeting with a woman with an eye for a handsome man. You're the only person I trust not to report me for sexism in the workplace. I'm desperate; would you mind working your charms on her?'

Luddy didn't seem to mind at all. In fact, he was glowing. 'You know me, boss, I'll take one for the team.'

'I don't want you to shag her, just win her around,' Ruby laughed. 'At the end of the day we're professionals, but I've got a feeling she'll see you as less of a threat than me. You up for it?'

Luddy opened his drawer and began to slip on his tie. 'Show me the way.'

CHAPTER THIRTY-FOUR

'Come in,' Hannah said, her face pale but immaculately made up. Her eyes were fixed on DC Ludgrove from the second he walked through the door.

'I'm sorry for the intrusion,' Ruby said, her voice echoing in the marble-floored hall. 'I know you've given us a statement, but we've got a few more questions that can't wait I'm afraid.' Ruby had read the paperwork that was uploaded to HOLMES the day before.

Hannah responded with a delicate smile. 'As I said on the phone, I'm happy to help in any way I can.' She was almost heavenly with her white blonde hair and floaty chiffon blouse. Her long tanned legs offset her short black leather skirt, and Ruby wondered if she dressed like that all the time or if she was going somewhere special. She slipped off her heels as she came to what looked like a reception room. 'Could I trouble you terribly and ask you to remove your shoes? It's a Jan Kath,' she said, pointing to a rug through the open door.

Ruby looked at her blankly as she stepped out of her shoes. The brown weave carpet looked as if someone had been let loose with a pink crayon and went a bit mad.

'I had it imported from New York,' Hannah said, by means of explanation. 'It's insured, of course, but I don't want it picking up any dirt.'

But Ruby was not impressed by Hannah's ostentatious decor. She was too busy smirking at Luddy's Harry Potter socks.

Having finally been allowed into the living room, DC Ludgrove sat on the end of the designer sofa, balancing his folder on his lap. Ruby cleared her throat, trying to catch Luddy's eye. She had prepped him to lead the interview, but as Hannah eased herself next to him, he seemed to have missed Ruby's cue. 'DC Ludgrove, would you like to begin?' she said, as his eyes wandered, taking in the grandeur of the room.

'Sorry,' he said, returning his focus to Hannah. 'Nice place you've got here.'

Ruby stopped short of rolling her eyes. Was he making small talk to develop a rapport and get her to open up a little more?

'Thank you,' Hannah said, gracing him with a smile. 'I'm very fortunate. All earned from the proceeds of my modelling career.' She gracefully crossed her legs, having seemingly forgotten all about her friend Cheryl as she swallowed DC Ludgrove with her eyes.

Luddy straightened, sliding a pen from his inside jacket pocket and taking his notebook in the palm of his hand. 'Is there anything more you can tell us that you haven't mentioned in your statement?' He gave her an inquiring look. 'The thing is, we've learned that the dating site that Cheryl was mixed up with was by invitation only. Somebody must have passed on those details. We know you mix in similar circles and were wondering if anyone approached you?'

Diplomatic, Ruby thought, when what they really wanted to know was if the invites had anything to do with her.

'I was hoping to keep my name out of this,' Hannah said softly. 'But Cheryl needs me, so I can't stay silent anymore.' She toyed with the delicate silver crucifix on a chain around her neck, her eyes smouldering as she parted her lips.

Ruby stood by the wall, blending into the full-length curtains in an attempt to remain as innocuous as she could. A woody smell with a hint of maple hung in the air. Her gaze wandered to the diffusers poking from a scent bottle on a table nearby. Something told her that, unlike hers, they did not originate from Poundland. She watched as Hannah flicked her hair then and continued to toy with the delicate silver chain. The cream chiffon top she was wearing slid from her shoulder, revealing another flash of tanned skin.

It's like watching a mating ritual, Ruby thought, *each of Hannah's movements choreographed to lure Luddy in.*

Releasing the chain, Hannah began to speak. 'What more can you tell us?' Luddy said, pen poised on his notebook.

'I had an invite pressed into my hand at a party a couple of weeks ago. When Cheryl told me about it I tried to act surprised.' She sighed, recalling the memory. 'I didn't want to steal her thunder. She was so excited, and usually lives such a dull life.'

'I thought the site was strictly for married users,' Luddy said, his face flushing as Hannah's leg brushed against his.

'Sorry,' Hannah said, uncrossing her legs. 'I can't seem to settle today. Now what were you saying?' She raised a finger as Luddy opened his mouth to reply. 'Oh yes. I was wearing a wedding ring because I didn't want to be hit on that night. I'd just been through a messy break-up and, well, you know how these soirées go. I just didn't have the energy that night.'

Ruby smiled, knowing Luddy's nights down the local boozer were as far removed from socialite soirées as they could get.

'And you say someone pressed the invite into your hand?' Luddy said, moving swiftly on. 'Can you give me a description? Tell me where it was you met?'

'I'd love to, darling, but I go to so many,' Hannah said apologetically. 'And I'd had quite a few glasses of champagne that night. All I remember is seeing a black card with the word debauchery in red letters. There was a website address, and some numbers underneath.' Hannah frowned as she raked her memory. 'What was it he said again? Something about a once-in-a-lifetime experience. I told him that I had just broken up with my partner so I was free to see whoever I wanted. He lost interest after that.' She tilted her head to one side. 'Come to think of it, he took back the card. I asked if I could keep it but he said it was very exclusive. I was a bit miffed because I don't like being kept out of anything.'

'FOMO,' Luddy smiled, offering up an explanation in response to her confused expression. 'Fear of missing out.'

Laughing much louder than necessary, Hannah gave his knee a brief squeeze. 'Oh, you are adorable, I do like you! Yes, you could call it that. I like to experience everything at its fullest. Don't you?' Her words slowed as she drew breath, her eyes on Luddy like a panther circling its prey. 'Life would be terribly dull if we didn't try something different every now and again.'

Ruby had heard enough. Sliding her phone from her pocket, she pretended to look surprised. 'I forgot I put this on silent. I've got a call coming in; I'll meet you outside when you're done,' she said, leaving them together.

Five minutes later, DC Ludgrove met her out by the front of the car. 'Finished already?' Ruby said, lowering the phone from her ear. Hannah waved politely from the front door.

Ruby got into the passenger seat, waiting until they were well out of earshot before she spoke again. 'Did she try to eat you alive?' she said, half joking. 'Did you "take one for the team"?'

Luddy smiled, looking like the cat who got the cream. 'She was a bit of all right actually, an ex-model too.'

'OK, Romeo, stick your tongue back in for a second. Did this ex-model give you any info worthy of our visit?'

Luddy checked his mirrors as he negotiated the car out of the driveway and onto the road. 'Yeah. After you left she remembered details of the party where the guy gave her the invite, so that's worth checking out.' He threw her a guilty look. 'And there's something else which I'd love to follow up on but can't.'

'Oh yeah? And what was that?' Ruby said, enjoying the banter, despite everything that was going on.

Luddy delivered a smug smile. 'Her phone number.'

CHAPTER THIRTY-FIVE

Swallowing, Mason Gatley could still taste the after-effects of the capsules he had been given half an hour before. They were slow releasing, administered to treat him gradually throughout the day. Modified release dosage they called it. For Mason, grinding the capsule between his back molars provided an instant kick. Tasted bitter as fuck though. He took a sip from the plastic cup of water and swished it around his mouth. The table wobbled as he leaned on it to face his guest. The room was nothing more than an 8 x 8 ft box. Cream walls, strip lighting and carrying the sickly scent of flowery disinfectant in the air. He missed the exotic smells of the outside world and thought about it at night when he closed his eyes. But now the man sharing his space breathed new life into a usually dull day. Even better, they had been granted privacy. It was just the two of them here today.

Matthew watched silently, keeping a close eye on Mason's every move. Mason supposed it wasn't easy to relax in the same room as a serial killer. The thought warmed him. He could see the undisguised admiration in his eyes. 'You know there's one thing I'm curious about,' Mason said, cocking his head to one side. 'You've never asked me if I'm sorry for what I've done.'

'Does it matter?' Matthew replied.

Mason thought it over. 'No, I suppose it doesn't, but I'm wondering why you don't care? I've watched my words take effect, seen your eyes burn with something deep inside.'

Matthew shrugged. 'I'm just grateful you chose to speak to me. I know how many people you've turned down.'

Mason smiled at the thoughts of the requests he had received to meet him. Before Matthew, they had dwindled to a trickle. He was old news, forgotten. A nobody. He could not allow that to happen. It felt good to be talked about. It made him feel alive. 'Oh yeah, I've had the do-gooders all right. The ones who want to save me, or give comfort to the victims if they can. Some just want to make money out of selling my story. But you're not like them. The fact you don't care about the victims pleases me. You know why? Because they're not really victims. By answering my ad, they dictated their own fate.'

'I agree,' Matthew simply said, his perfectly manicured nails drumming the table separating them. He seemed oblivious to the action, too wrapped up in what Mason had to say. 'The last time we spoke you told me about Becky. How quickly did you move on from her to your next victim? Did she stay in your memory or just evaporate?'

Evaporate. Matthew's choice of words was curious. The man had intrigued Mason from the start. Perhaps it was because he could recognise some of himself in his expressionless deep-set eyes. He spoke about people as if they were nothing. Perhaps that's why he had opened up to him. He had met a kindred soul. 'I have a special place in my memory for all of the people I met during that time.'

'So you've relived each kill?' Matthew said, a hint of a smile on his lips.

'Continuously, although it fades I'm sad to say. It's hard to keep the memories fresh.'

Matthew nodded knowingly. 'Keeping the memories alive is important – unless you plan on not getting caught.'

Mason snorted. 'Everybody gets caught in the end.'

'Not everybody.'

Narrowing his eyes, Mason's words took on a serious tone. 'You think you're better than me?'

The nail drumming stopped as Matthew withdrew his hands. 'Far from it. I can only aspire to be like you. I just wish you hadn't got arrested.'

'You wouldn't be sitting here across from me otherwise,' Mason replied, stony-faced.

'But I would have followed you with interest. Who knows the good work you could have done if the police hadn't cut it short.'

'Good work?' Mason said, failing to hide his annoyance. 'I wasn't interested in "good work" as you put it. I purely satisfied my own needs.'

'And I've enjoyed hearing about them,' Matthew said, steering the conversation away from his own motivations. 'I've spent many happy hours reading up on what you did to those sluts.'

'So now it's time for you to return the favour,' Mason said, his tongue darting from between his lips as he licked them. 'Tell me about your latest kill.'

CHAPTER THIRTY-SIX

Their banter was short-lived, as Ruby and Luddy returned to the station. The arrival of the third photo filled Ruby with a sense of despair. They were too late. Their time had run out. Cheryl was dead. They were dealing with a serial killer, and now their suspicions had been confirmed, the two incidents would continue to be investigated as one. Ruby paced the room as she spoke to DC Rutherford, the family liaison officer assigned to the families involved. Usually one officer would be involved with each family, but cutbacks meant that he was juggling both. It was the same everywhere in the emergency services. As Ruby had told her team several times, there was no point in complaining. They had to knuckle down like everybody else. She was grateful that they were keeping their heads above water staff-wise at least. She did not always see eye to eye with DCI Worrow, but her superior had her back when it came to allocating officers to her team. Ruby pressed her mobile phone to her ear to overcome the sound of background noise. Phone chatter, keyboards clacking and a tray full of empty mugs being carried to the sink were just a few of the sounds she had to contend with. Her office was no better, the noise of the busy streets filtering into her window, punctuated by the occasional siren as her uniformed colleagues rushed from job to job. Despite making the best of their resources, time was something they could not stall.

'At least we managed to intercept the photo,' DC Rutherford said, relief evident in his tone. 'It came from a courier, paid cash by all accounts. Her husband's asked to see it but I've told him that's not happening.'

'You can say that again,' Ruby said. Things were bad enough without him being put through that. The fact it had come by courier was a deviation from the original murders and could hopefully provide further clues. 'And the finger?' she said, dreading his response.

'We intercepted it at his workplace. Just as with Melissa, it came wrapped in tissue paper in a padded envelope. It was like he wanted her husband to find it; which is why, I'm guessing, he didn't send it to Cheryl's home address.'

'Bastard,' Ruby said, her jaw set firm to keep her rising emotions at bay. 'He copies the murders perfectly but the delivery is erratic and unpredictable. I guess he has more choices than Mason did back then. Or maybe he's honing his methods, seeing what works best.'

'And I take it none of this is known to the press?' DC Rutherford said.

'Not yet,' Ruby said, taking a break from pacing to lean against an unoccupied office desk. 'It's all the more reason to keep it quiet. How are you managing? You OK with all this? I know it's pretty grim…'

'You don't join this job for candyfloss and unicorns,' DC Rutherford said, his smile carrying on his voice.

Ruby snorted. Even during times like these, they could find a way of raising morale. It was the only way to deal with the horrors around them. It would have been too easy to scream in frustration, to allow the tears to come, but her team needed a strong leader and she would not let them down. 'If it all gets too much just let us know. At least you can cross reference the family tree with both cases, see if they've got any links with friends, work colleagues. We need to get to the heart of who's passing out these invites. There's got to be a link somewhere.'

'Leave it with me,' DC Rutherford said. 'I'll upload the pictures and email you a password protected copy. The finger is en route to Bones.'

Ruby wondered what clues the crime scene officer could gain from another severed finger, but was glad everything was under control. 'I take it the photo's similar to the last one? Same MO?'

'Yes. Hog-tied on the bed, seems like a hotel. That look on her face. I'd say it was snapped not long after she died.'

A brief silence fell as Ruby gathered her thoughts. She tried to push aside the feeling of helplessness that was coming in waves. She was not in this alone. She had to have faith in her team. She said her goodbyes to DC Rutherford and ended the call.

'Tea?' Luddy said, passing her a steaming mug.

'Cheers mate,' she replied, wearily accepting the brew. 'The third photo of Cheryl has come in; it looks like we're too late. Are we any closer to tracking down the hotel?'

From the moment DC Rutherford had informed Downes, he had requested a meeting with DCI Worrow to bring her up to speed. Not all briefings included the ground troops. Some were for high ranking officers only, and she knew Downes would be feeling the squeeze.

'We've marked out a perimeter and are speaking to hoteliers and guest houses in the area. It's tough though, they're very tight-lipped.'

'And I can't see any of them offering to check the rooms either,' Ruby said. 'The last photo is on its way to us now. Hopefully you'll be able to narrow it down. If not, I'll round up some ground troops, start knocking on hotel room doors.' An obvious police presence would persuade hoteliers to be a bit more receptive. Ruby had no qualms about involving uniformed officers. Their presence would be deemed bad publicity and the hotel manager would no doubt be more likely to comply.

CHAPTER THIRTY-SEVEN

Pacing the station car park, Ruby inhaled one last puff from the vaporiser in her hand. A quick phone call to her mother's care home left her satisfied that her presence was not needed. It made her smile to discover that Cathy, her daughter, was visiting that day. Taking a deep breath, she focused her mind on the case as she pushed her security tag against the panel on the wall. As she entered their office, she became immediately aware of the facts that her team looked like something out of the mannequin challenge. Figures sat unmoving at their desks, officers were huddled around the photocopier, and Luddy stood in the middle of the floor with a piece of paper in his hand. But her team had not become suddenly frozen in time: the muffled shouting coming from the office of DI Downes was what stole their attention. The high-pitched strident voice could only be that of DCI Worrow, because nobody else would speak to Downes like that. Usually calm and collected, it was a novelty to hear her lose her temper in such a way. It was hardly any wonder that her team were drawn to the argument, temporarily forgetting the urgency of their tasks. Unease at the top spread downwards. This was not going to help morale.

She coughed loudly, and it had the desired effect as everyone quickly returned to work. 'What's going on?' she said to Richard, as she crossed the floor to his desk. His was located nearest to the DI's workspace. Surely he had heard what the argument was about?

'Not my circus, not my monkeys,' Richard replied flatly, returning his attention to his computer screen.

'Fine,' Ruby said with begrudging admiration.

Creeping towards the office, she peered through the drawn blinds to see a sliver of Downes's arms waving in the air as he spoke. This was not a good sign. Normally he kept his temper in check and took whatever Worrow had to give him. But today it seemed that he'd had enough. She approached the office, wondering if she should interrupt. Things seemed to be escalating and he had his limits. It had been hard for him being supervised by someone less than half his age with a fraction of his experience. DCI Worrow was a strong woman and did not mince her words. Ruby turned away from the door. She would find out soon enough. If Downes was getting a telling off then it would most certainly filter down to her. Instead, she strode into her office and dialled his mobile number. She groaned as it rang off the hook, and his desk phone elicited the same: no response. That wasn't like him. Usually he would be glad of an excuse to be rescued. But today it seemed he was holding his own. A door slammed in the distance and Ruby watched as he left his own office in a strop. Ruby's head swivelled from left to right as she caught Worrow striding in the opposite direction, her arms swinging as she walked. She felt a pang of worry. Was Worrow going upstairs to report the state of play? Keeping their heads bowed, Ruby's team did not afford her eye contact as she trotted outside after DI Downes to find out what was wrong. After catching sight of him getting into his car, she ran across the car park and jumped into the passenger seat beside him.

Filled with fury, Downes's eyes lit upon her.

'Steady on, boss, everything all right?' Ruby said, her face creased with worry as she caught her breath.

Downes's muscles seemed to relax as he took her presence in. 'I thought you were Worrow,' he said in a terse exhale. 'Who the feck does she think she is talking to me like that?'

'Like what?' Ruby asked. 'What happened? What were you shouting about?'

Downes shook his head in disgust. 'It's not what happened, it's the way she talks to me. I'm sick to the teeth of her lack of respect. I have fillings older than her. Do you know what she had the cheek to say?' Downes said, his Northern Irish accent coming through loud and clear. 'That if I couldn't manage my team then she'd find someone who could. Well, I told her a few home truths to be sure, oh yes I did.'

Ruby grimaced. Words like that were bound to press anybody's buttons but she still wanted to know what had been said. 'What was she so pissed about?'

'That photo of Cheryl Barber for starters. She promised the command team we'd find her in time. Well she shouldn't be making promises she can't keep. And that's not all…'

'What else?' Ruby groaned.

'It's only going to hit the press, isn't it? Someone's blabbed, and all the details of Phillip Sherman's missus are going to be all over the tabloids. They've been ringing the press office before it goes on. Sherman's trying to put a stop to it, but if he can't… it might go global.'

'Shit,' Ruby said, feeling sick to the core. 'It doesn't mean it was us that squealed. In fact, I don't think it was. There's lots of other people who know about the case. You can't be responsible for them all.'

'I am according to Worrow,' Downes replied. 'You know what I told her when I left?' A satisfied smile was spreading across his face, which had now lost all of its colour.

Ruby groaned. Given Worrow's tight expression she knew it was not good. 'What did you say?'

'I told her to fuck right off. And then do you know what I told her?' A shallow laugh escaped his lips. Ruby knew this was serious but she could not help but join in. Downes's shoulders shook with laughter as he tried to relate the words.

'You're scaring me now,' Ruby said, smiling despite the awfulness of it all.

'I…' Downes laughed then snorted, before clearing his throat. 'I told her to stick her job up her skinny little arse and not to bother me again. Flamin' Nora,' he blurted another laugh. 'I'm really for the high jump this time.'

Ruby groaned at the scenario playing out before them. What she would have given to have been a fly on the wall. 'Jack, what have you done?' She shook her head in bewilderment. Worse things than this had happened in his career. Why was he so on edge now? He had put his job and future pension at risk.

Downes rubbed his chest, his face pallid. 'I bet she's marched up to the command team, as thick as two planks, repeating every word I've said. She's been wanting to get rid of me for ages. I've just given her the ammunition to do it. And you know what?' Downes said, 'I don't care. I've had enough of this place. This job. All I want to do right now is to go home and get pissed.'

'No, you don't,' Ruby said, placing her hand on his arm. She was all too aware of the problems he'd had with alcohol in the past. If he lost his job like this, things would take a turn for the worse in every aspect of his life. She needed to turn this around. 'Phillip Sherman likes you. Why don't you give him a call, try to find out who's been talking? He's got cleaning staff in the house; anyone could have listened in.'

'And what about Worrow?' Downes said. 'No doubt she's typing up my resignation letter as we speak.'

'She can't just sack you like that. Hell, if someone was sacked every time they answered back in this job the station would be empty. We've all been feeling the pressure. Nobody can blame you for letting off some steam. I'll go and speak to her, see if I can smooth things over, but you have to be prepared to apologise.'

Downes rolled his eyes at the very suggestion. 'Apologise my arse, she can feck right off.'

'Why are you suddenly starting to sound like an extra from *Father Ted*?' Ruby laughed, referring to an Irish comedy programme that was peppered with swear words from the off.

Downes shrugged his shoulders. 'I'm tired. Tired of taking everyone else's shit. Did you see the hours we put in last week and not an ounce of thanks from above? What's the point? We're just pissing against the wind.'

'But it's always been that way,' Ruby said. 'You know better than to expect recognition. Worrow's just frustrated because she's been getting it in the neck too.'

'Oh, I know she has,' Downes said, his laughter turning into a grimace as he gave his chest another rub.

'Are you all right?' Ruby said, horrified to see the last of the colour drain from his face, a blue tinge touching his lips.

His forehead beaded with perspiration, he grunted a response, his face tightening as he grasped the left side of his chest. 'My chest… pain…' Bent over in two, it was all he could manage, his teeth clenched as he spoke.

Filled with terror, Ruby fumbled with her job radio. 'I'm calling an ambulance,' she said. Taking a deep breath she notified control.

CHAPTER THIRTY-EIGHT

Ruby paused at the open doorway of the hospital room, watching a nurse she recognised squeeze Jack Downes's hand. She realised that it was the same woman who helped him get through his wife's illness before she died. It was not the first time Ruby had caught them chatting intimately, and she smiled as she entered the room. Quickly turning on her heel, the Ward Sister gave her a gracious nod.

'You old dog,' Ruby said, as soon as the woman left. 'There are easier ways of asking her out than feigning your own death.'

'Well it seems to have done the trick,' Downes joked, looking pleased with himself. Dressed in a grey T-shirt and jogging bottoms, he had declined the usual hospital robe. Sitting on top of the blankets, his long legs were crossed, with pillows supporting his back.

'Good for you,' Ruby said. 'There's more to life than work. But you gave me a hell of a fright back there.'

'It wasn't exactly a party for me either,' Downes replied. Rubbing his chest, the memory of the pain still etched on his face. After a barrage of tests, Ruby had been relieved to hear the conclusion. It was not the heart attack she had feared but angina, which is often brought on in times of stress. Her chair screeched against the floor as she pulled it beside the bed.

'I hope you're going to take some time off work,' she said, taking the weight off her feet.

'I feel a bit stupid now, but I honestly thought my number was up.' He raised his hand in a theatrical manner, looking up to the ceiling as he spoke. 'I remember thinking, just as the white light was about to swallow me, of all the ways I had to go, it would have be on the job with you.'

'You should be so lucky,' Ruby replied, her face breaking into a smile. 'But seriously, Jack, treat this as a warning. No job is worth compromising your health. If it's really bothering you that much then maybe you should consider early retirement, although I really don't want to see you go.'

'Och, I'm not going anywhere, ya daft mare,' Downes said. 'If anything, today might have helped. I can use it as an excuse, say I wasn't thinking straight when I told her to stick her job up her skinny arse.'

'She was probably pushing pins into her voodoo doll. I reckon she's got ones of us all.' Ruby smiled, her face growing serious as she thought about how close they'd come. Things could have been so much worse. 'What's really bothering you? Because it's more than Worrow losing her rag. She wouldn't have gone off like that if you hadn't blown your top.'

Downes rolled his eyes. 'Here I am after nearly popping me clogs and you're questioning me like a number one suspect. Jesus, woman, have a heart.'

'It's because I care,' Ruby replied. 'Please. Tell me what's wrong. You've had enough drama from me over the years, it's about time I returned the favour.'

Downes sighed as he conceded. 'All right then, you've worn me down. But at least close the door.'

As she did what he asked, Ruby was grateful that his insurance covered a private room. She took her seat and silenced her phone, devoting her full attention to what he was about to say.

Folding his arms, Downes gave her a cautious glance. 'This is just between us mind, I don't want anyone else to know.'

'You have my word,' Ruby said, wondering what could have driven him to the edge.

'You're right, I am moving on, starting to let go of my wife. But there's one thing that's resurfaced from the past and it's been playing on my mind.' He paused, his brow furrowed. In the hall, a trolley squeaked past, laden with medication. 'It all came to a head when I heard that the Lonely Hearts Killer had hit the press. Even if Sherman puts a stop to it, they're still going to run a "then and now" story, devoting coverage to Mason Gatley, with a mention to present-day dating sites.' Downes fell silent, lost in his thoughts.

'But we handle lots of cases,' Ruby interjected. 'What's so special about this one?'

Downes seemed to mull it over before delivering a reply. 'You know I worked some of the original case, don't you? I was just a DC back then, going through the evidence and reporting my finds. The wife and I, well we were going through a rough patch.' Downes looked at her ruefully. 'A rough patch that lasted about five years. I was working long hours, trying to prove myself. I neglected her; that's how it was with a lot of coppers' wives. It was when I was going through the letters, that I recognised her writing. It knocked me for six.'

'Wait a minute,' Ruby said, confusion crossing her face. 'What letters?'

'The ones written to Mason Gatley. A proper Lothario he was back then. He could pick and choose his victims. Most were lonely married women in need of a bit of attention. Some got more than they bargained for. And my wife could have been one of them.'

'You're joking,' Ruby said. 'Your wife wrote to Mason Gatley asking for a hook up?'

Straightening up in his bed, Downes nodded his response. 'It was just a letter, one letter, saying how lonely she was. I don't know if he ever replied. I don't think she would have gone as far as meeting up. Mason's ad offered to make things better, give them a boost, put things back on track. What a load of bullshit. I'm just grateful we caught him. She could have died.'

'What did you do about the letter?' Ruby said.

'The only thing I could do,' Downes replied. 'I destroyed it. I knew nobody would miss just one.'

Silence fell as his words hung in the air. Ruby could not believe her ears. All the times Downes had told her off for bending the rules and he had destroyed evidence in a murder investigation. 'Did you ever tell anyone?' Ruby said.

Downes shook his head. 'That's why I didn't want you visiting Mason. It's been keeping me awake at night. I don't know if he ever realised that he received a letter from my missus. He was a clever bastard and I wouldn't put it past him to stalk his victims before he moved in for the kill. To this day I don't know.'

'How would he know where you lived?' Ruby said, trying to place Downes's actions with the man she knew today.

'Because she gave her address, of course. How else was he going to write back? And yes, before you ask, she was that gullible. But that's what I loved about her. She wasn't hardened to the world like me. I only thank God I was able to find it and save her the embarrassment of it coming out.'

'What did she say when you confronted her?' Ruby said, feeling sympathy for the man before her. He looked tired and unshaven, but at least some colour had returned to his cheeks.

Downes gave Ruby a meaningful stare.

'You mean you never told her you knew?' Ruby said, utilising her ability to read his expressions.

Downes delivered a brief nod of the head. 'I took it as a warning. A chance to make things better between us. I booked a holiday, took some time off to treat her like she deserved. I know she hadn't been unfaithful, but she had come close. I made sure that wouldn't happen again.'

'So you never spoke about it? She must have been shocked to hear you were on the case,' Ruby said, trying to imagine herself in the same situation.

Downes tilted his head to one side as he resurrected memories long past. 'I think she came close to telling me a few times, and perhaps she was aware that I knew. In a way, it was the best thing that could have happened, me finding out like that. I didn't know that our days together were numbered, and we made every moment count. I still hung onto my job. I think she wanted it here as a backup for after she was gone.'

'I'm so sorry,' Ruby replied, feeling helpless at the futility of her words.

'Don't be,' Downes said simply. 'You've nothing to be sorry for. I was the one who drove her away. I'm only glad I got her back.'

Ruby nodded, trying to understand. She was hot-headed at times. She would not have been as gracious in such circumstances as DI Downes. 'So what now?' she asked.

Downes responded with a smile. 'I take my medication and go back to work. Now that you know, I don't need to get wound up about it any more. I was just worried that Mason would use it as ammo. I didn't want to think of him talking about her and disrespecting her name.'

'I'm sure if he knew he would have rubbed it in my face by now,' Ruby said. 'He wouldn't have passed up the opportunity to get a reaction. I'll have a word with Worrow, see if we can get things back on track with your job.'

'Have they found her yet? Cheryl? I presume they have.'

Ruby's expression was downcast. 'I wasn't going to say anything. The update came through when you were being taken in.'

'It's as much as I expected. I take it she's dead?'

'Yes, she was found by the hotel maid,' Ruby said. 'Just like Melissa, sitting up in bed holding a card. Only this time the word

"WHORE" was written in blood. Her husband's being updated as we speak. Which is why I have to get back, I'm afraid.'

Downes reached out and squeezed her hand in an act of thanks. 'Just catch this killer. We've got to get him, Ruby, we can't allow any more people to get hurt.'

CHAPTER THIRTY-NINE

Laura sat with her legs crossed, smoothing down her newly straightened hair. She had finally raised enough money to buy a pair of GHDs. It was only a matter of time before her sister took them, but at least she was coming to the helpline centre feeling good about herself. Gathered in a circle, she smiled at her fellow volunteers, ready to pick over the bones of this week's calls.

After ensuring everyone was equipped with a hot cup of tea, Ann, their team manager, took a seat in her swivel chair. Her face was taut. Just this once, the phones were off the hook. The silence was unprecedented, but calls would not go unanswered as they were diverted to the national line. 'Right. As you all know, we've called this meeting to discuss a case due to some concerns that have been raised. I've brought this meeting forward to discuss the ground rules, rather than an individual case. I know some of you are worried, but we're not meant to discuss calls in detail, much less take notes, as several of you have done.' She met Laura's gaze. 'I know you mean well, but if this gets out, then people may stop confiding in us. Worse still, our branch could be closed down because of failure to abide by the rules. Some of our callers are a hair's breadth away from suicide. We've got to put them first.'

'I don't see the harm in discussing it. There's only a few of us here.' Joseph Calleja, a long-term volunteer, cradled his mug of tea in his hands. His dark brown eyes were filled with sincerity as he spoke. 'We're not going to put it on Facebook or call the press.

And we've had quite a few calls from Matthew, each one more disturbing than the last.'

'I know you're worried about Matthew, but what do you want us to do about it?' Ann glanced around the room. 'We're not the police. We offer a listening service, and that's as far as it goes. You know that our usual callers pose harm only to themselves. We've no way of knowing if what Matthew says is true.'

'It's here in black and white. Everything matches up,' Laura said, her words filled with conviction as she held her newspaper aloft. 'They say there's a copycat killer on the loose. I'm sure Matthew has something to do with it.'

'Your imagination is running riot,' Ann interrupted. 'I've read that article. There's no victims' names mentioned, much less the fact your caller is responsible for their deaths.'

Laura frowned. 'But there's nothing to say that he isn't, either. I don't want to stop volunteering, but it's no great secret where the centre's located. I'm scared I'll come out some night to find some weirdo standing in the shadows, waiting to grab me.'

Ann exhaled loudly. 'Weirdos? I'm challenging you for that remark. Weren't you listening to any of the training when you came on board?'

'Steady on, girl,' Joan said, resting her hand on Ann's shoulder. The 65-year-old woman was the most experienced of the group and had seen and heard it all. 'She's just a teenager. That's how they talk these days.' She winked at Laura from behind Ann's back.

Laura bit back her smile, trying to appear as remorseful as she could. Her role as a volunteer had provided some much-needed experience and a reference from Ann would be needed when she decided to move on. 'Sorry,' she said, 'I didn't mean it like it sounded. I'm just worried. This Matthew... the stuff he's coming out with... dating married women then punishing them for being unfaithful – it's weird. Now he's started asking for me by name. It feels like it's coming to a head and I'm worried what's next.'

'Whose fault is that?' Ann reprimanded. 'You're feeding him information. You know the rules. We don't engage in two-way conversations, and you should never give your real name. People can be manipulative, and they'll prise information out of you in any way they can. To be honest, I'm beginning to wonder if this is the right place for you…'

Joseph raised his eyebrows. 'Well I've been in this game a very long time, and I think you're being a bit harsh. Yes, she is inexperienced, but she's doing her best and puts in more shifts than most. I've listened to her during some right dodgy calls, and she takes them in her stride. But Matthew is different. I've spoken to him too, and we have a right to be worried.'

Laura warmed from the inside out. Joseph was her dad's age and had barely spoken to her before. She had no idea that he valued her contribution to the team. Then again, perhaps he didn't want to cover her shifts if she left. Regardless, she acknowledged him with a gracious nod making a mental note to bring him in some chocolate biscuits as a gesture of thanks.

Ann rubbed her face, exhaling a long terse breath. 'OK, let's focus on Matthew then. So far we've gathered that he's local and seems to have a fixation on women who cheat on their husbands, but he's not made any direct threats to us.'

'Maybe not,' Laura piped up, 'but he mentioned teaching a lesson to a Melissa and a Cheryl. My uncle – he's working on the murder case mentioned in the paper. Two women with these names were found dead after meeting some guy from an online dating site for married men and women.'

Ann shook her head. 'Melissa and Cheryl are hardly unique names. You know most of our clients use pseudonyms when they call. Unless he's made a specific threat then you've nothing to worry about.'

But Laura did not look convinced. 'All the same,' she said, staring at the floor, 'I don't want to talk to him the next time he calls.'

Ann grunted. 'And how do you suggest we do that? We can't monitor the calls, and we certainly can't pass our callers to someone else if we don't like what they're saying.'

'I think we need to establish some positive action,' Joan said, raising her hand to stall the argument. 'We've laboured the point about ground rules. God knows I don't want to pick up the newspaper and find out some poor devil's been murdered, but I can't see how there's a lot we can do.'

'The police can log things as intelligence,' Laura said. 'It just comes up on their computer system, so it lets everyone know.'

'You've not been speaking to your uncle about this, have you?' Ann said, stiffening in her chair. The fact Laura's uncle was a police officer was well known within the group.

Laura shook her head vehemently; her straightened blonde ponytail swaying with her. She had been tempted to confide in him at the time, but wanted to speak to the group first. 'Of course not. It's just things I pick up. Mum said if I'm worried about something at work then I should be straight with you. It's better than just walking out. Seems to me, enough people have done that already.'

'We're not liaising with the police,' Ann said. 'I can tell you that for starters. I'm trying to protect what we have here. There are rules in place and we have to stick to them if we want to keep going. Sure we have funding now but if we get bad publicity as a result of something we've said then they could close us down.' She gave Laura a gentle smile. 'Of course I want to keep you safe. I want to look after all our volunteers. I'm just disappointed because you've interacted with the caller more than you should. From now on, don't be drawn in to conversation, focus on how they're feeling and put the onus on them. This could just be a poor tortured soul that's fabricating all of this as an excuse to speak to another human being. This society we live in, it makes us so very insulated. People are so caught up in the virtual world that they can go days without speaking to another living soul. That's what I love about what we have, real warm, human voices on the line. I don't think our caller is a threat to anyone.'

'What if you're wrong?' Laura said. 'What if another woman is in danger? What then?'

'To be honest, I don't think it's appropriate that your uncle has been talking with you about his investigation, but that's your business.' Ann sighed. 'I can't physically stop you talking to him, but if you break the rules again, then we don't have a place for you here anymore.'

Laura nodded dumbly, lowering her gaze to the floor. Her position had been made clear. Now she had to decide what to do about it. Would she stay and take the risk, or leave and report the caller to her uncle? Without proof, there wouldn't be much the police could do. 'I'll stay,' she said, speaking what felt like famous last words. 'You never know, we might not hear from him again.'

CHAPTER FORTY

Tapping lightly on DCI Worrow's door, Ruby awaited a response. A furtive shuffling noise from within signalled her presence, but she seemed in no hurry to respond.

'Ma'am, it's me, Ruby,' she said, slowly opening the door. She frowned as she caught sight of DCI Worrow with her back to her, her shoulders hunched. But she refused to be put off and slid inside before closing the door behind her.

'I'm busy,' Worrow said. Her words muffled with tears. 'Come… come back later.'

Ruby didn't move. She softened her voice, having left her judgement at the door. She was all too aware of the pressure DCI Worrow would have been under to have made her snap. It was hard getting to the top so young and not something Ruby envied. 'I've been to see DI Downes,' she said. 'They're letting him out later today.'

Plucking a tissue from her pocket, Worrow dabbed her eyes before turning around. Their puffiness told Ruby she had been crying for some time. She hated seeing her colleagues at each other's throats.

'Really?' Worrow said, having contacted Ruby for an update earlier in the day.

'He'll be fine once he gets a bit of rest. He…' Ruby paused, mentally assembling her words. 'He's asked me to apologise for his behaviour. He's been very stressed. Finding out about Cheryl and details of the case hitting the press just made things worse.'

'I know all about stress,' Worrow said. 'I'm being held fully responsible as to the direction that this case is taking. I promised results, and now another woman is dead. Then there's the press. If we can't trust our officers to keep this information to themselves…' She wrung the tissue between her fingers, trying but failing to keep calm. 'I mean, how many times have we told them? This is sensitive information. Under no circumstances are they to discuss it outside of work.'

'With all respect, Ma'am, I don't believe it came from one of our officers.'

'Yes, well, we're the ones getting the blame,' Worrow said. 'And the only way to make things right is to catch this killer in his tracks, before someone else dies.'

Ruby nodded, her hands clasped behind her back. Worrow always made her feel like she was walking on eggshells, and it could not be any more different to her relationship with DI Downes. 'We all feel the same way and we're working around the clock. DI Downes is going to smooth things over with Phillip Sherman when he gets out. Hopefully he can find out where the leak originated.'

Worrow's face thawed a little. 'As for the way he spoke to me, has he told you about that?'

'From what I gather things got very heated on both sides, Ma'am,' Ruby said diplomatically. 'But it's important to keep morale up as we work through the investigation.'

'It's all right for you,' Worrow said. 'You have the respect of your team, and Downes is your right-hand man. But if I died tomorrow, I'm sure that team of yours would be singing "ding dong the witch is dead" before my body was put in the ground.'

Ruby frowned. It was unlike Worrow to be so maudlin. But it wasn't as if she could put her arm around her and say that everything was going to be OK. Besides, she had a point. She was never going to win any popularity contests. The higher the rank the more distant you were from the rest of the team.

'You've always been a stable leader,' Ruby said, choosing to focus on the positives. 'We respect you for that. But it's important we keep a united front if we're to focus on the task in hand.' Ruby caught Worrow's expression of mild annoyance and remembered who she was talking to. 'Sorry. I don't mean to tell you how to do your job. I can only imagine how difficult it is, working with such tight resources and dwindling budgets. Then throw a celebrity into the mix and it becomes overwhelming for us all. But we will get through this and I'll use whatever measures necessary to find our suspect and bring them in.'

Worrow straightened her stature. 'I agree with keeping a strong front, and I'd be grateful if you keep the details of this meeting to yourself.'

Ruby nodded in agreement. She was hardly likely to go back and say she'd seen her DCI blubbing in her office due to an argument earlier on.

'Tell me, do you think Mason Gatley is involved?' Worrow said. 'I read your report. Is another visit worthwhile?'

'I think Mason's enjoying the attention but I may have a way of turning that around to our advantage.'

'Good,' Worrow said, the primness returning to her tone. Their conversation was interrupted by a ringing telephone. 'Dammit, I forgot. I've got a meeting scheduled. Perhaps we can finish this conversation another time.'

'Of course,' Ruby said taken aback by her supervisor's language. It was another chink in the armour of a woman they called the Ice Queen. Ruby tried to imagine herself in the same position. It only cemented the decision to stay where she was in the ranks. She turned to leave, reminding herself to sort out another visit to Mason.

'Oh and Ruby?' Worrow said, silencing her phone. 'If you're talking to Downes tell him we'll keep this morning between us. Draw a line under the whole thing.'

'Yes, Ma'am,' Ruby said, before turning to leave. She was beginning to feel like a UN peace negotiator by the time she left.

After a quick cigarette, Ruby walked to her office, surprised to see DI Downes sitting in her chair. She cradled the cup of tea Richard had just made, feeling pleased with herself that she had managed to avert Downes from suspension. Had that happened, he would be cracking open the bottle of whisky that she knew he kept in the cabinet in his house. It was very expensive fine malt, one he kept for the worst of emergencies but Ruby was equipped with the knowledge that once he started to drink from that bottle he would not be able to stop.

Such was the history between them: they knew of each other's weaknesses and learned to tap into each other's strengths. 'You're looking like the cat that got the cream,' she said, taking a seat beside him. 'And I didn't expect to see you again so soon.'

'Aye, that was a good idea of mine, giving Phillip Sherman a call.' His eyes glinted in the knowledge that it was Ruby he had to thank.

'Oh yeah?' Ruby said, giving him a wry smile as she tipped the mug to her lips.

'Turns out you're right. It was one of the housekeepers. Sherman had her followed, caught her accepting a payout from the newspaper that took the report. He threatened to sue the paper, citing slander if they mention his wife by name. Not just that, but he's going to get in touch with Worrow and apologise for his earlier outburst.'

'Blimey, how did you manage that?' Ruby said. Phillip Sherman did not seem like the type of man who apologised for anything.

'Let's just say I have my ways,' Downes said. 'Mind you, it could be all for nothing if I've lost my job. You've not seen her about have you? I came in to grovel.'

Ruby paused. She would have loved to have told him about Worrow's outburst and the fact the woman cried real tears. But she felt solidarity towards her female colleague, despite the fact they did not always get along. 'I spoke to her on your behalf. She's gone no further with it. Wants to draw a line under it all.'

Downes's face lit up in a smile as he clapped her heartily on the back. 'Really? You're a lifesaver that's what you are. A lifesaver!'

Ruby gasped at the display of strength. 'Steady on, I need my lungs for smoking. Don't want you dislodging them when we've so much to do.'

'You could be right there,' Downes said. 'They've tracked down Mason Gatley's son. He works in a coffee kiosk in Liverpool Street Station. Luddy's getting the tube over there now.'

'Not without me,' Ruby said, shrugging on her harness and clipping her radio back on to her belt.

CHAPTER FORTY-ONE

'What is it? What's wrong?' The young man glared warily at Ruby and Luddy amid the hustle and bustle of evening commuters. It had been quicker to come by tube, given rush hour traffic was in full flow. Having persuaded Mason's son, James, to leave his kiosk in the hands of his colleagues, Ruby was keen to take him to one side. The only resemblance Ruby could see between James and his father was his sandy-coloured hair, which was cropped short. The same height as his father, James stood with slouched shoulders and the composure of someone who preferred to be lost in the crowd. Ruby guessed it was due to the devastation his father had caused. After pointing out there was nothing to worry about, she asked James if they could find a quiet spot to talk.

'You're kidding me, aren't you?' James said, raising his voice over the sounds of the tannoy. 'I run a coffee kiosk and it's rush hour. Time is money. What do you want?'

'It's about your father,' Ruby said. 'Hence the need for privacy.'

James grimaced at the mention of Mason's name. 'Fine. We'll talk outside. But that's it. I'm not having you coming to my home. Five minutes and we're done.'

Liverpool Street housed both a train and tube station, making it one of the busiest places in London to be. Ruby was dreading the ride home on a packed tube. She dodged a woman wheeling a suitcase while carrying a baby on her hip. All around her, work-weary commuters hustled to their trains and tubes, desperate to get home. But respite was hours away for Ruby. As they walked up the steps to the main concourse, she focused her mind on what lay ahead. Having led him to the quietest space she could find, James turned to Ruby, grim-faced.

'Is he dead? Is that what you've come here to tell me? Because that would make my week.' Although several inches taller than Ruby, James lacked the commanding presence of his father.

Ruby took a strengthening breath of city air before relaying the recent murders, which held all the hallmarks of his father's case. 'We're concerned someone's emulating your father, but it appears to be a person with an intimate knowledge of his case. I was wondering if anyone had spoken to you about it recently?'

'Oh yeah sure,' James said, his lip arched in a sneer. 'I love talking about my darling dad to the press.' He twisted his forefinger around his index finger in a gesture of friendship. 'We're like that we are, I love journalists.'

Ruby arched an eyebrow as she gave him a withering glare.

'The press made our lives hell for years. My poor mum had to move away because they wouldn't stop knocking on our door. The endless phone calls... being stopped in the street. Why would I want anything to do with those bloodsucking vampires?'

'What about online forums?' Luddy said. 'Social media? Facebook?'

A crackle of laughter escaped James's lips. He stared at Luddy with humourless eyes. 'Yeah because I'm so proud to be the son of a serial killer. It's great for my pulling power. You just roll that out as a chat-up line and all the lads want to know you. You've no idea how much my family has gone through because, if you did—' He raised a finger to interrupt Ruby, who opened her mouth to speak. 'If you did,' he said, tears springing to his eyes, 'you would not come here and so casually start raking things up again. Those women weren't the only ones wounded. We all suffered because of what he did.' His hands trembling, he took a breath, the blood draining from his face.

Ruby wondered if such hatred could fuel a passion that could drive him to do terrible things as well. 'I'm sorry,' she said, 'I didn't mean to upset you. But whoever it is seems to know an awful lot about his case. We need to find out who's been sharing information. Women's lives are at risk.'

James sniffed, wiping the tears from his eyes. 'Look, I know you're only doing your job but I can't help you. I've been through years of therapy to get where I am now. I've got a steady life, my own business.' He looked from Luddy to Ruby, a look of horror dawning on his face. 'You think it's me, don't you? You actually think I've been walking in his shoes.'

'I never said that,' Ruby replied. 'But as investigators we have to explore all avenues. Perhaps it would be better if we spoke about this at the station in a voluntary interview.'

'If you want me to come to the police station, you'll have to arrest me first,' James spat, his face inches away from Ruby as he spoke.

Ruby stood her ground, noting his clenched fists by his side. 'There's no need for aggression,' she said calmly, giving Luddy a look to say that she was OK.

Stepping back, James raised his hands in the air and slapped them against his legs. 'Do you see? See what he's doing to me? I'm not normally like this.' The heat left his words as he spoke, and he seemed to be slowly coming back to ground. Turning his back, he plucked a small brown plastic container of tablets from his pocket and, tipping two onto his palm, swallowed them dry. Briefly closing his eyes, his lips moved as he silently counted backwards from five to one. 'In answer to your question, I've not spoken to my father recently. The last time I tried was five years ago when my therapist suggested we meet.'

'How did it go?' Luddy said, watching him intently for any sudden moves.

'It didn't. He disowned me years ago because of my... life choices. I'm gay. Therefore, I disgust him.' James smiled, bitterness lacing his words. 'After everything he's done, I disgust him.' He looked from Luddy to Ruby. 'And now I'm done with the whole thing. Please don't contact me again, not unless it's to tell me he's dead.'

'James, wait,' Ruby said, reaching out as he turned away. 'Isn't there anyone you could think of that might have in-depth knowledge of your father? Anyone at all?'

James turned to face her, pulling back his arm from her touch. 'Yes, there is actually. One very irritating woman who refuses to go away. I'm beginning to think I'm speaking a different language because she keeps asking me the same question over and over again. I've tried telling her the truth but she won't leave me alone.'

Devoid of words, Ruby sighed.

'Who?' Luddy asked, reaching for his pocket notebook and pen as James walked away.

'Me,' Ruby said flatly. 'He's talking about me.'

Hands in pockets, Luddy turned towards the station entrance. 'We'd better get our tube.'

Deep in thought, Ruby entered the bowels of the station, her attention drawn to the huge flashing screens overhead. Advertisements, movie trailers, all were shown in their colourful glory. Ruby paused. A rock in a sea of bustling commuters, she stared up at the screens.

'CCTV,' she spoke the words on an exhale. 'Cameras cover every angle of this place. I want you to seize all footage of James's comings and goings at around the time of Cheryl's death.'

'But we haven't pinpointed the time,' Luddy said, raising his eyebrows at the mammoth task ahead.

'We have, or at least close enough,' Ruby said, the presence of the screens triggering a finite detail she had missed out on when she read the statements the first time around. 'The hotel they found her in – The Grand. The maid said the television was on when she got there. Most likely to drown out any noise.'

'Yes, and?' Luddy said, confusion crossing his face.

'I'll bet money that it's on a timer. Two, maybe four hours before it switches off by itself. Which means the killer was there not long before the body was found.'

'So pinpoint the time and see if James was working that day,' Luddy replied.

Ruby nodded in agreement. 'And if he's not, we've got enough suspicion to bring him in.'

CHAPTER FORTY-TWO

'Since when did you own a car?' Ruby said, looking pointedly at the keys her daughter had placed on the glossy kitchen counter. Ruby pulled down two mugs from the overhead cupboard as she made the first cuppa of the morning.

'Frances bought it for me. I think she's worried that it'll take me too long to get to Chigwell by public transport and I might not come back.'

'Bribery's one way around it I suppose,' Ruby said, regretting the words as soon as they had left her lips.

Cathy looked pointedly around the luxury Dalston flat. 'I guess none of us are shy when it comes to accepting gifts from the Crosbys.'

Ruby took a breath and prepared to start again. The last thing she wanted was their first weekend together getting off on a bad foot. Not that she would be there very much, given her team's caseload. She'd barely had time for breakfast before going to work. 'Coffee?' Ruby said, taking the milk from the fridge.

'I'd much prefer tea,' Cathy replied. 'Strong, three sugars… what are you grinning at?'

'Nothing,' Ruby replied, biting back her smile. 'It's just… that's how I like it too.'

'Good,' Cathy said. 'It means you won't be lecturing me about my sugar intake like Nana.'

'Nana?' Ruby laughed. 'How do you get away with calling her that?' Frances may have been Cathy's grandmother but she would hardly appreciate the reference.

'I only use it when she's getting on my nerves. She hates being reminded of her age. It's one way of getting her off my back.'

Walking into the living room, Ruby rested their tea on the coffee table. 'It's really nice to have you here,' she said. 'I'm looking forward to getting to know you better.'

'I'd like that, too,' Cathy said, kicking off her boots before curling up on the sofa. 'And I'm not going to sponge off the family for ever. I'm going to get a good job, start paying my way.'

Ruby smiled gently, taking a seat next to her. 'Hun, I think you're entitled to some payback, given all the years you were away. I know it wasn't easy for you and I'm sorry. I wish things had turned out differently.'

'You want to know about the scars, don't you?' Cathy said, staring into her cup. 'I've caught you looking at them enough times.'

'Only when you're good and ready,' Ruby said, steeling herself for her daughter's reply.

'I've spent half my life thinking like a victim,' Cathy said. 'It's time to move on. I don't blame you for giving me up. I probably would have done the same thing at that age.'

Ruby stared, speechless, at her change of heart. 'When did you come to this decision?'

'Dad talked me through the whole thing. It's OK. I get it. I'd like to begin again.'

'And your past?' Ruby asked. 'Would you like to talk to someone about it? If not me, then maybe we could arrange for—'

'Counselling?' Cathy said, pre-empting her words. 'No thanks. I'm putting a lid on it. My scars are part of me now. They've made me strong. I'm going to get a tattoo, incorporate them in. It'll be tastefully done. Nobody will know they're there, except for me.'

'And your boyfriend?' Ruby paused to sip her tea, swallowing back her regret. She had believed in the system when she gave her daughter up, and it had let them both down.

'You know, I think he's more in love with you than me.' Cathy grinned, her eyes twinkling at the mention of his name. 'Look, Mum… can I call you Mum?'

'I'd love you to,' Ruby said, feeling warmth spread like a fire inside her.

'I'll tell you what happened but I need you to let it lie. Don't go poking your nose in. Do you promise?'

Ruby nodded silently by means of reply. A flicker of fear rose up inside her as she braced herself for what was to come. Was she ready to hear this?

Cathy cleared her throat. 'I was in and out of foster homes until the Connor family took me in at the age of ten. Peter, the head of the household, was big into corporal punishment and took his belt to me more than once. I took punishments for the other foster kids because I couldn't bear to see them suffer too. He said nobody would believe us if we told the truth. So when I was thirteen, I fought back.'

'No,' Ruby said, her hand slowly cupping her mouth.

Cathy shifted in her seat as she prepared to relay the rest of the story. 'One day Peter made me kneel in the corner of the garage. I stayed silent as he beat me across the back with his belt. Then he said he was going to administer a special punishment. I saw how he'd been looking at me, and something told me there was something far worse coming my way. I acted all meek, but he underestimated me. When he turned to lock the garage door, I picked up a shovel and whacked him over the head.' She grinned at the memory but Ruby did not share in her glee. Her eyes wet with tears, she placed her cup on the table before taking her daughter's hand.

'That's horrific,' she said, 'I'm so sorry—'

'It's not your fault,' Cathy interrupted, briefly squeezing her hand.

'What happened? Did you get help?' Ruby's stomach churned as she contemplated the pain her daughter had been through.

'I told the police it was self-defence. They couldn't argue with the scars on my back, all courtesy of his thick leather trouser belt, buckle side up.' She sighed as she recalled the memory, the smile stiff on her face. 'We got help, the other kids found new homes. But I didn't get on anywhere after that. When I was old enough I got a flat. But I wasn't what you'd call responsible. I didn't cope very well on my own.'

'I knew things were tough when you found us,' Ruby said quietly.

Cathy did not disagree. 'I fell in with a bad crowd, got into drugs. Slept with people I shouldn't have. I'm one of the lucky ones: I got out in time. Others – they weren't so fortunate. I dread to think how some of them ended up. Dead, probably.'

'You're so strong. Coming out the other side.'

'Dad said I get that from you. From what I've seen, you're both pretty ballsy. But I don't want to think about the past anymore. It's time to move on.'

'You know I'll support you in whatever you want to do.'

Cathy's expression lightened as they moved on to a brighter subject. 'Good, because I've been studying law.'

'Really?' Ruby said. 'Joining the dark side?'

'No, I'm joining the police.'

Ruby stared, wordless and expressionless, as she absorbed her daughter's words.

'Well? Say something,' Cathy said.

'When you said law, I presumed you were talking about becoming a criminal defence lawyer,' Ruby replied. 'Isn't that what your dad thinks you're going to do?'

'Yeah,' Cathy smirked. 'He thinks I'm going to get some of his old cronies off when I'm qualified. I was hardly gonna tell him the truth, was I? Not while I'm living with Frances. You know how much she hates the old bill; she'd do her nut.'

'She will.' Ruby grimaced at the thought. 'And you know who she'll blame? Me.'

'Since when have you been afraid of Frances Crosby?' Cathy said.

Ruby smiled. Her daughter had gotten to know her well.

Swigging back the dregs of her tea, Cathy lay her cup on her lap, placed her feet on the coffee table and turned to face her mum. 'I thought you'd be pleased.'

Ruby exhaled a deep sigh. 'After all you've been through… I just wanted you to have an easier life. What's made you want to join the job? I always thought you disapproved?'

'I only said that stuff to get back at you,' Cathy said. 'I didn't mean a word. If anything, I admire what you do.'

'And what about your dad?' Ruby said earnestly. 'Do you admire that side of the business?'

'He's trying to clean up his act. Seriously, you want to hear the rows Lenny has with him over the phone. He's sold off half the businesses, and after those prostitutes got killed, he's closed down the escort site too.'

Ruby tried not to act surprised. She knew Nathan had been affected by the murders of the girls who had once worked on his patch, but she was not made aware of this most recent development in things. Was Nathan Crosby finally going straight? He had always managed to evade being charged for his crimes. There was still time for him to turn things around. 'That's good to hear,' she said. 'I'll support you, if you can give me a good enough reason as to why you want to join the police.'

Cathy's focus turned inwards as she retrieved long-buried memories. 'When I turned the tables on my foster father and gave him a taste of his own medicine… it made me feel like I was worthwhile. One of the other foster kids was called Fiona. She was Down's syndrome. She couldn't fight back. I had to make it so he could never hurt anyone again.'

'How did you do that?' Ruby said.

'Peter came to punish Fiona that day, not me. I wouldn't let him take her away. So I wound him up, really bad. He forgot all about her and chose to teach me a lesson instead.'

'That's awful,' Ruby said.

'No, it was good, because this time I had scars. I'd already planned my escape. Without a proper beating, it would have been my word against his. Social care knew I couldn't have whipped my own back. They found the belt in the garage; it still had traces of my blood on it. It was thanks to the police and my testimony that he was locked away for what he did.'

'And Fiona?'

'She was adopted. A sweet kid. I often think about her now.'

A sudden thought shot across Ruby's consciousness. 'Does your dad know about this?'

'No,' Cathy said, shaking her head. 'And you can't let him know. He'd find him and string him up by the balls.'

'I thought you'd welcome it,' Ruby said, prising more information from her.

'Once, I would have. But not anymore. Seeing Lenny in action is enough to put me off.'

Ruby frowned. 'What have you seen?'

Cathy tapped her finger to the side of her nose. 'Nothing for you to worry about.'

'God, you remind me of your father,' Ruby said, making a mental note to find out later.

'I'll take that as a compliment,' Cathy replied. 'Don't worry, it works both ways. I don't report anything I hear from you either.'

'What have you heard?' Ruby said, wishing she could stay and chat a little longer.

'Oh, just that Dad's arranged for you to speak to Mason Gatley. Or rather Lenny has. Made up, he was. But I think you need to be careful there. I know he's my uncle but I don't trust him an inch.'

'I'm glad you have the measure of him,' Ruby said. 'Because he knew exactly who you were when he took you on in the club… long before he told your father.'

'I know, and I've spoken to him about it. He said it wasn't his place to say.'

Ruby frowned, reminding herself to keep things light. 'Well you don't need to be getting involved in police business. Leave that to me.'

Cathy cocked her head to one side. 'I know who this Mason Gatley is. The Lonely Hearts Killer, right? If you need any help finding his copycat then I'm happy to get stuck in.'

Ruby paled at the thought. 'You're joking me, right?'

'It was just an offer,' Cathy said, picking up the cups to bring them to the sink. 'Word has it that he's been hitting the clubs.'

The thought of her daughter getting involved in her case sent a cold shiver down her spine. She checked her watch, preparing to put this conversation to the back of her mind. Now was time to focus on leading her team. But not before she issued a warning to her daughter. 'No involvement. Nothing. Do you hear me?' she said, in a stern voice.

'Your face!' Cathy laughed, flicking her head back as her dark hair tumbled into her face. 'Chill your beans. I was joking. Besides, he only goes for married chicks.'

Ruby pulled on her blazer, frustration spearing her words. 'We'll talk about this later. Promise me you won't have anything to do with this case.'

'Relax, all I've planned for tonight is a hot chocolate and a chick flick on the box.'

But Ruby was not convinced. The sooner she got this killer off the streets, the sooner they would all be safe.

CHAPTER FORTY-THREE

Pressing her palms against the interview room door, Ruby took a moment to pause. She had barely reached her office before being notified of another missing person case. The speed at which the killer was working was frightening. First Cheryl, then Melissa. Was there a third victim already? Yesterday's conversation with Mason's son, James, had left her unsettled. With just four hours' sleep under her belt, she felt barely able to face the world again. Pressing down firmly on the door handle, she gathered up all of her strength to deal with what lay ahead.

Lisa Crawley's missing person report had been fast tracked as soon as she mentioned a photograph of her husband had arrived at her home. Slid through the letterbox of the three-bedroom semi, it was met with confusion by his wife. From postal workers to couriers, the choice of delivery seemed random each time. To them, they were simply doing their job. They had no idea of the devastation they were delivering as they walked around from door to door. Ruby wondered how many more people were getting photographs of their partners. Were there more, unreported, crimes?

One thing at a time, she told herself. It was a mantra she used when she began to feel overwhelmed. Dressed in yesterday's trouser suit, her hair straggling from her ponytail it was most certainly the case today. The briefing room was filled with enquiries. Crime scene pictures, maps, suspects, theories, and that was just on one board. She had no doubt that the discovery of the body of Matthew Johnson had meant the perpetrator had taken over his role. Filling his shoes, he had taken his online profile as his own.

Keeping a neutral expression, Ruby introduced herself to Lisa. She was an attractive woman with a pixie nose and cropped mousy brown hair. In her early forties, she had described herself as happily married when asked by attending officers, and Ruby wondered if she knew her husband had an interest in men.

Pleasantries over, Ruby launched into her line of questioning. She could have asked a detective constable to get the measure of her, but Ruby wanted to see for herself. 'You told the officers your husband was expected home yesterday, but didn't return home, is that right? Has he ever done anything like this before?' She was aware she was trawling over the same questions she had asked Cheryl's husband not long before.

Lisa sat with her fingers intertwined, her knuckles white from the effort. 'Thomas is very punctual. If he says he's going to be somewhere at a certain time then he'll be there. He sent me a text at five o'clock to say he was going to some meeting after work and would be home by nine that night. Even that's unlike him. He doesn't text because he's never late.' She gave Ruby a weak smile. 'His father was in the army, you see. Thomas grew up in a regimented way of life. This is so out of character for him.'

'Have you any idea as to where he might be?' Ruby said.

Tears brimmed Lisa's eyes as she shook her head from left to right. 'When I told my friends he didn't come home they just smiled at me, saying he was probably out on the prowl. But Thomas isn't like their husbands. He's not interested in other women. He doesn't get drunk and, no matter what happens, he always finds his way home.'

'When you say he isn't "interested in other women", what do you mean by that?' Ruby said, finding an opening and using it.

Lisa released her fingers and began dry washing her hands, as if wanting to cleanse herself of Ruby's words. 'Nothing,' she said sharply. 'He's a one-woman man. That's all I meant.'

'What about men?' Ruby said, gauging her reaction.

'I beg your pardon?' Lisa replied, her features creased in a frown.

Oh well, in for a penny in for a pound, Ruby thought, no stranger to rubbing people up the wrong way. She could not sugar coat it. She did not have the time. 'Has he ever been sexually attracted to men?'

'Of course not. What does that have to do with him being missing? Have you got the right to ask me questions like these?'

'Sometimes,' Ruby said, 'if it pertains to the investigation. Please, Lisa. It's important. Has Thomas ever dated another man?'

'What relevance has that got to him not coming home?' Lisa asked.

Ruby exhaled. 'There's a line of enquiry in a similar case that we're following, but I can't give you any details at this stage. The photo you've been sent is significant, and I need you to cooperate with us because there's a chance more pictures may be sent to your home.'

Ruby watched Lisa's face crumple as she spoke. 'What do you mean, more? Is Thomas in trouble?' She began to nibble on a jagged thumbnail, and Ruby noticed it had been bitten to the quick.

'Can you answer my question, please? About his previous relationships. I promise I'll be discreet,' Ruby said firmly.

Lisa returned to wringing her hands, her legs crossed beneath the table. It was like every inch of her was tying itself up in knots. 'Once he told me that when he was eighteen, he had a crush on his supervisor; Michael, I think his name was. They both knew about it but it didn't go any further. People experiment at that age. It was nothing. He's not looked at another man since.'

Ruby nodded, fighting the rising internal sense of dread. She could see it all in front of her. Thomas fulfilling his fantasies with a one-night stand. Flirting at a party, a card being slipped into his hand. *Debauchery.* She could only hope that his wife avoided reading the stories bound to filter into the press.

'What do I do now?' Lisa sniffed, her words dissolving into a whine. 'Please. Is he in some kind of danger? Why can't you tell me any more? How am I meant to go home after this? What will I tell my kids?'

Ruby reached out and lightly patted Lisa's hand. Her wedding ring glinted from beneath the strip lights. It carried a design, and Ruby hated herself for wondering if Thomas had a matching band. She tried not to allow it in but the image came just the same: a thick gold engraved band dangling from a chain.

'Don't panic just yet,' Ruby said, grateful Lisa could not read her thoughts. 'Your husband's disappearance may not be connected to our other case. You might go home and find him sitting there, wondering what all the fuss is about.'

A gloom descended on the room. Given the presence of the photo, Ruby knew this was unlikely to be the case. 'All I'm asking is that you don't open any post over the next couple of days. We'll assign someone to come to your home and open it on your behalf just in case there's any more photos. Oh and Lisa, can you tell me, is your husband a member of a golf club?'

'Golf club?' Lisa said. 'No. I told you, we don't really go out. He lives for his work.'

'So he's never been to the Highfield Country Club then?'

Lisa frowned. 'No, wait… that name rings a bell. He's an airline pilot. They had a works do there recently. I had a migraine, so Thomas went on his own. It was an awards ceremony. He was nominated so he couldn't wriggle out of it. Why? What's that got to do with it?'

'Nothing at this point,' Ruby said, wishing she could tell her more. But after Worrow's recent outburst on information sharing, it was too great a risk to take. 'It's only been a day. Your case is being given priority. Most missing people return home safe and well.'

Ruby's reassurances seem to have done the trick at least enough for her to calm Lisa down. 'I'm sorry, I don't mean to be snappy. I know you're trying your best. My brother's a police officer in Suffolk.

He's told me how hard you all have it at the moment. It's the same on the NHS.' The briefest of smiles passed her lips. 'I used to be a nurse. But by the time I paid the childminder, it wasn't worth going to work. It's a shame because I loved what I did.'

'It's definitely a labour of love,' Ruby said, conscious of the time as she rose from her seat. More than ever she wanted to reunite this woman with her husband. 'Officers will need to seize any laptops or computers your husband had access to. Again, it's just a measure of precaution. Is that OK with you?'

Lisa's shoulders slumped as she met Ruby's gaze. 'It will have to be, won't it? I'll do anything to get him home.'

CHAPTER FORTY-FOUR

'Back so soon?' Mason said, in a voice that somehow suggested they were friends. 'Couldn't you stay away? Or are you admitting yourself as an inpatient and have come to say hello?' He sat at the table in his normal manner, his long legs sprawled underneath. Ruby edged her crossed legs beneath her wooden chair, physically distancing herself from his presence. She buttoned her jacket as a sliver of cold air made goosebumps rise on her skin. The room seemed gloomier today, and a creeping sense of menace infiltrated Ruby's senses. In the corner, Norman stood, keeping a watchful eye. It was a repetitive loop as far as Ruby was concerned, and her frustration was evident in her tone.

'I'm in no mood for games. We've had another missing person reported. All thanks to you.' Ruby delivered a hard stare. She had not expected a return visit to the psychiatric unit, but in the absence of any firm leads, DCI Worrow had instructed her to go.

'Really, officer, I'm offended,' Mason said, clearly animated by her presence. 'The bloodlust was there to begin with. I merely provided the inspiration. How many people have you inspired today?'

'You can shove your inspiration where the sun doesn't shine,' Ruby said, her eyes darting to Norman, who was standing by the door. It was taking time to obtain Mason's full medical records; all Ruby knew was that he was admitted due to what was termed a psychotic attack and a threat to self-harm. She did not doubt the man had problems, but she could not help but feel he was putting on his recent illness. Her team was still speaking to people likely to come into contact with him. It was quicker to come and see for herself.

'So I take it my elusive impersonator is still on the loose?' Mason's lips curled in a smile. 'After me working so hard to give you a clue. A clue you've failed to decipher.'

'You're wasting my time,' Ruby quipped. 'I'm only here because my DCI wanted me to appeal to your better nature. I've told her you don't have one, which is why I'm not staying long.'

'Such a shame,' Mason said. 'I've come to look forward to our little visits.'

Ruby swallowed. She could physically taste her dislike for this man as sourness on her tongue. 'I can see that. You've set all this up solely for your own amusement.'

'My hands are clean. No blood here.' Mason raised his palms. 'As much as I'd like to, I can't take the credit for the murders.' He raised his eyebrows and emitted a short chuckle. 'Or can I?'

Ruby's pulse raced as he teased her with the answers but she tried hard to hide the turmoil she felt inside. 'Enough with the games. If you won't tell me who's responsible then at least tell me where victim number three is.'

Rubbing his chin, Mason appeared to mull it over. 'I could, but you have to do something for me first.'

'I don't trade with killers,' Ruby said, deadpan.

'You do when it suits you. You forget. I know all about your relationship with Nathan Crosby. What's wrong? Is this victim not special enough for you to bend the rules? I was only asking for a phone call. Does she deserve everything she gets?'

She, Ruby thought, a light-bulb moment flicking on in her brain. *If Thomas really is the next victim then Mason doesn't know.* An idea turned over in her head. It would be risky, and involved bluffing to some extent. But what did she have to lose? She bit her lip as she thought it over. Mason appeared far too calm. She needed to inject some emotion into the proceedings first. 'We don't all share your way of thinking,' Ruby said, conveying an expression of disgust as she eyed him up and down. 'You swagger around like you're some kind of celebrity, whereas all you are is a pathetic loser who gets your rocks off from watching other people do what you can't.'

Mason jumped forward, grabbing Ruby by both wrists.

Shocked by the sudden contact of his cold flesh, Ruby untangled her crossed legs and jerked back in her chair.

'You cheeky bitch,' Mason snarled, spittle landing on her face. 'When I get out of here I'm going to skin you alive.'

'That's enough now!' the man at the door shouted, striding towards them.

Ruby shook her wrists as if to discard his DNA from her skin. 'It's OK,' she said speaking with more confidence than she felt. Mason's eyes had bored through her as he made his threat, revealing every ounce of hatred he felt inside. She knew all the light banter, compliments and niceties were only skimming the surface. His real personality lay beneath. Personality that housed a monster. It was a timely reminder of the sort of man she was dealing with, but she could not afford to stop now. She was glad she had invoked a reaction because now the real work could begin.

Norman Jennings stood over them, looking to Ruby for reassurance. She knew everything about this member of staff after Mason had mentioned him previously. He had come up clean after a thorough check. All the same, she found her eyes falling on his neckline, looking for the tell-tale bump of wedding rings on a chain beneath his clothes. Mason raised his hands in mock submission, his earlier smile returning to his face.

'Sorry, I got a little carried away. I'll behave myself from now on, I promise.' He gave Norman a winning smile but neither of them were fooled.

Ruby nodded that she was OK and, reluctantly, Norman took three steps back.

'So,' Ruby said, keeping her tone light. 'Whatever you want, I'm not giving you any more. Just remember that, without me, you'll have no knowledge of the damage these murders are causing your reputation. It does make me wonder though, why did the killer make a variation to the routine this time? What does he know about you that we don't?'

'What deviation?' Mason said, his interest restored.

'Yes, it's strange that one,' Ruby responded, preparing to deliver her bluff. 'You see, I always thought your murders were sexually motivated, because you raped your victims and masturbated while you were there. But with the current victims, there's no evidence to suggest the killer has been sexually active in any way. At first, we thought it was down to lack of evidence. Like you, our suspect found these women attractive and that's why he chose to do what he did. But now it seems that there's a bigger picture.' Ruby crossed her ankles beneath the table. 'It's all slotting together now. We found semen at the crime scene. We have DNA.'

'You just said he wasn't sexually active,' Mason said, narrowing his eyes.

'He wasn't, except for this one victim,' Ruby replied.

Mason shrugged. 'So? It won't be any value to you unless he's already on your system, and if you knew who it was, you wouldn't be visiting me.'

'True,' Ruby said, 'but what was it about this particular person that turned him on? Made him so overcome that he forgot himself.'

Mason's eyes narrowed. You could almost see the cogs in his mind turning as he tried to work out just what she was getting at.

Reminding herself of who she was dealing with, Ruby slowly straightened her posture. It would not do to be caught off guard should Mason rise up again. She sighed. 'It makes me wonder if he's delivering a message about you.'

'So, he wanked off. Big deal,' Mason said.

Ruby prepared to deliver the bombshell. 'I'm not the only one unable to work out clues. Don't you see? This one was different. The victim wasn't a woman, it was a man. In fact, it was the man he killed so he could take his place. The one from the dating agency, *Debauchery*. Very handsome by all accounts too.'

The darkness returned to Mason's face as the implication of her words became clear.

'Funny, isn't it? It's like he's getting back at women by murdering them. Maybe he hates them full stop. But men… that's where his real fantasies lie. Is he trying to tell us the same thing about you?'

The comment about finding semen was a lie. Ruby could not care less about Mason, or Matthew's sexuality, but what she did care about was making Mason mad. His breathing was elevated now, the colour rising from his neck to his cheeks like a temperature gauge. He clenched his teeth, but yet Ruby continued to speak.

'You see the thing is that everything Mason does, oh, sorry, I meant Matthew, it's easy to get you two mixed up these days…'

Mason's body tensed and the man at the door took a step forward.

Ruby continued. 'Everything he does reflects on you. It's certainly going to provoke a great debate in the media. That's if we don't catch him in time.'

'You've got it wrong,' Mason said. 'This is bullshit. He wouldn't deviate from the plan like this.'

'Don't take my word for it,' Ruby said. 'If we don't catch him soon, you'll be able to read about it for yourself. And yes, we could have got it wrong. The man who was murdered could have been seeing someone else. But you know what proves it? What really leaves me in no doubt that your impersonator is gay?'

Mason sat back in his chair and folded his arms. His biceps strained against his sleeves as they tensed.

'It's that victim number three isn't a woman. It's a man,' Ruby continued, forthright in tone. 'So I think it's time you revise the idea of helping us out.'

CHAPTER FORTY-FIVE

Ruby paced the hospital corridor as she waited to be allowed in. Her stomach was tied up in knots, her body still trembling from the come down of adrenalin flowing through her veins. Units had raced to find Thomas at the hotel Mason disclosed. It had proved one of two things: Mason knew the killer's next move, and he cared enough about his reputation to want to stop him dead. Thomas was not just alive, but conscious. Although dehydrated, his fingers were still intact and officers had reached him with time to spare. With the hotel room under constant surveillance, Ruby prayed the killer would return. She could have arrested Mason for the offence of assisting him in his crimes, but like a game of Jenga, that would send their carefully constructed relationship tumbling down. He was on the precipice of giving her the killer's identity. An arrest at this time would serve to shut him up. She tried to imagine the killer returning to the hotel room and discovering a police officer in Thomas's place. Would he be caught just as Mason was before? She had lied to Mason. No semen had been found. She smiled, barely able to believe that he had fallen into her trap. Her visits to the prison had been worthwhile, and she had Nathan to thank for getting her a foot in the door. But now she had made Mason's acquaintance, she knew he would not let it go. She had seen the hatred in his eyes, felt the firmness of his fingers as they dug into her skin.

Downes's honeyed voice carried in the air as he sweet-talked his friend the Ward Sister into letting them in to Thomas's hospital room. Ruby watched as she tilted her head to one side, her eyes twinkling in response to the lilt of his Northern Irish accent. Ruby looked away as a tiny pang of jealousy bloomed. She still had feelings for him, even now. What they had was more than friendship and she supposed that it would never go away. In truth, she did not want him to retire because she did not want him to go. The future felt uncertain and she hated it. Why couldn't things stay the way they were?

Ambling towards her, Downes wore a satisfied grin. 'We can visit for a few minutes. He's traumatised and tired, but should be all right to speak. Let me do the talking,' he said, his hand gently resting on Ruby's back as he followed her into the room. Rank was meant to take precedence but sometimes Ruby forgot. To her, it was about the best way to get the job done. She dreaded to think who would be her senior officer once Downes had left. Unless she took the post herself. She pushed such thoughts aside as they entered the private room, grateful his wife had gone home to bring him in a change of clothes.

A weary man, he lay back on the bed, his expression still carrying fragments of the horrors of his ordeal. Pressing a button, he elevated the bed. He winced as he made himself comfortable, the rope burns on his wrists and neck covered by a thin transparent gauze.

Ruby thought of his wife and wondered what she was going through. Yes, he would have some explaining to do, but surely she would be happy just to have him in one piece? Ruby reminded herself that it was not for her to contemplate how his marriage was going to survive. She was here to glean as much information as she could. Memories of Melissa's autopsy came back to haunt her. Now Cheryl was due on the mortuary slab. It was good to see Thomas pink skinned and alive. Taking out her notebook and pen, she prepared to take notes as Downes introduced them both.

But Thomas seemed keen to get something off his chest. 'You're the officers that saved me,' he croaked, his voice hoarse.

'Yes,' Downes replied, giving Ruby a sideways nod. 'Sergeant Preston here was instrumental in finding your hotel room in time.'

Thomas nodded solemnly, tears welling in his eyes. Squeezing them tight, he tried to blink them away. He looked at Ruby, his face filled with gratitude. 'Thank you,' he said, his chin wobbling. 'I was sure he was going to kill me. He threatened to do it when he…' His voice broke off as sobs wracked his body.

'Here.' Ruby plucked a man-sized tissue from the box at the end of the bed.

'Thanks.' Thomas sniffed, wiping his nose and eyes. 'I tried to scream but it built up in my throat because he'd shoved a rag in my mouth. But then his phone rang, and he left me alone in the hotel. When the door opened, I thought he was coming back to kill me. I was in a horror movie and there was no way out.'

'Can you tell us from the beginning what happened?' Downes said, nodding at Ruby to take note. She remembered the voice recorder in her pocket, preferring it to her scribbled notes, which she would struggle to decipher later on. Turning it on, she introduced the people present, along with the time, date and case number for reference later.

Barely pausing for breath, Thomas described his first meeting with Matthew and the online details that had been given to him by a stranger at the golf club party he recently attended. 'I'm so ashamed,' he said. 'I've never tried anything like this before and now my wife has to come to terms with what I've done. I hope she can forgive me.'

'When you got to the hotel room, what happened?' Downes said, encouraging him to carry on.

'I'd already had a few drinks for Dutch courage, and to be honest I was having cold feet.' Thomas picked a thread from the hospital blanket, his words laced with regret. 'Matthew reassured me his discretion and said I could back out any time I wanted. I've never been unfaithful to my wife. I can't imagine what you must think.'

'We're not here to judge,' Ruby sighed, wishing he would worry a bit less about what they thought and get on with the description.

Thomas nodded, looking a little more reassured. 'Of course, sorry.' He drew in a deep breath before continuing. 'We got to the room and we kissed a couple of times. I went to the bathroom while he cut us a few lines of coke. Again, it's not something I've tried that often,' he said, throwing them a guilty glance. 'I felt awful afterwards. It's never affected me that way before. Then Matthew started tying me up and I just presumed it was part of our night. Then he just stopped and turned on the television like I wasn't there. I must have passed out, as there was something else on the television when I came to, and Matthew had eaten a meal. I couldn't believe he'd ordered room service while I was tied up on the bed.'

'Can I interrupt you there,' Ruby said, forgetting her promise to Downes to allow him to take the lead. 'When Matthew was with you, was he sexually excited?'

'Yes, he had a whopping great erection,' Thomas sniffed. 'Which is why I couldn't understand why he suddenly stopped.'

'You were saying that he'd ordered room service,' Downes said, giving Ruby a look before bringing him back to his account.

Thomas nodded. 'I asked him what the hell he was doing, but I don't remember his response. I kept blacking out and coming to, missing great big chunks of time. It had to be the drugs. Eventually he told me that if I didn't shut up he'd gag me. I tried to get off the bed but I was tied to the posts.'

Ruby frowned. That wasn't the way the victims were displayed in the pictures. She hated to interrupt as Thomas was looking tired and she knew they had only a little time. 'Did he take any photos?' she said.

'Yes,' Thomas replied. 'He snapped one with his iPhone when we got to the hotel. I told him I didn't want any pictures taken but he just laughed it off and said he'd delete it. He took the second one when I was tied up. He'd untied me from the bed posts by this time, but because the rope was around my neck, I was still in no position to move. That's when he got the phone call and left.' Thomas's fingers touched the gauze on his neck as he relived the memory. 'I'm sure I was minutes from death.'

Ruby did not argue.

'What about a description?' Downes cut in. 'Could you work with a police sketch artist?' 'Yes,' Thomas said. 'He was about 5' 11", just looked like a regular guy. Average build, brown hair, nothing special but he had a way about him, you know? He was very charismatic, almost commanding.' He paused, pressing a button that lay on the bed by his side.

'Are you all right?' Ruby asked, as the colour left his face.

'Just a bit of pain,' Thomas said, his features relaxing as the morphine kicked in.

Ruby felt genuine sympathy for the man whose life had just imploded. She knew that this would be the first of many times he would relive each painful memory. But the most accurate information was that gathered directly after the event. Soon the minute details of such a horrific event would begin to fade.

As the Ward Sister slid the door open, it seemed that their time was up. She looked at Downes as if he were the only person in the room. 'The doctor is on his rounds, come back later when he's had some rest.'

'Thanks, love,' Downes replied, before turning to Thomas. 'We'll arrange a sketch artist. Have him drop by to see you later on.'

Ruby followed him out, feeling hope at last. With a description to follow and having saved their last victim, their killer was running on borrowed time.

CHAPTER FORTY-SIX

Abby's voice crumbled as she acknowledged her appointment. Her long dark lashes wet with tears, she hunched over her mobile phone. Her size ten jeans felt loose around her hips as she paced her bedroom, a direct result of the mounting stress that stemmed her appetite and made her feel ill. Sheer panic was guiding her actions, but she found herself pressing the self-destruct button just the same. It would have seemed odd to most people, unless they had been through a trauma of some kind. Abby's life had been one headlong collision after another. She had fooled herself into thinking that she could be happy, just for a little while. She was wrong. Nothing this good could last for ever. It was time to accept that she could not have what was granted so easily to others. She was soiled. Damaged goods. The flashbacks of her past served as timely reminders, fuelled by the constant worrying thoughts bouncing against the walls of her mind.

Up until Steve, she had ended relationships just as they began to blossom. She had to get there before they did, to soften the blow. Steve was her constant, her happy ever after. But now, as she stared at the test resting on the side of the bath, she felt sick with fear. *A baby.* They were going to have a baby. Something she desperately wanted but never believed she could have. She was always forgetting to take her pill. Was it on purpose? A tiny spark of hope whispered that everything would be OK. She shook her head, dispersing the thought. Nothing good could come into her life without ending in tragedy. What if she had a little girl? What if she was subject to the pain and degradation she had been through? Back and forth, the argument raged inside her. She was doing Steve a favour. The sooner he found out what she was like the better it would be all around. But Steve was not one to give up, which was why she was making it really easy for him.

The acceptance email had pinged into her email inbox and the timing was impeccable. She had not been able to resist the site, having been given the invitation by an old friend. For an hour Abby had bent their ear with drunken ramblings about how her husband was too nice and everything was just too perfect in her world.

'Have a blowout,' her friend had said flippantly, looking glad to be rid of her as she rose to leave. 'Get drunk, have a shag and then get back to normal for everyone's sake. A night of single life will make you realise just how lucky you are.' It seemed like fate when she found the invite to *Debauchery* in her handbag later that night.

Her cheeks puffed as she exhaled a heavy breath. Being unfaithful and then an abortion? Was she strong enough to go through with it all? It made her heart ache to think of the growing baby inside her, already equipped with DNA – a little bit of her and Steve. She picked up the test and stared at the double blue line. Dropping it into the bin, she reminded herself to be strong. Soon she would return to her old life. The one that held no promises and even less hope. Returning her attention to her laptop, she typed an instant message confirming her illicit date. Matthew had come with positive feedback. An ordinary guy who would see to her every need. Paying on Steve's credit card made a nice touch. *What a bitch,* Abby thought. *Financial as well as emotional abuse.* She wiped her cheek as a tear made a path down her heavy foundation. She had paid extra for the brand because it hid the scar running down her cheek. But some wounds you could never heal. She had been stupid to lower her walls of defence, and had warned Steve she would hurt him in the end. And now she had, in the worst way possible. Her finger hovered over the green button. With one click she determined her fate. Her computer made a whooshing sound as she finally pressed send.

CHAPTER FORTY-SEVEN

'Laura. Good to hear from you. I've been thinking about what you said.'

'What's that?' Laura said, her heart picking up a beat in her chest. Matthew's voice crept across the phone line like a millipede, driving a chill up her spine. Since her meeting with the rest of the team at Sanity Line, she had begun to relax. But hearing him speak brought back all the old feelings of dread. Why did she agree to work late? Would he be standing in the shadows, waiting for her to finish her shift? Steadying her breath, she tried to focus on the call, but helping such a disturbed mind seemed too big a task.

Matthew seemed brighter today, bordering on cheerful. 'You told me to examine my hatred towards people who cheat. I've been thinking about it a lot. You're a bright girl, Laura. Probably brighter than people give you credit for.'

'So what did you come up with?' Laura said, trying to keep the onus off her. She bit into the fullness of her lip, her heart racing in her chest. Across the way, Joseph rose to put the kettle on. Giving him the thumbs up, Laura responded to his gesture to ask if she wanted tea. She placed her hand over the receiver, taking a deep breath as she willed herself to calm down.

For now, Matthew was reposeful and in the background the low drawl of country music played. Laura pressed her phone tightly to her ear to try to decipher his location. Was it a radio? Television? Or was he in a bar? She jumped as Matthew's voice boomed down the line.

'I've been thinking about my past. Perhaps I have my father to thank.'

'Would you like to talk about that?' Laura said, grabbing a pen to take forbidden notes. If she could not trace his location, perhaps his background would provide a clue. A surge of excitement bubbled up inside her. Yes, this was dangerous but it was exciting too. She imagined her uncle's face as she provided him with answers. She could do this. She had to.

'My mother did her best,' Matthew said. 'She was away a lot for work while Dad stayed at home to look after me. Sometimes she'd be gone overnight, sometimes the whole weekend. My parents were wealthy. I didn't go without, but my father couldn't stay faithful for very long.'

'And you were witness to this?' Laura said, quickly glancing around before scribbling on her pad. Joseph smiled as he placed a cup of tea on her desk, the persistent ring of his telephone calling him away before he could glance at her notes.

'I saw everything from a very early age. They weren't business colleagues he brought home either, they were hookers, flea-bitten slags. He did things to those women that you wouldn't believe.' Matthew exhaled a bitter laugh. 'But don't worry, I won't taint your innocent ears.'

Was he telling the truth, Laura wondered, or fabricating an explanation in the hope she would see him in a better light? She tried to listen for clues in the background, but the music had died, and all she could hear was Matthew's breathing as he paused for thought.

'I used to watch them you know,' he said. 'Sometimes he would have two or three at a time. He called it letting off steam. He didn't care if I saw them. He was off his face on coke by then.'

'I'm sorry to hear that,' Laura said, scribbling his words down.

Matthew continued to speak, without acknowledging her response. He took a breath, exhaling it slowly, as if the act required more effort than he was able to give. 'As I got older the visits continued. Then I began to wonder if my mother knew – if her time away was to give him the outlet he needed because she would not give in to his demands.'

'That's a lot of big thoughts for such a young person,' Laura said, as Matthew fell quiet. 'Did you have any family members you could confide in?'

Matthew sighed. 'I was too ashamed. As I grew older, their visits became oddly fascinating, and sometimes…'

'Go on,' Laura encouraged.

'Sometimes they tried to get me to join in. I can still hear the sound of my father's laughter as they yanked down my trousers, my cheeks burning with humiliation. They revolted me, all of them. I didn't know where to turn.'

'When did it stop?' Laura said, resisting the urge to question his identity.

'When my parents divorced I thought things would get easier, but I still carried a lot of anger inside. Mum got me a therapist, and for a while it helped, but I can't seem to move on from the past.'

'Have you tried speaking to your dad?' Laura said, thoughts of Mason Gatley firmly in her mind.

'He's not around anymore. My biggest regret is not confronting him at the time.'

'That must have been awful for you, growing up like that,' Laura said. But in truth, she had little sympathy for the man on the other end of the line. Uncle Owen was depending on her. Nobody was safe until the killer was caught. She gripped her pen, trying to gather the courage to ask if Mason Gatley was his dad.

'When someone's unfaithful, nobody asks the rest of the family how they feel,' Matthew said. 'But I care. And I'm going to make it stop.'

Laura nibbled on the tip of her pen, wondering for the hundredth time if he was being honest. At points during his conversation, he seemed sincere, heartfelt. But other times, as his voice waned, she wondered if he had veered from the truth. 'Did you tell your mum how you felt?'

'She'd been hurt enough. We both were. Besides, Mum couldn't bear to look at me because I reminded her of him.'

A door opened and closed in the background as Laura heard Matthew move from one room to another. He cleared his throat, his words still trailing down the phone. 'Then I found myself in a place with like-minded people. For the first time in my life, it was like I belonged. I met a man like me, who understood how I felt. We made plans. I knew what I had to do.'

'Who was it? A relation? A friend? Someone who lived nearby?' Laura said, cursing her inability to ask a direct question. But even across the phone line, his presence intimidated her. Her uncle's words played on her mind. Had Matthew really killed those women? Throttled them until the air left their lungs? Laura's fingers found the base of her throat as his response was returned.

'He was my *only* friend, well, apart from you,' Matthew chuckled. 'He's Mason Gatley. I thought you would have guessed that by now.' His voice slowed to a crawl. 'Don't you know who I am?'

'You're Matthew,' Laura said, clutching the phone so tightly her fingers began to ache.

'That's not my real name,' he said. 'But you know that already, don't you? So why don't you just come out and ask me who I am?'

CHAPTER FORTY-EIGHT

'Mr Forbes, I'm afraid I can't spare you a lot of my time,' Ruby said, feeling harried as she brushed a strand of hair from her face. 'I'm sorry to hear about your wife's disappearance, but DC Ludgrove will be dealing with this.'

'I know, which is why I've insisted on talking to you. And please, call me Steve.'

Steve Forbes was nothing but insistent, having come to the front counter of Shoreditch police station, demanding to speak to her alone. But she could hardly afford the time.

'Come in here,' Ruby said, leading him to an empty interview room. She stood with the door open slightly, distracted by the cacophony of voices on the other side. The police station was a hive of activity today, which only served to increase the pressure even more. At the other side of the door, a wailing toddler's cries pierced the air, while his mother complained loudly of her husband's arrest. The place stank of stale alcohol, which was carried on the breath of a small group of homeless people waiting to be seen. Pressing her back against the door, Ruby pushed until it clicked shut, and turned to the man with an enquiring glance.

'What can I do for you?' she said, knowing it was quicker to get this enquiry out of the way than to argue as to why he had kicked up such a fuss. As much as she would have liked to discuss his wife's disappearance, she had a hundred other things demanding her attention. The police sketch artist for Thomas Crawley for one.

Steve half sat on the interview room table, declining Ruby's offer to take a seat. Unlike the queue of people waiting at the front counter, he was dressed in a suit and tie. Carrying an air of self-assurance, he looked Ruby squarely in the eye. 'If you're investigating Abby's disappearance it means there's something seriously wrong. I want you to tell me what that is.'

'With all respect,' Ruby said, mildly annoyed at being pulled out of her enquiries, 'we have our reasons for being involved and that's not something I can share at this time.'

'You can tell me,' Steve said. 'I'm an ex-copper myself, served five years on the force before being kicked out. I know they don't like calling it "the force" these days, but it felt very much like it when I got the elbow.'

Ruby tilted her face to one side as she examined his features. The strong jawline, his tightly clipped brown hair. 'I thought I recognised you. Have we worked together?'

'Only briefly,' Steve replied, with a half shouldered shrug. 'I didn't expect you to remember me. But I know something's going on here and I'm not leaving until I know what it is.'

Ruby did not appreciate the hint of arrogance in his tone. Ex-police officers were a pain in the neck when it came to being victims of crime. 'Given your experience you'll be well aware of the reasons why I can't give you full disclosure. Is that what got you kicked out in the end? Information sharing?' Her eyes raked over his form for clues. Steve was groomed, wearing expensive cologne and a designer watch. For someone who had been sacked, he appeared to be managing well.

'It was an inappropriate relationship, actually,' he said, maintaining eye contact. 'My wife was a victim of historic sexual abuse. I was the officer in charge of her case. The job took a dim view of me seeing her in work time. I was given an ultimatum and I chose her. It was the biggest favour anyone could have done me.'

It was a situation Ruby could empathise with, being constantly faced with a similar choice herself. The difference with Ruby was that Nathan was not a vulnerable victim and her superiors weren't involved. 'A favour? How do you work that out?' Ruby asked, temporarily forgetting the urgency of her case.

'Because the job made me choose, and I chose Abby. We married six months ago. I won't say it's been easy, but up until now, life has generally served me well.'

'So what do you do now? As an occupation, I mean,' Ruby said, her thoughts on the killer's previous victims who had all been financially secure. How would an ex-police officer gain wealth in such a short space of time?

A hint of a smile touched Steve's lips. It was as if he were waiting to be asked the question all along. 'I invented an app; it's something I was working on while I was still in the police. Getting the sack made me make some big life changes. Investing in my product and getting it to market was one.' Steve seemed to absorb Ruby's curious glance as he explained the invention that had brought him so much wealth. 'It's a personal security app. You can use it on any smartphone to track your loved ones. The user can call the police by voice command, even use code words if they need to. Helps people sleep a little more soundly when their children or loved ones are out alone.'

'Sounds a bit stalker-ish to me, what's it called?' Ruby asked.

'*Companion Keeper*,' Steve replied, a touch of smugness in his smile.

Ruby raised her eyebrows. Not only had she heard of the app but it was one that the force recommended to victims of crime. No wonder he was looking happy with himself. She knew the creator had made a fortune when it first hit the market and it came as standard on some brands of phone.

'I take it your wife isn't using it?' Ruby said, genuinely perplexed. How strange that given the nature of his invention, his wife had disappeared.

'That's what makes this so odd,' Steve said, his smile fading. 'Abby always uses it because she knows how worried I get. She'd have had to go to a lot of trouble to disable it from her phone.'

'And you watch her night and day?' Ruby asked, small alarm bells ringing in her head.

Steve folded his arms. 'The app just runs in the background. I'm not constantly checking her whereabouts, but it does reassure me to know that she's safe.'

'And does she do the same with you?' Ruby said. 'Check your whereabouts on her phone?'

'I work from home and I don't socialise without her.' Steve's face creased in a frown, his voice becoming terse. 'This isn't a domestic abuse case. I've come here looking for help.'

Ruby drew back on her line of questioning, reminding herself of his concerns. 'I'm just trying to get a clearer picture of your relationship. If you're saying that this is uncharacteristic then it's something we need to take into account. Did you have any arguments before she went missing?'

'I know exactly why she left,' Steve said. 'But it's more to do with her past than with me.'

The vibration of Ruby's phone told her she was in demand. She should leave this to Luddy to investigate but she had a feeling that the conversation may be of value. She could not walk out now.

Steve crossed his ankles as he leaned against the table. 'Abby's had a horrific childhood, but she didn't report it until two years ago. She warned me that she'd end up hurting me when we first got together. It's a safeguard mechanism: do the worst before the worst happens to you.'

'And you think her disappearance is related to how she's feeling?' Ruby said, the backs of her legs growing tired from standing up.

'It could be,' Steve replied, twiddling his wedding ring on the finger of his left hand. 'Abby was unfaithful on the night before our wedding. The next morning she told me what she'd done.'

'That can't have been easy to hear,' Ruby said.

'It was hard, but I forgave her. I know she got no enjoyment from it. Sex is just a tool she uses to push me away. God!' he said, driving his fingers through his hair. 'I don't know why I'm telling you all this. I only came in to report she'd not come home.'

'It might help,' Ruby said, her weariness forcing her to lean against the door.

Steve nodded, encouraged. 'After the wedding, she was really happy. Then a fortnight ago we had a good result with the court case against her parents. She was turning her life around. But now this.' His words grew thick with emotion. 'It's starting all over again. She's arranged to meet some guy called Matthew on a dating site.'

'Matthew?' Ruby said, a chill snaking down her spine. Up until now, it had seemed like this was just another regular missing person case. 'How do you know?'

'I found messages on her laptop. The thing is, she left them open for me to read.' He risked a glance at Ruby. 'I bet you think I'm a right doormat. But at the end of the day it's just sex. That's not important to me. Compared to Abby, it holds barely any meaning at all.'

Ruby nodded in understanding. Her phone vibrated in her pocket but she could not draw away from the story unfolding before her. 'What else do you know about who she's gone to meet?'

'Not much,' Steve said. 'I only saw screenshots of their emails. Now I'm pretty clued up when it comes to computers and from what I could see, they were like Snapchat: messages that were set to self-destruct. She would have had only seconds to take a screenshot before they disappeared. And before you ask, there's no meeting place or times, just the name Matthew and what seems like a dating site. The infidelity I can deal with, it's the rest of it…' His voice broke away and he cleared his throat.

'What else?' Ruby said. She was all too aware of the dangers that Abby could be finding herself in but Steve's knowledge was something new.

'It was in the bathroom: the real reason why she's doing this. She'd tried to hide it, but I know my wife and I went looking. I wasn't prepared for what I found.'

'Which was?' Ruby said, ignoring the tannoy in the hall persistently calling her name.

Steve looked at her imploringly. 'She's pregnant. Abby's pregnant. You've got to find her before she does something stupid. I need to tell her that everything's OK.'

CHAPTER FORTY-NINE

Ruby sat in the briefing room, feeling like she had been punched in the gut. She stood with her team in the airless space that was only ever too hot or too cold. Each evidence board bore the status of the investigation to date: CCTV stills pinned next to crime scene locations along with the details of suspects whose alibis had been checked. On another board, disturbing images of their victims as, trapped and tortured, they waited for help that would never come. Ruby's breath caught in her chest. She could not bear for another picture to be added to this line-up. None of Mason Gatley's victims were pregnant. Just how would Abby's pregnancy affect this case? She relayed Steve's visit to the rest of the team. The thought of not just one victim losing their lives but two was too devastating to contemplate. Their relationship was a strange one. Steve had taken ownership of a traumatised and vulnerable young woman, while being in a position of trust. 'Can we delve into Steve's history while we're at it?' Ruby said, adding to their long list of tasks. For the team, it was easy to see why he faced dismissal for what he did.

The fact that Abby had been unfaithful once before danced in Ruby's thoughts. Had Steve really gotten over her infidelity as he had said? To watch your partner so closely… to constantly monitor their day. Like all abusers, he believed his actions were normal yet he was fully aware of how it looked to the police. Such behaviour was commonplace in domestic abuse cases that she had dealt with in the past. Ruby needed to find Abby, not just to keep her safe, but to ask why she had run away. It was odd to think of someone being unfaithful and then returning to their fiancé the day before their wedding and confessing all. Was Steve's hold over her so tight that she was unable to escape? And now, a pregnancy. The fact that Steve was an ex-police officer could have made her feel there was nowhere to turn.

It seemed Ruby was not the only person with such thoughts, as DC Eve Tanner tentatively raised her hand. She dropped it as Ruby acknowledged her, resting it back on her bump. Eve's pregnancy was progressing to mid-term and the latest development would hit her hard.

'You mentioned screenshots of Abby's conversation, yet any useful details have been cut out,' Eve said.

'Go on,' Ruby encouraged.

'Steve said his wife wants him to know what she's done. It seems strange that she screenshot the conversation but kept the details private of where she's hooking up.'

'Maybe she didn't want to be interrupted,' Luddy said.

'Maybe…' Eve replied. 'Or maybe all of this is a ploy to make us think she went on a date. What if they're role playing and Steve is the one who turns up? You said it yourself that she's been unfaithful before. Maybe he's killed our victims then decided to get to the root of the problem. What if all of this has been about getting revenge all along?'

Ruby's head swam with conflicting thoughts. As soon as Steve was told serious crime were involved, he kicked up a stink to speak to her alone. Why would he do that unless he was genuinely worried about his wife? He was not hiding the intricacies of their relationship. Unless it was one big bluff.

'From ex-copper to serial killer… I'm not sure about that,' Downes said. 'I suppose it would explain why he's given us the slip so far. But the good news is we have DNA. Crime Scene Investigators have picked up saliva on Thomas Crawley's face.

We believe the killer's been using wet wipes to clean his other victims as traces of chemicals were found on Cheryl and Melissa's skin. Looks like he didn't have time with Thomas, although he's kept his wedding ring.'

'If Steve's a suspect then his DNA would be on our database from when he joined the police, wouldn't it?' Luddy said.

'I'm afraid not,' Downes replied. 'As per policy, it's been destroyed.'

'What about the sketch artist?' Ruby said, clinging on to a vestige of hope. 'He must have produced something by now.'

Downes shook his head. 'It's not good news. Thomas Crawley's suffered from a stroke and is in intensive care. He won't be talking to anyone for some time.'

Ruby pursed her lips, trying to contain the swear words building up in her throat. Why didn't she take a more detailed description when they'd had the chance? She thought back to his pallid complexion, the pain crossing his face. Had their visit contributed to the stress that caused his illness?

She arched her back as it delivered a dull throb of pain. There were so many people involved. Soon she would need a spreadsheet to keep check of them all. Yet, at the beating heart of this investigation was a pregnant woman who had already been through so much. To have her life end like this just when she was beginning to claw it back was more than Ruby could bear.

As if reading her mind, Downes spoke. 'Right, I know there's a lot to get through but here's an overview of where we are so far. Melissa Sherman, Cheryl Barber and Thomas Crawley are linked socially through parties they've attended and the invites for *Debauchery*, an online dating site. It's vague as to how they've received the invites, but there's an online code which brings them directly to Matthew Johnson's profile page.' Downes pointed to the board, his fingers hovering over the crime scene picture of Matthew's bloated body.

'DC Moss has been working with the tech unit and Matthew's page has now been closed down.'

'How have you got on with your background enquiries on these social events?' He looked pointedly at Luddy, having heard of his recent visit to Hannah Phillips, Cheryl's friend.

Luddy gazed up from his notes. 'We've spoken to a good seventy per cent of people that move in the same circles. Nobody's saying anything and CCTV of the golf club has produced nothing so far.'

'Keep looking,' Downes replied. 'See what links Abby to our previous victims. Someone knows more than they're letting on.'

Ruby glanced around the room. Double shifts and cancelled rest days was taking its toll on her team. She knew that somewhere in the hundreds of items seized, statements taken and CCTV to be viewed, therein their answers lay. But time was their biggest enemy and she had to go straight to the source. Like an arrow, her thoughts focused on the person with the motive and capabilities to carry out such vicious acts.

'Right, what about our persons of interest?' he said, pointing to a picture of Mason's son, James. We know that Mason is homophobic. James has issues. How did you get on with the CCTV of him coming to and from work?'

'I've requested it but I've not had the chance to follow it up,' Luddy said.

'Richard can you deal with that?' Downes said. 'Luddy's got enough on his plate for now.'

Ruby nodded in agreement. James had refused to provide a voluntary interview. They had only held off arresting him so they could keep an eye on his movements. 'Do it today,' she said. 'Find out when he's last visited his father. Look at his friends and family members to make sure he wasn't communicating through them.'

'We've gone as far back as the last year,' Luddy said. 'No visits either in prison or where he is now.'

Downes turned his attention onto DC Ludgrove. 'Maybe not as himself, but it's possible he's posing as someone else. Our killer's a chameleon – no stranger to taking other people's identities. James is currently a person of interest, but if you can find a shred of evidence to raise it to suspicion, then he's coming in.'

CHAPTER FIFTY

The Night Before

From the first minute he met Abby, Matthew knew she was different. The bubbly and giggly Melissa had done this sort of thing before, while Cheryl was nervous and easy to dominate. As for Thomas… he was just an idiot with luck on his side. But Abby – she carried an air of mild aggression that set him on edge. His efforts in persuading her to dabble in drugs had been fruitless. Her long black hair had shone beneath the flashing lights of the nightclub, her body pulsating to the music until her skin glistened with sweat.

Matthew had not been able to resist the club after reading its description online. Cargo promised 'the ultimate in late-night debauchery with DJs and dancing to boot'. But dancing was not the only thing on Abby's mind. After finding a dark corner, she had pressed herself onto him with a sense of frenzy, before demanding he take her to the hotel. After pushing through the sweaty bodies, they made their way outside.

But when they walked beneath Kingsland Viaduct to catch a cab on Shoreditch High Street, a cold, ominous feeling made itself known. *What if he got caught?* He would rather die than face imprisonment. Sweat beaded his brow while he stood on the pavement; fear twisting his gut as heavy-footed pedestrians pushed past. How had he expected to get away with it? It was central London for God's sake. There was CCTV everywhere. A red double decker bus rumbled by, making him blink as a gush of warm night air blasted against his face. His near miss with Thomas had unnerved him. *Should he cut his losses and choose again or carry on?*

The question seemed to answer itself as Abby's fingers laced through his. Pulling him towards the taxi, she flashed him a cautious smile, instructing him to get inside. The sight of two armed policemen in the distance made his heart skitter in his chest. Jumping in beside her, he told himself not to be stupid. The streets had been heavily policed since the terrorist attack. After blurting out the hotel address, he sat forward on the back seat, a trickle of sweat rolling down his back.

Abby's silence in the cab was in stark contrast to her behaviour just minutes before. He observed her twirling her wedding ring, her hands jittery as if moving without thought or instruction. The silence was maintained until they got to the hotel. Matthew's thoughts were one step ahead. By checking in that afternoon, he had hidden his rucksack to save any awkward questions later. He congratulated himself on his foresight. She was obviously the sort of person who would notice these things. The thought gripped his intestines as they strolled down the hotel corridor to their room. Could she be a police officer? Yet she was wearing so little, dressed in a pair of sequin hot pants and a sleeveless black vest. Her jewellery dictated wealth, but these things could be easily replicated.

Once inside, Abby slammed the door behind them and hungrily pressed her body against his. He stiffened as the force of her passion banged the back of his head against the door. Briefly he accepted her kiss before drawing away, a frown crossing his face.

'What's wrong?' she said.

Matthew swiped the remnants of her lip gloss from his mouth. 'Are you a cop? It's just that the site is run underground and we don't need any involvement from—'

Abby threw back her head and laughed. It was a loud shrill noise, followed by a snort as tears welled up in her eyes. If she was acting, she played her part well. 'Police?' She tittered, bringing her fingers to her eyes and wiping the wetness away. 'You're joking, aren't you?'

'A journalist then,' he said, hating the doubt in his voice. How dare she laugh at him? She was the one in the wrong and he despised the way she made him feel. He thought of a time in his life when such laughter was commonplace. But it was not a merry laugh. It was a sly and shallow amusement gained from his humiliation. His anger burned. He would make her pay for this.

'Why on earth would I be either? What would they want to do with the dating site?' Abby asked. She had already told him she did not read newspapers or watch current events on TV. If there were something to be concerned about, she would be the last person to know. 'Besides, I was invited.' She paused to take in his expression. 'Why are you so mad? Have you done something wrong?' She curled her arm around his waist. 'I do like a bad boy,' she whispered in his ear, before driving her tongue inside.

Matthew gasped. He had never felt so disarmed by one person. He needed to get on with things. Make things right. Clasping her left ring finger, he put it in his mouth and sucked hard. Now it was her turn to look surprised. He pushed her back on the bed. 'Just checking,' he said, as he clambered on top of her. 'I like to know who I'm fucking.'

'Just a piece of married totty,' she said, the laughter evaporating from her voice as she tugged at his belt buckle. 'Now are you going to get on with it or what?'

Matthew reached into his pocket. 'We've got all night. How about a bit of pre-sex coke?'

'I told you a million times, I don't do drugs,' Abby said. 'Are you on commission or something? Because if you don't get your kit off, I'll be giving you a one star review.'

Sex with Abby was the last thing Matthew wanted. Forced into a corner, he tried to work out his next move. He was not ready for this; he was never ready for this. He had come here intent on making her pay.

'How about we play a game?' he said, as Abby fiddled with the catch of his trousers. He could tie her up with her permission, then gag her when he had control.

'How about you screw me like you've been paid to do,' Abby sneered, her hands clasping his buttocks. 'Because I'm not into playing games.'

There it was again, that underlying current of anger. Just what was she up to? His outrage grew as she squirmed beneath his weight.

'You stupid slut,' he spat, stilling her movements. 'Do you really think I'd lower myself to sleep with you?'

'But we came here for sex,' Abby replied, her eyes wide with astonishment. 'The site—'

'Was just a tool to bring you here. I was hoping we could do this the easy way. But now I've got to shut you up.' The words were delivered in a growl. He drew back his clenched fist. His blood felt on fire as it raced through his veins.

'No!' Abby screamed. 'Please—' but her words were cut short as Matthew's punches rained down.

CHAPTER FIFTY-ONE

A low, guttural sound rose from Abby's throat as a wave of pain hit her with force. Every muscle in her body seemed to cry out in pain. She took a deep breath through her nostrils, the sticky sickly smell making her gag. It was tangy, almost like rust, and was followed by a sharp searing pain in her hand which was bound tightly behind her back. Last night had gone wrong – horribly wrong and she realised with horror that she was trussed from her neck to her ankles. Each jerk of her wrists pulled her limbs backwards, each movement of the rope tearing into the flesh around her throat. Biting down on the rag, she caught her tongue between her teeth, swallowing the trickle of warm blood that followed. But the pain of a split tongue was nothing compared to the white-hot agony searing from her left hand. Blinking, she struggled to cope with the invasion of senses. Her breath froze as she caught sight of Matthew watching her intently from his wingback chair. Leaning against the wall, a piece of white card caught her attention. Splashed across it in deep red was one word: 'SINNER'. Abby gulped back her tears. She wanted to cry, but shock had pervaded her system. It was all too surreal.

'I had to use red marker this time,' Matthew said, following her gaze. 'There were too many letters to write it in blood.' A freakish smile froze on his face, his eyes barely blinking as they drank in her form. He seemed to be taking great pleasure from her distress, absorbing her muffled cries with obvious delight. 'Are you sure you wouldn't like to take the drugs now?'

Blocking out the pain, Abby withdrew into herself just as she had done so many times before. The beatings in her childhood never made much sense. Equally, there was little point in trying to understand the motives of the man before her. She knew when she met her husband that her life would end badly because happy endings didn't exist for girls like her. She remembered her father's cruel words as he tore into her room, the stink of beer on his breath. *You can scrub your skin clean but you never remove the dirt from deep inside.* Because that's what she was: dirty. Something to be used and disposed of afterwards. People like her didn't lead normal lives, much less die a peaceful death. Abby closed her eyes, relinquishing herself to the situation. Then she remembered what brought her here in the first place. Her baby. The tiny heart beating inside her seemed to strengthen her own. A flame lit from within. She had more than just herself to think about and this baby had come from love. Just what had gotten into her when she booked a termination? Was this her punishment? Forcing her breathing to calm, Abby focused on the man before her. He was representative of everyone in her life that had hurt her. Her drunken parents, the teachers who did not listen and the care workers who abused her when she was finally taken in. She would not go quietly. She had someone to fight for. A tiny little person who was better than her.

Matthew surveyed her curiously, his head tilted to one side. It was as if he could see the internal struggle taking place and he regarded her with caution as he approached. 'You look so lovely lying there, how about I take your picture?' he said, his phone in his hand.

But Abby's thoughts were ticking over, trying to make sense of it all. She thought of the night before, and how he had refused to have sex. How he had drawn back his fist and punched her to the side of the head. Her gaze return to the piece of board where he had written the word 'Sinner' and she recalled the dating website, the ones set up for married people to use. She made a quick assumption of his motives. She needed to play against the persona he had created for her in his head.

He raised his phone to use its camera, disappointment etched on his face when she refused to scream or cry.

Abby forced her face in a neutral expression and stared blankly ahead.

'Don't you realise what I'm going to do?' His breath was hot on her skin as he lowered his face to hers. 'I'm going to tighten the rope around your neck until you stop breathing.'

Still he waited, before taking the snap. 'Why aren't you afraid? What's wrong with you? Can you feel your finger? Because it's not there anymore.' His eyes darted left and right as he searched her face for a reaction. Such a thought was enough to invoke a scream of terror, but Abby simply froze.

She despised this man with all of her heart and she would not give in. Her throbbing hand, her aching muscles, and the terrifying threat that was being made; she pushed them all aside, focusing on the two words that could turn everything around. Calmly, Abby tried to speak, but the cloth in her mouth muffled her words.

'Be sensible,' Matthew said, tugging on the frayed material. 'If you scream I'll finish you here and now.'

'I'm pregnant,' Abby blurted, delivering her words with haste. 'Why would you?…' she gasped for breath. 'Why would you kill an innocent baby? None of this is their fault.'

There was a loud clunk as Matthew's phone fell to the floor. 'You're lying,' he said, stepping back as if she were diseased. 'You can't be.'

'Why do you think I wouldn't drink or take drugs? I got scared when I found out I was pregnant. I came out on a date for one last fling. I know it was wrong. I shouldn't have done it. But my baby doesn't deserve to pay the price.'

'No,' Matthew said. 'You can't be. I don't believe you.' With each sentence, he took a step backwards, his eyes wide with disbelief.

'Look in my bag,' Abby croaked, grateful that she had kept one of the many tests she had taken the day before. She thought about the one she had thrown in the bathroom bin. Had Steve found it? Guilt and shame surged through her. What had she been thinking of, coming here? She could not bear for him to go through the pain of losing both a wife and a baby should she die today.

His hands shaking, Matthew rifled through her bag, throwing make-up and tissues onto the floor. His fingers found a plastic holder the size of a pen in the crumpled cardboard box she had kept.

She had not thrown it out because a small part of her didn't want to lose this baby, even then. She was certain of it now. Right now, her baby was the most important thing in the world.

'No,' he shouted staring at the test. Ripping open the instructions, he glared at it before returning his attention to the blue cross in the middle.

'Please,' Abby said, fighting the biting pain. 'Don't hurt my baby.' She closed her eyes, whispering what she could remember of the Lord's Prayer. It was a cheap test, only cost a couple of pounds, but there was a small chance it may have just saved her life.

CHAPTER FIFTY-TWO

Taking a deep breath, Ruby drew in the late spring air. It was good to see daylight. So much of her time was spent in her office with her window opened a crack as the sounds of traffic and pedestrians rose up from below. Standing in the station car park, she blinked against the sun, taking in a few more seconds of daylight before returning inside.

As her eyes adjusted to the gloomy corridor, she barely noticed the desk assistant coming towards her at full pelt. Pink faced and smiling, the woman stood with her hands on her hips, catching her breath. She reminded Ruby of a sprite, with her sky blue eyes and cropped blonde hair. But it was at odds with the accent that grated on her tongue.

''Ere, Sergeant Preston, I put a shout out over the tannoy but the blooming thing's on the blink.'

'Everything all right?' Ruby said, giving the woman a comical look. She was new to the post and tended to get herself into a flap.

'There was a witness. He came in asking to speak to the person in charge of the case. I said, "which case" and he said he had information about someone going around lobbing off women's ring fingers. Straight away I thought of you and told him to wait.' She paused for breath, her East London accent adding colour to her words. 'Anyways, when I turned round to call someone, he'd only gone and left. He's not gone far if you want to catch 'im.'

'I think that's unlikely,' Ruby said. 'By the time I check the CCTV, he'll be long gone.'

'Just go out the front and turn left. Oh!' She touched her forehead, 'I didn't tell ya, did I? He's a priest. Not that old either, about early thirties, dark hair, a bit tall and gangly.'

'C'mon then,' Ruby said as she followed her down the corridor. 'Lead the way.'

Just a minute later, Ruby had found him. In his black trousers and shirt, his priest's garb stood out from the crowd. He glanced at her curiously as she followed him down the street.

'Sorry, Father, can I trouble you for a minute?' she said, falling into step beside him.

'What can I do for you?' he said, looking her up and down.

A spot of rain touched Ruby's face, and she pulled her blazer around her. The weather was changeable, as if it could not decide if it were winter or spring. 'My name is DS Ruby Preston. I'm the officer in charge of the case you were asking about.' She paused, reading the confusion on his face. 'You came into the station. I saw you on CCTV.' It was a lie. She'd not yet had time to view it, but she did not want to give him the excuse to back out a second time.

'Father McElroy,' he said, extending a hand as he introduced himself. 'You can call me Isaac. But I'm sorry, I've changed my mind. I can't help you after all.'

'Please, Father,' Ruby said, still gripping his hand. 'Come back to the station with me. You came in for a reason.' She released his fingers as she realised she was holding on a little too tight.

'I'm sorry,' he said, 'I want to help you, but I can't risk my vocation. If I tell you what I know then I'll be thrown out of the church.'

'This isn't the right place to talk about it,' Ruby said, as shoppers dodged them on the busy streets. 'Please, give me five minutes of your time, if only to explain.'

Following her back, he was led into a witness interview room as he explained the reason behind his earlier visit. The room comprised a desk, computer, two chairs, and some posters about neighbourhood watch on the walls. Windowless and compact, it was a temporary but private space.

'I shouldn't have come.' Isaac shook his head. 'Even if I could tell you, I can't break the Sacramental Seal.'

'Let's start again,' Ruby replied, taking a seat at the interview table and gesturing at Isaac to do the same. 'How do you know so much about the case?'

Resigning himself, the priest pulled out a chair and sat. 'I provided confessions to one of my flock. But what he told me… it shook me to the core.'

'So you came here to help us?' Ruby leaned forward across the table, her eyes on Isaac's. 'The desk assistant said you had knowledge of amputations. What else do you know?'

'The man I spoke to seems like a disturbed soul,' Isaac said, sadly. 'Sometimes I sit at the back of the church and meditate. It can be enlightening, picking up on people's prayers. This man had been in several times and he seemed very torn. So, one day, I slid into the pew beside him and offered guidance. I gathered he must be in trouble of some kind. I'm quite new to the priesthood as you might have guessed,' he smiled, 'but I like to think that people can relate to me.'

'What did he say?' Ruby said, picturing the scene.

'Nothing, at first. I offered to take his confession, which he accepted. He unburdened his soul by confessing his sins in the Sacrament of Penance. But with such sacrament, a sacred trust is formed. No court in the land can force me to disclose what was said.'

'It must have been bad for you to come here and risk breaking the seal,' Ruby said, trying to work out a way in which she could prise the information from him. 'You do know we're dealing with a serial killer, don't you?'

The priest quietly responded with a knowing nod of the head. Silence fell between them as they contemplated the seriousness of their words.

'He's kidnapped another victim,' Ruby said. 'This doesn't just involve her, there's an unborn baby's life at risk too.'

Again, another nod of the head. Ruby drummed her fingers on the table before bringing her attention to the computer. She clicked on the mouse, her actions lighting the screen up before her. 'All we want to do is find them and keep them safe. You can tell me anonymously. I'll log it as intelligence. A description. An address. Please give me something. Help me save his next victim. Surely you have to think of her and her baby too?'

'I wanted to help you. It's why I came here earlier today.' Isaac's face creased as he relayed his frustration. 'But it's too big a risk. People rely on me. I have to think of the rest of my flock.'

'Wait,' Ruby said, logging onto the system and turning the screen around to face them both. She was taking a chance showing him this, and evidentially it would not stand up in court, but the only other option was allowing him to walk out the door. Swiftly she clicked through the images, watching his face for a glimmer of recognition. As she brought up James Gatley's image, Isaac's face froze.

'It's him, isn't it?' Ruby said, pointing to the image of Mason Gatley's son. The fact the colour had drained from the priest's face told her all she needed to know.

'I'm sorry, I've got to go. I hope you find him soon.'

'Him? Do you mean James?' Ruby said, touching his arm as he rose to leave. 'Please, Father. I'm not talking about the confessional, so you're not breaking the seal. Is this the man you sat beside in the church pew?'

With a faint nod of the head, Isaac turned and headed for the door.

CHAPTER FIFTY-THREE

'We're bringing James Gatley in,' DI Downes said, responding to Ruby's update on her meeting with the priest. 'What you've told me just confirms that we're right.' She was standing in Downes's office, her eyes roaming over the two bar heater plugged into the corner of the room.

'Where did you get that?' she said, an amused smile touching her lips. 'Don't tell me you're cold.'

'It's borrowed from lost property. Gets nippy in here after midnight,' Downes said, bringing his attention to the paperwork on his desk.

'Would you like me to bring in a pipe and slippers too?' Ruby teased. 'Or maybe you could go home of an evening and ask matron to keep you warm.'

Downes dropped the pen in his hand and exhaled a terse breath. 'Have you just come here to take the piss or was there something you wanted to ask me?'

'Sorry,' Ruby said, looking anything but. 'Has new evidence come to light?'

Downes nodded. 'That CCTV you asked for, it shows James leaving his kiosk and getting a tube a few hours before Thomas was found. Then it shows him returning to work around the time the police reached the hotel.'

'You think someone tipped him off?'

'Perhaps Mason had second thoughts after he gave you the hotel address. Who knows? He lied about speaking to his father too.'

'Oh,' Ruby said. 'I wasn't expecting that.'

'Well, it's all grounds to bring him in, see what he has to say.' He leaned back in his chair. His tie was loosened, his top shirt button undone. 'Well done. You've worked hard on this case. We may just have our man.'

'Team effort,' Ruby replied, before her attention was drawn to a knock on the door.

'Have you got a minute, sarge?' Luddy said, walking in.

Ruby's eyes fell to his empty hands. 'Sure. Fancy putting the kettle on first?' she asked, and was met with a smile.

Placing the chipped mug on her desk, Luddy cradled his own before taking a seat. Normally one to hover, he wore an expression of concern that told Ruby all was not well.

She rose to shut the door. As she took in Luddy's guarded expression, she had a sinking feeling that a private conversation was ahead. 'What's wrong? Have you had a development?'

Staring at the froth floating on top of his coffee, Luddy seemed barely able to meet Ruby's eye. 'I might be in a spot of trouble,' he said, his words barely audible.

'Spit it out then,' Ruby said. 'You're worrying me now.'

Luddy nodded, taking a sip from his coffee before placing his mug on the desk. 'It's my niece, Laura. She's a volunteer in a helpline called Sanity Line. It's a bit like the Samaritans except they work mainly with ex-offenders, but they're available for anyone that needs to talk. Lately she's had some worrying calls. I think it's our killer.'

Ruby raised an eyebrow, leaning forward in her chair. 'Really? What's he said?'

Luddy relayed the calls, as well as Laura's meeting with her supervisors and their warnings to keep things quiet. 'She wanted to tell me sooner, but she was pressured to keep it to herself. She just wants to do the right thing.'

Ruby nodded as he spoke, waiting until he was finished before she raised her concerns. 'There's one thing bothering me about all this. You said that Laura realised early on that she was talking to the killer. But how did she know Cheryl and Melissa's names? We've done really well to keep them out of the press.' It was true. Thanks to Phillip Sherman threatening to sue, the recent spate of reports focused mainly on Mason Gatley's historic murders, with sparse details about the present-day copycat.

Luddy lowered his head, avoiding her gaze. 'That's where me being in trouble comes in.'

Ruby frowned as she pre-empted his confession. It was unlike Luddy to cross the line. 'Please tell me you've not told her about the case. You know what Worrow's been like; she lost her nut when she thought the ins and outs of it was going to hit the press.'

A line deepened between Luddy's brows. 'We were all at a family do. I'd had a few drinks and let it slip that I was investigating the case. I mentioned the names Cheryl and Melissa and the fact the killer had used a dating site to lure them in.'

'Hells bells!' Ruby slammed her cup onto her desk before rising to her feet. 'You do know you could get the sack for this, right?'

'I'm sorry,' Luddy replied, heat staining his cheeks. 'It was stupid, I know. Laura wants to be a police officer one day. She asked me about work. I guess I was showing off that I was working on such a high-profile case.'

'Exactly, high profile,' Ruby said her voice rising an octave. 'The clue is in the name.' She slipped the blinds shut as heads began to spin in their direction. 'For fuck's sake, Luddy, if Worrow finds out she'll have your balls for breakfast. I'd expect that sort of crap from some of the others but not you. Right in the middle of your sergeant's exams too!'

'I've never spoken about work with anyone before, I swear. Laura's very discreet. I thought it wouldn't go any further.'

'Or you were drunk and shooting your mouth off,' Ruby fumed.

'I'm really sorry,' Luddy said, looking up at Ruby as he sat, glued to his chair. 'Is there any way I can keep my job by the end of the investigation?'

'What investigation?' Ruby said, slowly coming to ground.

'Well… I presume PSD will be getting involved.'

The mention of professional standards department made Ruby grimace. 'Why did you admit to this? You could have told me the caller filled Laura in on all the details. You didn't need to say she got this first-hand from you.'

'Because it's the right thing to do,' Luddy said.

Ruby shook her head. 'You've got a lot to learn if you think that putting your job on the line over a stupid indiscretion is the right thing to do. Did it make you feel good impressing your niece? Do you hold your head a little higher now she thinks you're the big man?'

Luddy drove his hand through his hair. 'No, of course not. I'd had too much to drink. I wasn't thinking…'

But Ruby was not ready to let him off the hook just yet. 'Do you know how many suspects I've heard use those very words? "I didn't mean to murder my wife; I had too much to drink when I drove into that child…"'

His face reddening, Luddy leapt to his feet. 'With all respect, I'm not the only one in this team who's made mistakes.'

Ruby's expression hardened. She knew he was referring to her relationship with Nathan. Along with Downes, he was one of the few people who knew. What else could it be? 'Don't you see?' she said. 'I'm not talking about me, or the police as a whole. I know I've messed up my chances of promotion, but you have what it takes to go far. Don't fuck it up now.'

'I'm sorry,' Luddy replied. 'I shouldn't have said what I did. I respect you as a sergeant…'

'There's no need to brown-nose me.' Ruby rested her hands on her hips.

'I wasn't. This is my fault and I'll hold up my hands to it. I'm ready to come clean when you want to make the call.'

'There won't be any investigation,' Ruby said, her voice dropping. 'Heaven help me, I need you on my team. But you need to come up with a different version of what happened, should we end up involving your niece.' She paused, giving it some thought. 'We'll say that you told me your niece is a call taker from Sanity Line who has asked you for advice.'

'But the murders?—'

Ruby finished Luddy's sentence. 'Were brought to light during the last call. Laura's come to you as her uncle, and you, without any comment about your current caseload, have taken this information and reported it to me. Isn't that right?'

'Yes,' Luddy said, staring at the floor.

'Make it more convincing next time,' Ruby replied. 'We'll need to take a statement. Arrange a visit. I need to speak to your niece in person, see if we can tease any more information out of this guy.'

'Will do.' Luddy turned to leave, the relief evident on his face.

'Detective Ludgrove?' Ruby said, pointedly using his official title.

Luddy turned to face her. 'Yes?'

'Don't ever let me down like that again.'

CHAPTER FIFTY-FOUR

Creeping in to the darkened room, Ruby found DI Downes hunched over the computer screen. It made for interesting viewing, as James, Mason Gatley's son, was interviewed on tape. He was dressed in a uniform of black trousers and logo-bearing white shirt and Ruby wondered if he had been arrested at work. To say the young man was angry would have been an understatement. But unlike previous suspects, he was not refusing to sit down or banging his fists on the table. His anger was simmering beneath the surface, ill-concealed by the expression on his face. Pressed together in a thin line, his lips were white and bloodless as he delivered a furious scowl.

Ruby would have loved to lead the interview, but she had to give her officers free rein. It was the role of the detective constable to interview their suspects, and on far too many occasions, she found herself butting in. They would never learn to progress in their career without taking the lead in a major investigation. Interviewing James would hone their skills.

DC Richard Moss was leading, with Eve by his side making notes.

'How's it going?' Ruby said, craning over DI Downes's shoulder as she watched.

'They've come to a stand-off,' Downes said. 'Want to listen?'

Ruby nodded. She did not need to be asked twice. Pressing on a spare set of headphones, she homed in on Richard's voice. *Good timing,* she thought, as she heard him say her name.

'You told Sergeant Preston that you hadn't spoken to your father in the last year. Is this true?' Richard fixed him with a stern stare.

'No comment,' James replied, exchanging a glance with the duty solicitor sitting next to him.

Ruby frowned. Apart from her, Mason Gatley did not have any visitors from the outside world. She pressed the headphones closer to her ears, not wanting to miss a word.

Richard came across as confident in interview and was dressed professionally in his suit and tie. But Ruby was not thrilled that DC Eve Tanner was present, in case it all kicked off. She had always been petite, but today she seemed all bump, her black shift dress doing little to hide her advancing pregnancy. Richard glanced at his paperwork before continuing in a strident tone. 'What about phone calls? Have you had any kind of communication with your father this year?'

James's forehead creased as he mulled over the question, his arms tightly crossed across his chest. 'No comment.'

Richard barely skipped a beat before continuing. 'Recently it was discovered that your father, Mason Gatley, had smuggled a mobile phone into his cell. We discovered several calls between the two of you over this last month.' Richard slid a piece of paper across the desk. 'I refer to Exhibit JH03, the call log taken from the seized mobile phone.'

Ruby sucked in a breath, relieved she had not given in to Mason's demands to speak to her in private. An unwelcome thought entered her head. He would blame her for this. She had failed to report Mason's phone to the authorities in case she needed to use it later on. Having refused to call him from home, Mason would think she tipped them off. Returning her focus to the interview, she watched closely as James's expression transformed from anger to fear.

'*He* called *me*,' James said. 'Check the log. No return calls were made.'

'So what did you talk about?' Richard said. 'His previous murders? Gave you inspiration, did he?'

Ruby winced. It was best not to lead their suspect. Let him speak for himself.

'No, of course not,' James replied. 'Sometimes he'd get bored. He'd ring me when he was stoned, just to tell me what a disappointment I was.'

'Why didn't you tell Sergeant Preston that?' Richard said, keeping the pressure on.

'I have advised my client to respond no comment,' the duty solicitor interrupted.

'It's OK,' James said, turning to face Richard. 'I didn't say anything because I was embarrassed. He's a monster, and communicating with him is not something I like to admit to. I told her that I visited him once. Those phone calls – they were just him degrading me. It's humiliating being treated that way.'

Stony-faced, Richard delivered his next question with force. 'I'll ask you one more time: where were you on the night Melissa Sherman was killed?'

'At home, alone, reading a book. I've already told you,' James said, his earlier confidence evaporating.

'Are you sure about that?' Richard glared at him. 'Because uniformed officers are searching your flat as we speak.'

'They're… they're in my home? Nobody asked me for permission.'

'We don't have to,' Eve interrupted. 'This is a multiple murder case. If you've any knowledge of these women's deaths or the dating site we spoke about, then you're best telling us now.'

James's Adam's apple bobbed as he swallowed hard. Exchanging a glance with his solicitor, he replied, 'No comment.'

'Do you know the whereabouts of Abby Forbes?' Richard asked, sliding another photo across.

'No comment,' James replied.

Ruby slid the headphones from her head, unknotting her hair as she did. 'Bloody hell, go Richard,' she said, her admiration for the newest member of staff growing rapidly.

'He's good. Calm under pressure,' Downes said. 'Hopefully he'll get him to crack. Where are you off to?'

She paused. The last thing she wanted was to get Luddy into trouble. The presence of her harness beneath her jacket must have given it away. 'We've had a call from a woman at Sanity Line. She's convinced she's spoken to our killer. We're taking a statement but I just want to have a quick word.'

'Aye, we're going to need more evidence if we're to charge. Right now, all we have is hearsay. Get what you can.'

'I'd also like to speak to Mason Gatley one more time. See what he has to say.'

'You might not need to if we can get James to confess. On the one hand, I'm thinking that if he is our man, then we're keeping Abby safe. But on the other—'

Ruby interrupted, finishing his sentence: 'On the other hand she could be bleeding out on a hotel bed, taking her last breath. Are you arranging surveillance if he's NFA'd? I can't see CPS giving you a charge on this.' The likelihood of no further action was a worrying reality, given the absence of a confession and forensic evidence so far.

'Let's see what you come back with. The team are working full steam ahead. We need results today.'

CHAPTER FIFTY-FIVE

'Hello, Laura, I presume Owen has told you why we want to speak to you today?' Ruby was sitting in Laura's dining room, using DC Ludgrove's first name in order to relax the nervous-looking young woman before her. The three-bedroom semi was like many on that estate: council owned but cared for, and a stone's throw away from shops and schools. Ruby did not like involving Luddy's niece, but given the seriousness of the crimes, she had little choice.

'Yes, he has,' Laura said, shifting nervously in the dining room chair. Dressed in a T-shirt, and leggings, she had time to spare before her next shift in Sanity Line. Her mother, Luddy's sister, had sensibly left them to it.

Ruby hoped she had enough time to clean up the mess that Luddy had found himself in. She was no stranger to bending the rules and had gone as far as discussing cases very briefly with Nathan, but she could handle her own indiscretions because they were for the good of the case. Bragging was not her scene, and she did not need her ego inflating. The victim's welfare was always at the heart of her actions. It was up to Ruby to keep her team in line. If they messed up then the fallout would rightly come upon her. She was always conscious that they worked as a team.

'Don't look so scared. You're not in any trouble.' Ruby watched Laura twiddle the ends of her long blonde ponytail.

'Oh, I know that,' Laura said, her dimples on display as she smiled. 'I just feel bad about discussing clients. My supervisor said that I'd lose my job. It's only voluntary, but I'm hoping to apply to the police, and a reference from Sanity Line would really help.'

'She doesn't need to know that you've spoken to us,' Ruby said. 'And at the end of the day, we're talking about murder. Anything we can do to speed up the investigation is surely worthwhile.' She rested her elbows on the table, gesticulating with her hands. 'Now it may be that this person is what we call a false lead – someone who wants to draw attention to themselves. Usually they have mental health issues. Sometimes they're just trolls. The problem is, with so many time-wasters, a genuine caller can be overlooked. That's why we have to examine each one on its own merit. Owen's filled me in on the nature of the call. Have you any idea of where your caller is based? And secondly, are you absolutely sure that you're talking to a man?'

'Yes, he's definitely a man,' Laura said, flicking her ponytail out behind her. 'I'm a hundred per cent sure of that. He's not said where he's from, but he always calls the local line instead of the national one.'

'What about background sounds?' Ruby said. 'Does he call from inside or outside? Shared accommodation? A house, workplace, or even a classroom? It's surprising what you can hear if you really tune into it.'

Laura looked upwards to the left, her fingers tapping the tablecloth as she searched her thoughts. From the kitchen, a kettle whistled and the clink of a cup against teaspoon ensued.

Her mother's head popped around the door. 'Can I make you a drink? Tea? Coffee?'

'No thanks,' Ruby said, answering for them all. James Mason's custody clock was ticking. They had up to twenty-four hours to hold him. After that, they could charge him, apply for an extension, or let him go. Ruby felt the pressure build. She prayed it would not be the latter.

Laura glanced at Ruby, her eyes alight. 'Come to think of it there *have* been sounds in the background. I've always imagined him calling from a house, maybe a flat. Sometimes I hear him make a cuppa in the background, just like Mum is now. At least, I can hear cups rattling and a kettle boiling so I always imagine him making a drink. Cupboard doors open and close. Sometimes I hear a television in the background. She paused as she searched her memory for answers. 'Let me think. Yes, now I remember. I don't think he lives alone. He says that sometimes it's hard to find peace and quiet to talk. He's definitely used us in the past. When he first rang he was very aware of the questions I had to ask, such as finding out if he's suicidal. It's something we have to work into each and every call.'

Ruby nodded in acknowledgement. 'Do you ask more than once? If the caller rang you again later that day would have to ask them again?'

'Yes, it's policy. Our training manual is very specific about it. We have to enquire about it every time. Sometimes when people suffer from depression it's the one question their families are afraid to ask. We bring it out into the open from the offset and it usually gives us a good indicator of where the call is going to progress. We also tell them that the call is confidential and that helps people relax. It's why I feel so bad now.' Laura frowned. 'I'm so out of my depth though. The last time we spoke, he challenged me to ask him who he really was. But when I opened my mouth to speak, the line went dead.'

'I see,' Ruby said. 'When it comes to identifying someone by voice alone, there are lots of factors to take on board. Does he sound old or young? What about a stutter or a speech impediment? Perhaps health issues such as a cough or breathing difficulties? Does he have an accent? Think about the quality of his voice when he's speaking. What clues does it give?'

Laura nodded in understanding. 'His health seems fine, although he has mood swings. One minute he seems OK, but say the wrong thing and he flies off the handle really quickly. Sometimes he hangs up with little warning. I think he likes to shock me. Talking about what he's done gives him some kind of release.'

Ruby leaned forward. 'Sorry to deviate from my questions, but when you say release, do you mean sexual release? Does he masturbate while you're on the phone?'

Laura glimpsed at her uncle, a pink bloom rising to her cheeks. 'No. It's happened with other callers but not him. If anything, I get the feeling that he's sexually frustrated. I think he's had problems in that department in the past. It could be down to what happened in his childhood.'

'He might be lying,' Ruby said. 'If you're hoping to be a copper you must never assume anything.'

'I know.' Laura broke into a grin. 'Uncle Owen said they teach you that in training school: Never assume – it makes an ass of you and me.'

Ruby returned her smile. It was obvious that Laura worshipped Luddy, and easy to see how he had played up to that role. 'So let's keep this on track. With regards to my questions about his voice and accent, are there any clues as to his age range or identity?'

Laura puffed out her cheeks as she exhaled a breath. 'Well I don't think he's old, and I wouldn't say he's a teenager either so maybe between twenty and forty years of age? I don't like to put a number to it because it can be hard to tell. He hasn't got a deep voice. It's kind of ordinary, but sometimes I pick up a little hint of a Scottish accent when he gets angry. His breathing's fine and he seems well. I've never heard anybody in the background, apart from the TV.'

'OK,' Ruby said, making a mental note to listen back to James's interview. Perhaps her superiors would allow her to play Laura a voice clip. *One thing at a time,* she told herself, focusing on the young woman before her. 'Would you say that given the nature of his calls he's spent time in prison? It's just that you mentioned his connection with Mason Gatley. He told you he's learned things from him. Is this right? Did he actually mention Mason by name? Or is this something you put together later on?'

Laura nodded profusely. 'Oh, he definitely mentioned Mason Gatley, because it gave me a fright. That's when I knew I had to ask Uncle Owen for advice. I remember writing it down, even though we're not meant to take notes. Then I got scared because Matthew started asking for me. The last thing I wanted to do was to talk to a serial killer. I already had my suspicions from what Owen told me about the case. He mentioned the names Cheryl and Melissa. When Matthew talked about punishing them I felt like I was on high alert.'

Ruby resisted giving Owen a stern look. She had made her point and would let things lie. For now, her thoughts were with finding their victim in time. 'I think it's best for now if we just focus on what your caller has said rather than what you've heard from outside sources. We all work in jobs in which confidentiality is key.' Ruby smiled. 'Do you understand what I'm saying?'

'So if anyone else asks I just mention the content of the calls?' Laura said.

'Yes. You're not lying or being dishonest, you're just focusing on what Matthew has said. I do think you should get your work reference sooner rather than later though, in case this all blows up. This might not be our man, but there's a chance that he's using you as a sounding board to relive what he's done.'

'What do I do if he calls again?' Laura said, nibbling her bottom lip.

'Don't allow him to draw you into any kind of conversation about your personal life. Don't sound judgemental, and if you must speak to him, try to keep him calm. I'm sure you know all this anyway, given your experience.'

'We offer a listening service,' Laura said. 'Although he does get angry when I use automated responses such as asking him how he's feeling about things. I'm not supposed to but sometimes I do draw him out just to find out a bit more.'

Ruby gave her a knowing look. She would have done the same in her shoes. 'As I said, be careful. This guy may be a time-waster or you could have a direct line to our killer.' She rubbed her chin. The last thing she wanted was to put Laura's life in danger. 'I'm going to speak to my superiors about this, make an official record. Is there any way you can get picked up at the end of your shift? How secure is the call centre?'

'Now they've closed off the drop-in centre, it's a lot more secure.'

'Good,' Ruby said, running through a tick list in her mind. 'I take it the door is locked while you're on your calls?'

'Oh yes. They've even installed a buzzer system with a camera and CCTV. It's just when I'm going home on my own that I feel nervous.'

'Her mum is going to pick her up from now on, and she's only working two shifts a week,' Luddy interjected. Up until now, he had chosen to stay quiet, allowing Ruby to take care of things.

Ruby nodded in response, returning her attention to Laura. 'If you do end up speaking to Matthew, act exactly as before. Your safety is our main priority and my advice has to be to decline the call. If this is the same person we're dealing with, he is unpredictable and dangerous. If you decide to go ahead then I'd be grateful if you could forward any notes you make to me.' She slipped a business card from her pocket and laid it on the desk. 'Anything urgent, take a snapshot with your phone and text me. If he threatens you then report it to your supervisors straight away.'

'I don't think he'll threaten me,' Laura said, taking the card. 'If anything, he's put me on a pedestal. He often says that I'm the only one who understands. It's a bit worrying but I think I'll be OK. It's only over the phone.'

'He doesn't know where you live, does he?' Ruby said.

'No. I gave him my first name because I always get mixed up when I give false ones. Laura is common enough though, isn't it?' Laura looked at Ruby for reassurance.

'As long as you've not discussed details of where you live or socialise,' Ruby replied. 'Is there anything else you can glean from your calls that we've not discussed so far?'

Laura returned to fiddling with her ponytail as she gave the question some thought. 'He might be religious, or was maybe brought up in that background. He's mentioned it before. Something about suicide. I can't remember exactly what he said. I got the feeling that it mattered to him though.'

'I take it he's not mentioned visiting church?' Ruby said, recalling her meeting with the priest. Would James be likely to return for another confessional?

'Sorry.' Laura shook her head. 'I can't remember any more than that.'

'That's OK,' Ruby said, 'You've been really helpful. More than you know.'

CHAPTER FIFTY-SIX

'Sanity Line, how can I help you?' Laura smiled as she answered the phone. Today had been a good day and she was enjoying her evening shift. She got things off her chest with Detective Preston and, as if fate had intervened, her application to join the police had progressed to the next stage. It felt great to be moving on to better things. Her dealings with Matthew had given her the dig in the ribs she needed. Life was short, and her conversation with Ruby had put things in perspective. But her smile faded as a man's voice responded on the other side of the line.

'It's me, Matthew,' he replied, the words crawling off his tongue. 'It's so good to hear your voice, Laura. I really need to talk.'

Laura's stomach lurched at the sound of his name. She swallowed back the bile rising in her throat and told herself to calm down. The killer had been arrested. Her uncle had told her. So how was he calling her? She reminded herself that she was safe, tucked away in a building covered by CCTV. She was anonymous. Wasn't she? The sound of her name rolling off his tongue made her shudder in her chair. Quickly, she reached for the plastic bottle of water on her desk. 'Hello, Matthew,' she said, tipping the liquid down her throat as she awaited his response. Her eyes scanned the desk for a paper and pen. No answer. She had to keep the chatter up. 'How are you?' she continued, but her voice sounded strangely high-pitched as she spoke. She reminded herself to act normally. She had made a promise to her uncle that she would try and glean any information that she could. She listened for background sounds but all she could hear was the sound of his feet shuffling back and forth.

'I'm bad, real bad,' Matthew said. 'I feel sick to the core.'

Laura put a hand over the telephone mouthpiece as her breath shuddered in response. Was he with the victim now? Calling from his hotel room? Was that where he had been calling from all along? Her heart pounded a warm beat behind her ribcage, and more than ever, she felt ill-equipped to deal with this call. But Matthew was too caught up in his own emotions to pick up on her anxiety. She took a calming breath then started again. 'Would you like to talk about it?'

But all she could hear were Matthew's muffled sobs.

'I thought I was doing the right thing, but now everything has changed and it makes me sick. I don't know what to do.'

'You can talk to me,' Laura said, resisting the urge to ask him who he was. She could not spook him. *Slowly, slowly catchy monkey,* she told herself, listening in for every sound.

'I met this girl, from the dating site. Her name is Abby. God, I shouldn't be telling you this…' Matthew's voice died off into a strangled whine.

'It's OK,' Laura said, soothingly. 'It's just you and me here.' She wanted to create a sense of intimacy between them, make him believe he could confide anything in her. Today he sounded needy, so different to his call before. 'I won't be shocked, whatever you say. What happened with Abby? Where did you meet?' She looked over her shoulder to check that nobody was listening to her call. They were short-staffed, as usual, with only Joseph manning the other lines. Sitting across from her with his head bowed, he seemed too wrapped up in his own caller to pay any attention to hers. It was just as well. Asking for an address was against protocols. She crossed her legs beneath her chair, feeling her muscles tense.

'We…' Matthew stuttered, 'we went clubbing in Shoreditch but we didn't stay long. She was desperate to get to our hotel room.

She wasn't drinking. She didn't want drugs. She just wanted sex. There was a real urgency to it, like it was something she had to get over with. I've never met anyone like her before.'

'And you didn't want sex?' Laura said, her heart beating so hard she could almost feel it through the thin layers of her blouse.

'No, I didn't. But when we got to the room, she pounced on me, pulling at my trousers to get them off. When I didn't respond, she turned nasty, saying I was at fault. The dirty slag. She was the one cheating on her partner, not me!'

'What happened?' Laura said, bracing herself for the answer.

Matthew's response was immediate, his voice gaining in strength as he relayed what he had done. 'I hit her, and kept hitting her until she passed out. Then I tied her up. I took some drugs. Took some photos. I didn't do anything she didn't deserve.'

Laura wondered if he had amputated Abby's finger but it was a question she couldn't bring herself to ask. Should she tell Matthew that what he did was wrong? Would her judgement make him hang up the phone? She remembered DS Preston's words. *No judgement.* 'What happened next?' she asked, choosing the safest response of all.

'I did what I had to do. The next part of the plan. Afterwards she came to. I took off her gag. She didn't scream. But she told me… she told me…' a muffled sob crossed the line. 'I didn't know. I didn't know.'

'What did she say?' Laura said, her arm rigid as she pressed the phone to her ear.

'She said she was pregnant. I was minutes away from killing an unborn child.' He gasped for one breath, then another.

'Slow your breathing,' Laura said. 'Tell me where she is. We can make all of this OK.'

'How can you?' Matthew said, panic driving another sudden inhalation of breath. 'She knows who I am. I'll go to prison. If Mason gets a hold of me, he'll kill me for what I've done.' He exhaled loudly down the line. 'It's bad enough I got involved with a man, but now a pregnant woman? I'm done for. There's no point in living any more.'

'No wait, we're friends, aren't we?' Laura said, her pulse racing. She could not let him go. Not now. 'You've confided so much in me, please don't go, let me help you. Tell me where she is.'

'It's too late for that now,' Matthew said. 'I have to finish what I started. I don't want to kill her or the baby, but what choice do I have? I'm sorry. I wanted to explain that I'm not a monster. God forgive me, I'm going to do this, I've got to.'

'No Matthew, wait!' Laura shouted, but it was too late. All she could hear was the low hum of a dead line.

CHAPTER FIFTY-SEVEN

'This is my last visit,' Ruby said, her gaze firmly on Mason Gatley. The piped music and floral scents of the psychiatric unit were just a memory as they sat on their hard, unforgiving prison chairs.

'Really?' Pushing up the sleeves of his sweater, Mason displayed an array of tattoos on his skin. 'And here was me, thinking we'd become best friends.'

Ruby felt tense, unsettled. She had not expected this kind of whimsical response. But people like Mason could explode without a moment's notice. She had to get this out of the way. 'I heard you had a cell search. It wasn't me who dobbed you in.'

'I know that,' he said. 'At least, I know now.'

Ruby frowned. She had come here to ask for Abby's whereabouts, but his words drew her in. His stay in the psychiatric unit had been short-lived. Was his illness part of an elaborate ploy? 'How so?' she said, her words steeped in cynicism.

'I had a visit from your boyfriend. He set a few things straight.'

'Nathan came here?' Ruby's eyebrows shot up. Was he bluffing? Nathan hated institutions of any kind. It would take a lot for him to come in person. How did he gain entry for starters?

'You're not the only one able to pull strings around here,' Mason said. 'No need to worry. Boundaries have been laid. We didn't come to blows over you.'

'Look, I don't have time for this. There's another woman missing and I need to know where she is.' She hated the pleading sound of her voice but she had switched tack for a reason. She had to take the focus off her personal life and onto the task in hand. She could speak to Nathan later. Nothing else mattered while Abby and her baby were at risk.

'You don't have time?' Mason said, his chair creaking as he leaned forward and delivered a chilling stare. 'Baby, time with me is all you have. If you haven't caught the killer by now then I'm the best lead you've got.'

'Really?' Ruby said, amused that, for once, she knew something he didn't. But Mason was still talking. A speech he had no doubt rehearsed before she came.

'While I'm holding all the cards you are at my mercy. So let's cut to the chase. I've come up with a list of demands. Something to put me in the mood to talk.'

'You can keep your list,' Ruby said, 'because I don't need it. Our suspect has opened up about you; he's having a good laugh at your expense.' She pursed her lips. She could have told him about his son's arrest, used that angle to taunt him. But sharing such sensitive information at this stage of the investigation could have her removed from the case. She was not done squeezing Mason Gatley yet.

Mason's expression darkened as Ruby's words had the desired effect. 'He's not called the filth. He wouldn't dare.'

Ruby gave him a knowing glance. She knew she was playing with fire, but with James still in custody, what did she have to lose? Mason gave her a hotel address once before. Could she fool him into helping her again? 'I didn't say *who* he was in touch with, just that he's opened a line of communication. I think he's missing the attention. He feels he deserves more media coverage than he's been getting.'

'So he's been speaking to journalists,' Mason said bitterly. 'Trying to make a name for himself.'

Ruby did not correct him. 'He's had plenty to say.'

'You're bluffing.' Mason's mouth curled in a sneer. 'I warned him not to contact the press.'

Slowly Ruby inhaled a breath, instilling her best poker face. She was not surprised Mason Gatley told his protégé to stay out of the limelight. He wanted the attention reserved solely for himself.

'I wasn't bluffing when I told you about Thomas,' Ruby said. 'Seems you've backed the wrong horse to carry on your name. I have some of the transcriptions of his calls. Apparently he falls into a little Scottish accent when he gets passionate about things.'

Mason was shaking his head, but Ruby knew by the thunder crossing his face that her comment about the Scottish accent had hit home. Did James have a Scottish drawl? There was nothing in his background to suggest he had ever lived there. All the same, she had hit a raw nerve. She licked her lips, trying to remain calm while her heart was beating double time. 'He really opened up. Used the child abuse angle, can you believe it? Turns out he wants us to feel sorry for him. They say abuse runs in families. I know you said you killed for fun but who knows what the press will make out of this one?'

Ruby jumped as Mason brought down both his fists on the table. A broad shouldered member of staff took two steps towards them only to pause as Ruby raised her hand to implore for a few seconds more.

'I'm the one in control here, not you,' Mason raged, his eyes alight with fury. 'I am not some pathetic weakling begging some journo for scraps. Did you see the pictures of my victims? That's nothing compared to what I could do to you.'

Ruby held up her hands in a gesture of mock surrender. She sat tall, her voice firm, but beneath the table, her leg trembled as a shot of adrenalin flowed through her veins. 'Would you prefer that I say nothing? I'm doing you a favour. It's better you're prepared, before all the juicy details hit the press.'

The air seemed to thicken between them as Mason clenched and unclenched his fists. 'It's not going to. Because you're going to stop that little bastard before he goes any further. If you weren't so incompetent you would have arrested him by now.'

Ruby snorted. 'You're the one withholding information. If you want him stopped then you know what you have to do.' She prodded the table with her finger. 'Think about the headlines. They'll print a story about abuse victims and tar you both with the same brush.'

'You're lying. Why the fuck would a cop want to help someone like me?' Suspicion narrowed Mason's eyes.

Ruby gave a one shouldered shrug, resisting the urge to recoil. He had leaned in so close to her that she could smell his last meal on his breath. 'You know who my boyfriend is. Call it honour among thieves. In prison, reputation is everything. The press is baying for a story. I can stop it, but only if we catch him in time.'

'He's nothing, nothing but a plaything.' Mason's frown deepened as he turned his thoughts inward. 'I'm not having that little runt making out he's better than me.'

'Give me the name and a hotel address. I'll shut this down for good. Soon you'll be talking to them face-to-face. I give you my word,' Ruby said. They were big promises but time was running out. She could feel the answers drawing near. Mason would not have cooperated if she told him his son was in custody. He would not have cared about the woman tied up in a hotel room. The only way to get answers was to make Mason feel that he would be made to look a fool.

'Don't you see?' Mason said. 'Talk about dropping clues. I've been talking to him face-to-face all this time.'

Ruby shook her head. 'No, you haven't. I've drilled down through all of the patients, visitors and inmates that you've shared time with, and none of them were released that recently. They couldn't have been there to carry out the crimes.' She thought about Nathan's visit and imagined his name being added to that list.

'They're not inmates or patients,' Mason said. 'They never were.'

Ruby's mind was racing now as she searched for answers. 'We've interviewed the staff. None of them worked both the prison and the mental institution.'

'Who else has free passage, someone who can come and go as they please. Someone who doesn't need a visiting order? Someone who could talk to me alone.'

Precious seconds ticked away as Ruby worked it out. She inhaled sharply as the answers finally dawned. 'I know who it is,' she gasped, the answers becoming clear. 'But it can't be. Not him.' She cupped her mouth with her hand. She had spoken to the killer face-to-face. The very last person she imagined to be involved in such a thing.

'But it is. The person you'd least expect,' Mason replied, eerily voicing her thoughts. 'It was fascinating dealing with him, watching him become aroused when I confessed my crimes. 'There was no censorship between us. I even inspired him to do more.'

'But now he's gone too far, filled with his own sense of self-importance,' Ruby replied. 'I can't believe he played me.'

Mason leaned forward, his eyes ice cold. 'And now I want you to take him down. I would so love to see him again.'

CHAPTER FIFTY-EIGHT

Blinking through her encrusted eyelids, Abby tried once again to focus on the room. Her eyes swivelled from left to right in their sockets as she took in her dim surroundings. With the curtains closed and the bedside light on, she had lost all sense of time. *Oh yeah... ooh... that's it.* What was that sound? Had Matthew gone out and left the television on? Abby craned her neck to the flat-screen television on the wall. Two women and one man writhed naked on a sofa, their bodies slick with sweat. It was the porn channel and, with frightening clarity, she realised it served a double purpose. Anyone listening on the other side of the door would not disturb them. Any moaning noises she forced through her gag would be mistaken for something else. She was used to such movies, having been exposed to them from an early age. It was merely background noise. Nothing could shock her, at least until now. But why was she still here? He said he was going to kill her. In her experience, such people had a total lack of conscience. Had her pregnancy meant that much to him? She thought about the abortion she had booked in. The baby may have saved her life. It was time to return the favour and give the poor mite a chance.

She strained to listen, pushing past the pain of her throbbing hand. A bout of nausea rose up as she came to grips with the burning, meaty scent infiltrating the room. Her nostrils flared as she inhaled another breath, the sickly clammy smell of dried blood and urine making her stomach heave even more. *Jesus Christ,* she thought, *what has he done to me?* She could not afford to vomit.

With no outlet, she would choke before anyone could find her. *Steady*, she told herself. *I'm going to be OK. I'm in a hotel. The room will be cleaned. It's only a matter of time.* Outside her door, a low thrumming sound made her heart flicker in her chest. It was a hoover. Someone was cleaning the corridor. She wriggled against her bindings, her muffled screams drowned by the *ah, ah, ah,* filtering from the television in the room. She had to get out. But the noise from outside faded as the cleaner slowly walked down the hall. Each movement of Abby's hands and feet tightened the rope around her neck. She could edge herself off the bed and fall onto the floor but what then? Was it worth killing both herself and her baby in the process? Surely, she should wait it out? But the decision was taken away from her as a voice spoke outside her room door. It was Matthew, passing polite conversation with the cleaner. Abby stiffened, her heartbeat cranking up a notch in her chest.

Unshaven and with red-rimmed eyes, he slid his body through the door, quickly closing it behind him. 'Phew!' he said, waving his hand over his face. 'Stinks in here. We need to turn that air con up. Have you wet the bed?'

Blinking furiously, Abby stared up at him, the soiled sheets the least of her concerns. Had he returned to finish her, or was he going to set her free?

'I'm sorry,' he said, reaching out to touch her hair. 'But you've come to the end of the road.'

Abby flinched, her stomach clenching as she thought about the life she carried inside. Was her baby picking up on her distress? Could it feel that something was wrong? Being alone had granted her with time to enrich her view of the life growing inside her. It was no longer just a pregnancy. It was her little girl or boy. In the long hours with pain and terror pushing in from every side, Abby had forced her thoughts within. She had chosen baby names, picked their school and their vocation when they grew up. But now, as she stared into Matthew's eyes, she knew it had all been a dream. She had dared to look into the life of a woman far better than herself.

Matthew loomed over her, his features twisted. 'I would never have chosen you if I had known you were pregnant. This is all your fault, putting your baby in danger like that.'

Abby bit back the whimper rising in her throat. The coldness of Matthew's fingers raised goosebumps on her skin as he paused to stroke her cheek.

Sighing, he reached into his pocket and pulled out a plastic bag. 'I really am sorry though. This wasn't the way it was meant to be. But I can't let you go, not now you know who I am.'

Laying the bag on the mattress, he gently undid the rope around her neck. But he was not releasing her, he was merely delivering a different method of death. 'I'll make it as kind as I can. You should pass out in a few minutes after inhaling enough of your own breath.'

Whimpering, Abby tried to wriggle away. Mascara-stained tears formed streams down her face. She was unable to hide her fear any longer because she placed more value on her baby's life than her own. 'Please,' she said, her words a muffled garble. But all she could see was the clear plastic bag as it was placed over her head. Taking a shuddering breath, she accepted her fate. *I'm sorry,* she sent a silent message to her baby, mourning the life inside her. *You deserved better than me. I'm so sorry I let you down.* The sound of her heartbeat thrashed in her ears and she drew up her knees to her chest.

'Shhh don't cry…' Matthew said, winding the base of the bag around her neck. He paused to direct the television remote control. 'Let me put on some music. Something peaceful. Then we can say a little prayer.'

CHAPTER FIFTY-NINE

Blasting the car horn, Ruby sped through the city traffic. She had never envisaged when she first met him how helpful Mason Gatley would become. It was not as if she had lied during their conversation. It was not her fault he presumed she was talking about the press being called rather than the helpline. She flicked the button on the car dashboard to listen to the voicemail she had missed. It was Luddy, and the sound of his voice delivered a flurry of panic. Was his niece OK?

'Sarge, I just wanted to update you. James has been released to his home address. CPS refused to charge on circumstantial evidence. Laura's had another call. She said he was suicidal and he's going to finish Abby off. He said they went to a club in Shoreditch last night, and on to a nearby hotel. I've tried calling DI Downes but I can't get through to him.'

The message ended as Ruby drove, leaving her painfully aware of the minutes ticking by. As always in such investigations, time was a precious commodity, and she had already alerted units to the location of Abby at the Willow Street Hotel. She could only pray that Mason had been telling the truth and officers reached her and the killer on time.

As officers took the lift to Matthew's room, Ruby thought about the contents of Laura's call. It sounded as if he had given up on life. He must have known that Mason Gatley would kill him should he ever step foot in jail. And now, the sight of police entering the five star hotel would drive Matthew just one way. Mason Gatley had been caught as he recovered his bag that had been hidden on the hotel roof. His attachment to the rope used in the murders had been his downfall as well as the inability to stay away. Would history repeat itself one more time? Such thoughts entered Ruby's mind as she sprinted out of the lift and up the single flight of stairs that brought her to the hotel roof. She could barely hear the updates filtering through her police radio over the clamour of her own heart. There were enough bodies on the ground. The only way was up.

'We're with the female now, ambulance required,' a uniformed officer informed control on a channel set aside for the team's search. As she took in the rest of the message, Ruby gleaned that Abby was alive. Lying on the bed with a bag over her head, they had found her with seconds to spare. But as further updates filtered through, it seemed their killer was nowhere to be found.

Tearing onto the rooftop, Ruby was immediately blindsided by a strong gust of wind. As she clawed back the strands of long dark hair from her face, her vision cleared to reveal a man in the distance. Rucksack on his back, he held onto the hotel flagpole as she clambered onto the roof ledge. All of London seemed laid out before her, with lights twinkling in the distance amongst the skyscrapers that formed a breathtaking backdrop that she knew and loved. In any other circumstances, it was beautiful. But it was all lost on Ruby as she approached the man before her.

He glanced back, his features contorted as he grabbed the flagpole beside him that ruffled in the breeze. 'Put the radio down,' he shouted, the wind catching his words.

Ruby held her hands out before her, gently lowering her police radio and harness to the floor. 'It's me, Ruby,' she said, having met him before.

'I know who you are.' The man frowned. 'How did you find me?'

But Ruby did not answer quickly enough.

'I said: how did you know I was here!'

'Mason Gatley,' Ruby replied. 'Please, Father, come away from the edge so we can talk things through.'

The priest turned his head to face her, the wind ruffling his hair as he clung onto the flagpole. 'He told you about his confessions?'

'Yes,' Ruby said, 'and how they turned into something more. He encouraged you, didn't he? Got pleasure from hearing about your kills.' Up until her conversation with Mason she had been convinced that the killer was James. Spurned by his father, eager to please. He seemed the most obvious suspect. She had justified the lack of sexual intercourse with the victims because James was gay. But Isaac was different. He did not kill these people with lustful intent. He took his vow of celibacy seriously. Men or women, they were all sinners in his eyes. A theory grown from a past that would not let go.

Isaac raised a palm to his hair as his fringe danced in his eyes. The breeze on the rooftop was sharp, despite the clement weather. 'Stay where you are,' he shouted the wind whipping his words. 'Don't move another step.'

'We've got Abby,' Ruby shouted, taking another step forward. 'Officers found her just in time.' She tried not to think of how high up they were as she approached the flagpole with caution.

'I don't believe you,' Isaac said. 'She's dead. But you can't pin it on me. All you have is the word of a killer and nothing more.'

'We know everything,' Ruby replied. 'Your phone calls to Sanity Line, your troubled childhood. It's why you came to me, isn't it? To try and put things right. But then you got afraid and backed out. I showed you the pictures. You put the blame on Mason's son instead.'

'Get back!' Isaac shouted. 'I was making things right. Don't you see? All these sinners, they need to be taught a lesson. Nobody listens to sermons any more. I had to take action. I had to make them pay.'

'I'm not here to discuss morality,' Ruby said. 'I'm here to bring you in. You have to account for the murders of Melissa Sherman, Cheryl Barber and Matthew Johnson. The abduction of Thomas Crawley and the attempted murder of Abby Forbes.' Ruby thought she could appeal to his better nature, but the priest's eyes had glazed over as he took a step towards the edge of the building. Gradually she moved closer, the wind chilling her skin. A low mumble followed as Isaac began to pray.

'Please, take my hand,' Ruby said, placing one foot onto the ledge while she tried to keep her balance. She was all too aware that he could grab for her, should he wish to take her over the edge.

'There's only one way this is ending and it's *not* with me in prison,' Isaac said. 'I'd rather take my chances with God.'

Ruby's eyes widened as she realised he was serious. She needed a negotiator but time was not on her side as he shifted closer to the edge. All she could do was try to delay him until units realised where she was.

'At least I made an effort during my time here. I tried to put things right,' he said, giving her one last glance.

'Is that why you joined the priesthood?' Ruby asked. 'Surely this wasn't what you intended? You're not Mason Gatley. You've been hurt too. It's time to face up to what you've done.'

'You're right,' Isaac replied. 'Yes. I need to be judged for my sins.'

Ruby exhaled in relief as she held out her hand. 'Good, then come down from there. Please.'

'You misunderstand me, detective. Only God is fit to judge me.' Closing his eyes, he released his grip from the flagpole and surrendered his body into the air.

CHAPTER SIXTY

Lurching forward, Ruby wrapped her fingers around the cold metal flagpole as she grabbed the priest's rucksack with her left hand. Life seemed to pass in slow motion as she made the decision to jump, but in those nanoseconds, she forged the strength of conviction that saving his miserable life was the right thing to do.

In a strange moment of enlightenment, her senses awoke in a blaze. Hanging over the edge of the building with one hand gripping the pole, the sounds and smells of city life erupted around her. The feeling of her heart freezing in her chest as fear took hold. The sudden rush of air into her lungs as she inhaled a breath to scream his name. Panic had overcome her as she jumped onto the ledge, screaming a warning to pedestrians on the streets below. She had seen the look in the priest's eyes before he closed them, resigned to his fate. But she was not alone. Having pressed the panic button on her airwave radio before putting it down, she had given the control room an open mike.

Her colleagues reached the rooftop just seconds before Isaac had let go. The church was an angle that Ruby had been keen to explore when it came to giving him a reason to live. She had not expected him to turn it on its head and use his death as a means of facing his maker.

Her fingers wrapped around the straps of his backpack; his eyes snapped open at the sudden jolt. Ruby winced as the priest dangled against the ledge, struggling against her grip. As her fingers began to slide on the flagpole, she refused to relinquish her hold. She had never been so relieved when DI Downes's strong arms wrapped around her and her colleague's steady hands guided them back on to solid ground. His eyes wide in disbelief, Isaac screamed in rage. Bundled to the ground, he was handcuffed before he could do himself any more harm.

It was not that Ruby cared enough about the killer to risk her own life. Sickened by his actions, she could just as easily have watched him hurtle to his death. But she could not deprive the victims' families of justice. The horrors of his acts would haunt them for years to come.

But DI Downes did not appear in agreement as he pulled her to one side. 'What the hell were ya thinking? You could have got yourself killed! And for what? To prevent a death in custody? You should have let the bastard jump.'

'I saw you coming from the corner of my eye,' Ruby said, her heart still hammering in her chest. 'I knew you'd have my back.' But her grip on the rucksack would only have lasted for seconds before he pulled her down. Furiously her captive had wriggled, depriving her of every last ounce of strength.

'Christ, woman, you nearly gave me a heart attack – for real this time. You're mad, completely off your head!' Downes shook his head, his eyes wide with disbelief.

'You would have done the same thing to bring him in,' Ruby said, but the look he returned told her this was not the case. After getting Isaac to his feet, the officers dragged him to the stairwell, ignoring his outrage at being saved.

'How did you know it was him?' Downes said, as they both followed from behind.

Ruby pointed to the sky, relieved but happy. 'Call it divine intervention,' she smiled. 'I went to the prison thinking it was James, but I came out with the priest's name.'

A glint of admiration crept into his gaze. 'It's thanks to you that we found Abby alive. Now let's get this waste of space in custody where he belongs.'

CHAPTER SIXTY-ONE

'Are you sure this is wise?' Luddy asked, pulling the car up on the immaculate tarmac drive. 'Shouldn't we have brought uniform as backup just in case?'

'It's about pride,' Ruby said, her face taut. 'We started here so we'll end here. No fanfare, no police units, just the satisfaction of a job well done.' Events from the day before were still fresh in her mind. Closure was what was needed now.

'But it's not well done, is it?' Luddy said, turning off the ignition. 'Three people have died.'

Fiddling with her police radio, Ruby pressed the code to update her time of arrival at the address she had logged. 'Can you look me in the eye and say you did your best with the resources that you had?' She clipped her airwave radio to her belt before meeting his gaze. She could see his thoughts were tainted with guilt for the lives they had not been able to save.

'Yeah,' Luddy nodded. 'I couldn't have done any more.'

'There you go then. Thomas Crawley's alive because of us. Abby and her unborn baby are too. The killer only stopped because we disrupted him. It could have been so much worse.'

'You squeezed the info out of Mason Gatley, not us,' Luddy said, his hands resting on the steering wheel of the car.

Ruby laughed incredulously. 'You're kidding me, aren't you? Who's put together the file for the CPS? Who's trawled through the mountain of statements and evidence to make the case strong? It's teamwork. Always has been, which is why I asked you along.'

Luddy delivered a lopsided grin. 'It's a good thing I threw away her phone number, eh? That would have made for an awkward first date.'

'Yes well, looks like she's expecting us, there's some serious curtain twitching going on,' Ruby said, before stepping out of the car.

'This time she's all yours.' Buttoning his suit jacket, Luddy followed Ruby as she approached the house. They would not be removing their shoes. Today their attention was not on the lavish surroundings, it was solely focused on the occupant within.

The front door was opened before Ruby was able to press the gold-plated doorbell. Hannah greeted them with a 14-carat smile.

'Owen, Ruby. I didn't expect to see you again so soon.'

'Can we come in?' Ruby asked, unimpressed with the use of their first names. 'We need to speak to you about Cheryl's case.'

'Of course,' Hannah said, wiping the flour from her hands onto the apron tied around her waist. 'You'll have to excuse me, I'm baking. Come into the kitchen. We can talk there.'

The smell of freshly baked sponge cake filled the hall, teasing Ruby's senses.

'It's a family recipe,' Hannah said, 'my sister's grandchildren begged me to make some for the school fete.'

'You wouldn't happen to have a file in one of those cakes, would you?' Ruby said, unable to resist the quip.

Hannah frowned, creating distance between them as she turned her back to peep through the oven door. 'I'm not with you, officer,' she said, but her tone was strained, and after composing herself, she turned to face her.

'We know about Isaac – Father McElroy. Change his surname when he joined the priesthood, did he? No wonder we couldn't trace him. What did you do, put him up to the murders?'

'What?' Hannah said, her eyebrows shooting up. 'I've no idea what you're talking about…'

'Oh come on,' Ruby said. 'Cut the crap. We know he's your son. And as for giving him an alibi… did you think we wouldn't check?'

Hannah whipped off the apron and threw it on the side. 'You're wrong. Isaac comforted me in my grief. Cheryl was my best friend. I was devastated when she died.' Her fingers crept to the crucifix around her neck, but today her eyes were filled with fear.

'Devastated enough to be eyeing up my DC just days after her death? Why did you give Owen your phone number? Were you scared that things with Gordon wouldn't work out, or were you trying to lead us away from the trail?' Ruby advanced towards Hannah, sliding her handcuffs from the pouch on her shoulder harness.

The sight of the handcuffs sparked further terror. 'I don't know what you mean,' Hannah said, stepping backwards until she hit the kitchen units.

Ruby gave her a knowing look. She was not buying her innocent act. 'I know about your affair. Your son, he's a real chameleon, isn't he? Giving sermons during the day and murdering his victims by night. Provide him with the coke, did you? Can't see there would be much call for it where he lives with the other priests.'

'That had nothing to do with me,' Hannah said. 'It was Mason Gatley that put the idea in his mind.'

'Yet you were kind enough to pass out invites at the golf club to his *Debauchery* page. Your friends were very reluctant to dob you in – that is, until your son was arrested and they saw how much trouble you were in.' Ruby slowly advanced, DC Ludgrove one step behind her. 'You knew he was under Mason Gatley's influence, yet you hinted that Cheryl was a woman who didn't deserve to live. Then you set up a date with Matthew Johnson, and killed him so Isaac could take his identity. With everything in place, all you had to do was to reel Cheryl in.'

Under the blinding light of the truth, Hannah's expression changed. With nowhere left to go, she glared at Ruby with undiluted hatred in her eyes. 'Cheryl didn't deserve Gordon. She stole him away from me. I was just reclaiming what was rightfully mine.'

'By killing her?' Ruby said, inwardly warmed by Hannah's admittance.

'I never touched her though, did I?' Hannah's mouth turned upwards in an ugly smile. 'It's not my fault if my son felt compelled to take it further. You'll never pin this on me.'

'We'll see about that,' Ruby said, grabbing her by the wrist.

'Ow!' Hannah yelled. 'What are you doing?'

'You're under arrest on suspicion of the murder of Matthew Johnson and perverting the course of justice. We've got new witness testimony – someone who saw you leaving his flat.' As Ruby began to recite the caution, Hannah pulled away.

'That's not happening,' Hannah grimaced as she jolted backwards, her fingers wrapping around a breadknife on the kitchen counter. Her hand shook as she held it aloft, staring from Ruby to Owen as they stood either side. From the oven, a plume of grey smoke filtered out as the last of her cakes began to burn.

'Don't be stupid,' Luddy said, unclasping his baton from his shoulder harness and releasing it to its full extent.

'It's OK.' Ruby shot Luddy a reassuring glare. 'Everything's under control. Drop the knife, Hannah. You really don't want to go there.' In the hall, the smoke alarm began to beep, but Ruby's attention was on the blade of the knife glinting in Hannah's hand. A single stab wound was what had killed Matthew Johnson. She had murdered once already. Ruby would not underestimate her again.

'You're not taking me,' Hannah said, her voice taking on a hysterical tone as she swiped the air. She carried a manic look in her eye – a trait that she no doubt had passed on to her son.

Having investigated Isaac's background, Ruby discovered that Hannah was the mother he had told the helpline about. After spending a few years in Scotland, he had come to live in London and joined the priesthood upon his return. But Hannah had been cocky, providing him with an alibi when officers asked about his visits to Mason Gatley in the psychiatric unit.

'Put the knife down,' Ruby said firmly, taking another step forward. It felt like déjà vu as she persuaded yet another killer to hand themselves in.

'You're not arresting me,' Hannah screamed, raising the blade in the air. 'I'm not going to prison. Not for Isaac, not for anyone.'

'Hannah?' A voice trailed from the doorway behind them. 'What are you doing?' He paused to cough as the smell of burning cake filtered through the air.

'Darling… I…' Hannah said, her gaze diverted.

Coming down hard with his baton, Luddy swung for Hannah's right arm. As the knife clanged against the tiled floor, Ruby pulled out her cuffs, risking a quick glance over her shoulder. It was Gordon, and he was standing, frozen, in the doorway, his face pale, and his mouth open in shock.

'You've broken my arm!' Hannah screamed, clutching her forearm miserably.

Ruby clicked on the handcuffs, barely able to hear Gordon speaking over Hannah's howls of despair.

'What's going on?' he repeated, making no move to comfort the screaming woman who had crumpled onto the floor. 'Why are you arresting her?'

'Like you don't know?' Ruby said, pulling Hannah to her feet.

Turning off the smoking oven, Gordon seemed mystified by their presence, his eyebrows raised. 'You're not saying…' he paused, trying to gather his words. 'You're not saying Hannah had something to do with Cheryl's murder… are you?'

'We can talk about it down the station,' Ruby said. 'You'll need to come in too.'

Gordon stood, still open mouthed. 'You've got this all wrong. I didn't kill my wife.'

'Just the same, we need to talk,' Ruby said, holding onto Hannah as Luddy took her other arm. 'We've arrested Isaac. He's told us everything.'

'Isaac who?' Gordon said, his frown deepening in confusion.

'Hannah's son,' Ruby said. 'The man who murdered your wife. Cheryl wasn't the only victim caught up in all of this.'

'I didn't mean him to kill the others; you can blame Mason Gatley for that,' Hannah wailed.

Gordon stared in disbelief. He spoke between his fingers. 'No. Sweetheart, you're not thinking straight. Tell them it's not true.'

'It was the only way we could be together,' she said miserably as Ruby led her to the door. 'Tell her to loosen these cuffs, they're really hurting me.'

Ruby shook her head. Even now, she was thinking of herself.

CHAPTER SIXTY-TWO

Ruby was feeling pleased with herself, having bagged an outside seat at one of her favourite cafés. Based on Redchurch Street, Franze and Evans was situated right at the top of Brick Lane. As the sun warmed her face, she reflected that soon summer would be upon them. Her life had changed beyond recognition in the last year. She was glad to see the back of her grubby little flat, and struggling to pay for her mother's care. Nathan had been a lifesaver. It was only now, when she could see how hard he was trying, that she could accept his help without being plagued by guilt. Nobody knew what the future would hold but having both her family and her job was more than she could have dreamed of.

A month had passed since the murders, enough time for people to come to terms with events and for wounds to begin to heal. As Abby joined her, Ruby knew she had made the right decision. She had risked her life to save Isaac's, but now he and his mother had been charged, justice had been done.

'Let me get you a coffee,' Ruby said, as Abby graced her with a smile. The welts around her neck had softened in time. Ruby had yet to look at her hand. It was missing a finger: a gruesome reminder of how close she had come to death.

'I'm OK, thanks. I saw you had a drink so I ordered myself a green tea on the way in.'

'Their French toast and bananas is to die for,' Ruby said. 'Can I tempt you? My treat?'

'I'm fine, thanks,' Abby replied. 'Besides, it should be me treating you. Ian… I mean, DC Rutherford, he told me what you did. I felt that I needed some…' She tapped a varnished finger against her lip. 'What's the word?'

'Closure?' Ruby replied.

'Yes, that's it. Closure. That's why I asked to meet. If it wasn't for you I wouldn't be alive today.' Her words faded as thoughts of the past filled her mind. 'If he hadn't looked out the window and seen the police—' Abby's words were cut short by her tears. She fell silent as staff placed her tea on the table, and taking out a tissue, dabbed the wetness from her eyes.

'I'll pass on your thanks to the team,' Ruby replied. 'How are you coping? It must have taken a lot for you to meet me today.'

'I'm good,' she said, pausing to pour her tea. 'If anything, Steve and I are closer than before. I came so near to death. Steve said nothing else mattered; he just wanted to get me and the baby home.'

'Congratulations,' Ruby said, keeping her reservations about Steve's controlling ways to herself. The domestic abuse team had already offered Abby assistance and was politely told to go away. 'I hear the pregnancy is going well.'

'It is,' Abby nodded. 'I was so blind back then. I didn't trust myself to handle it. But now I know I'm strong enough for anything. We're putting the past behind us and moving on.'

'I have a feeling there's something more you want to know,' Ruby said, noticing her hesitancy as she stirred her tea.

Abby's lips turned upwards in a soft smile. 'I could ask questions for ever and never be satisfied. I'm glad he's pleading guilty though. At least I'll be spared the embarrassment of testifying in court.'

'You've nothing to be ashamed of. He's admitted everything and the evidence against him is strong,' Ruby said, keen to put her mind at rest.

Abby sipped her tea, her little finger poised in the air as she raised her cup. 'I heard he had a rough childhood.' It was true. Isaac had put his mother on a pedestal, but he did not know her at all. He was too focused on his father's misdemeanours to realise that she was using him for her own gain.

'Doesn't justify what he's done,' Ruby said, pausing to take a drink. From reading through her research, Abby's childhood had been far worse. But it was not something she wanted to dwell on today. Abby was a survivor. She was moving on. 'You want to know why I saved him, don't you? Why I didn't let him jump.'

'You're a very perceptive person,' Abby said. 'But yes, sometimes it keeps me awake at night. I feel so angry for what he did to me. I bought a new wedding ring. I wear it on my right hand.'

'What about a prosthetic finger?' Ruby asked, finally daring a glance at her left hand. The stump looked red and sore, out of place on such smooth and unlined skin.

'I'm having one as soon as everything's healed. It's a small blessing that he cauterised my hand after amputating my finger. I could have bled out.'

'You're a strong woman,' Ruby said. 'Most people would have fallen apart.'

'I'm not the only one,' Abby replied, giving her a respectful nod. 'They told me you pulled him back off the roof with one hand. Why risk your life for him? I don't understand.'

Ruby swatted an inquisitive fly from their table. 'I wanted you to have justice. It might not feel like it now, but after he's convicted, you'll be glad that he served his time and paid for what he did. Death is too easy an option for the likes of him.' She met Abby's gaze. 'Do you know, he closed his eyes and smiled, actually *smiled* as he let go. I remember thinking that he didn't get to choose how it ended. It wasn't up to him.' Ruby could feel her passion rising, the old emotions coming to the surface once more.

'Now I understand. Thank you,' Abby said, draining her tea.

'Don't get me wrong, I was tempted to push him off myself,' Ruby smirked. 'But it's better to play things by the book. It was the right thing to do.' A look of understanding passed between them. Ever the rule breaker, she sometimes surprised herself by working inside the law.

As Abby said her goodbyes and left, Ruby caught sight of Nathan, strolling down Brick Lane with Cathy by his side. A flutter rose in her stomach as he approached. His white shirt was open at the neck, perfectly fitted to flatter his muscular form. Hands deep in his trouser pockets, he smiled as he returned her admiring glance. Ruby could not catch Cathy's words, but they had the effect of making him laugh. In her Top Shop jeans and billowing white blouse, she looked as carefree as Ruby had ever seen her in a very long time.

'Have you decided yet?' Nathan said, stretching his hand out to take Ruby's. Their afternoon excursion was yet to be chosen.

Briefly kissing him on the cheek, Ruby laced her fingers in Nathan's as she walked between him and Cathy. Finally, she felt confident enough to go public with their relationship and face whatever lay ahead. 'What about taking in a show? Think we can get any decent tickets at this late stage?'

'I know a man who can.' Nathan winked.

'Oh Dad, what are you like?' Cathy replied. 'Why sit in some stuffy theatre when we can have some fun instead? I fancy the Tower of London, the dungeon tour.'

'You choose then,' Ruby said. 'We've got the whole day to ourselves.'

As they strolled to Nathan's car, Ruby was not complacent enough to believe they were home and dry. Experience taught her that danger lurked around every corner. But courage in danger was half the battle. With her family by her side, she would get through whatever was to come.

A LETTER FROM CAROLINE

Dear Reader,

I would like to express my heartfelt thanks for choosing to read *Murder Game*. DS Ruby Preston has been so enjoyable to write, although given the darkness of some of the scenes, I totally understand if you question my idea of fun.

If you did enjoy it, and want to keep up to date with all my books, just sign up at the following link. Your email address will never be shared and you can unsubscribe at any time.

www.bookouture.com/caroline-mitchell

I hope I've been able to take you out of your everyday lives for a few hours as you have turned the pages. I also hope that my ex-police colleagues forgive me for the freedom Ruby sometimes is afforded as a sergeant. I'm sure they will agree that it makes for very entertaining reading, if stretching the truth just a little bit. I am only too aware of the days in which paperwork prevails, or the times when you're handling so much work that you feel as if your head is going to explode. The emergency services will always have my unfaltering admiration, and I always try to capture the human side of such demanding roles.

If you did enjoy this book, do check out my backlist on Amazon. I would also be truly grateful if you would write a review. Are you on social media? I love to hear from my readers and you can find my social media links and my website below.

Thank you so much for your support – until next time.
Caroline Mitchell

www.caroline-writes.com

CMitchellAuthor

Twitter.com/Caroline_writes

#MurderGame

ACKNOWLEDGEMENTS

I am hugely grateful to the people who have helped bring this book, the third in the DS Ruby Preston series, to fruition.

To Oliver Rhodes and the growing Bookouture team – thank you as always for your support. In particular, thank you to the very special Kim Nash and Noelle Holton for your time and devotion, and my editor Natasha Harding for making my book the best it can be. Thanks also to the fantastic cover designers who made this series stand out, and all those working in the background to get it seen.

To the wonderful supportive group of authors, without whom I would have lost my marbles years ago – thank you for being there, both online and at the occasional author event I'm lucky enough to attend. It was with great sadness that we lost one of our group, the lovely Helen Cadbury, to whom this book is dedicated. To the fabulous Angela Marsons, Lindsay J. Pryor and Mel Sherratt – thanks for the giggles, never a dull moment!

I'd like to give a special thanks to my wonderful agent Madeleine Milburn and the fantastic #teamMaddy who champion my books. To the lovely Hayley Steed whose tweets make me laugh. Your boundless energy and enthusiasm leave me in awe.

To the amazing book clubs and bloggers who have supported me, thank you so much for spreading the word. I'm sending virtual hugs to you and my readers. It's been quite a journey and I can't believe I'm about to write my tenth book! None of this would be possible without you. Thank you, from the bottom of my heart.

Last but not least, to my family and friends, words aren't needed, because you know just how much you mean to me.

10607499R00166

Printed in Germany
by Amazon Distribution
GmbH, Leipzig